RECLAIMED

Sarah Guillory

Spencer Hill Press

Contact: Spencer Hill Press, PO Box 247, Contoocook, NH 03229, USA

Please visit our website at www.spencerhillpress.com
First Edition: October 2013.
Sarah Guillory
Reclaimed : a novel / by Sarah Guillory – 1st ed.
p. cm.
Summary:

A girl determined to flee her small town finds a reason to stay when she falls in love with twin brothers, one who can't remember his past and the other who doesn't want him to remember..

The author acknowledges the copyrighted or trademarked status and trademark owners of the following wordmarks mentioned in this fiction: Band-Aid, Boy Scouts of America, Coca-Cola, Canopy, Crock-Pot, Diet Coke, Disneyland, Floaties, Ford Bronco, Formica, Frankenstein, Humpty Dumpty, Indiana Jones, James Bond, Jeep Cherokee, Little League, Peter Pan, Scooby Doo, Sheetrock, Shell, Technicolor, Walmart, Wonderland

Cover design by Jennifer Rush
Interior layout by Marie Romero

ISBN 978-1-937053-88-8 (paperback)
ISBN 978-1-937053-89-5 (e-book)

Printed in the United States of America

For Josh

BEFORE

JENNA

October had tremendous possibility. The summer's oppressive heat was a distant memory, and the golden leaves promised a world full of beautiful adventures. They made me believe in miracles.

The crisp air smelled like wood smoke, and I longed to lace up my running shoes. Fall was the best time to run—the air tasted better and was easier to move through.

In the fall, I could fly.

Instead, Mom and I were making the hour-long drive from our house in Solitude, Arkansas, to the hospital in Middleton. I drove. Mom kept picking at her cuticles and wishing I would do something with my hair other than a ponytail, and *surely* I had a pair of jeans that didn't have holes in them. Mom had a tendency to come apart in a crisis—or a minor inconvenience, for that matter.

I understood Mom's worry, but Pops was going to be fine. He'd promised. Just yesterday, he'd been sitting up and flirting with the young nurse who was checking his IV. Mom had poured him some juice and snapped at Mops for not doing it first, and Pops had told the joke about the bear, which had stopped being funny when I was six. I'd laughed anyway.

But today, when I got to his room, I knew Pops was worse. Instead of telling jokes, he gasped like there wasn't enough oxygen on the entire planet. I couldn't stand seeing him like that. Pops was supposed to be strong. He'd carried me on his shoulders until I was seven years old. Pops wasn't old, or sick, or frail. This wasn't Pops.

"Why didn't you call me?" Mom shouted at Mops. "We would have been here sooner."

Pops spoke up so Mops didn't have to. He was good at smoothing things over. "I'm fine," he said, but he barely got the words out, and I didn't know if he was.

I was glad when the nurses told us we had to wait outside. I stood in the hallway, grateful to be away from the beeping machines.

"This wouldn't have happened if you'd been at home with him," Mom said, glaring at Mops.

"Or if *you'd* answered your phone when he called you," Mops answered.

Mom paled, turning away. Mops ran a hand over her face and looked guilty. But neither of them apologized. They sat on opposite sides of the waiting room.

"I'm going outside," I said. I needed to breathe.

I escaped the tension into a cold north wind. I tried to convince myself that Pops was going to pull through. He always did. He'd been in the hospital three times in the past year, and he'd always come out in a couple of days, ranting about how they'd tried to starve him. He'd told me he was too ornery to die, and I believed him. Pops couldn't die in October. There was too much promise.

I grabbed my writing notebook from the car and sat at a cracked picnic table nestled in a cluster of trees. The ground was golden with pine needles, and the wind through the trees sounded like rushing water. I opened to a blank page and tried to change my worry into words, but I hadn't yet mastered that kind of alchemy.

"Ian!"

I turned to see a woman leaning out of the back door of the building, then noticed a guy about my age sitting on the ground behind the hospital. He was almost invisible in the shadows. When he saw me staring, he put his finger to his lips.

The woman shouted for Ian again, but neither the boy nor I moved, and she finally went inside. I tried to focus on my writing, but his behavior left me with a curiosity as deep as the gloom the boy was sitting in. I wrote a few words and crossed them out. I looked back at the boy. His head was bowed, and it took me a minute to realize what he was doing—whittling. Strange.

When he looked up, I dropped my head back to my notebook, embarrassed that he'd caught me staring. After another minute of gazing at the mostly blank page, I ventured another look. He was whittling again. This time, when he glanced up, he grinned, and I had to laugh.

The boy stood and peeked around the building. When he was sure the woman was gone, he walked over.

He was tall, his hands shoved in the pockets of his jeans and his dark hair curling at the edges of his collar. He gave me a crooked half-smile, and his blue eyes crinkled at the corners. "Thanks for that."

"No problem. What are you hiding from, anyway?" I asked.

His smile slipped away. "Everything. You?"

I admired his honesty. I wanted to tell him that I wasn't hiding, but it was a lie I wasn't sure I could pull off. I gave him the easiest piece of truth. "I just needed some air."

He nodded like I'd said something witty and wise instead of avoiding his question. The wind kicked up, and I hugged my notebook tighter to my chest.

"What's in the notebook?" he asked, sitting beside me on the picnic table.

Words and wishes and a way out. "My plan for world domination," I said instead.

"Does yours include the Bond girls?" His voice was deep, and the way he spoke made me think he wasn't from Arkansas. That made me even more curious.

I laughed. "No."

He looked surprised. "Must be just mine, then."

"You're Ian?" I asked. He nodded, his eyes seeming to ask a question I didn't know if I could answer. "I'm Jenna. What were you working on?"

He pulled a small piece of wood out of his pocket. At first it didn't look like anything at all, just some wood with the bark still on it. But when he turned it over, I saw it was a bird—a seagull.

"Whoa," I said, reaching for it without thinking. I stopped myself and looked up at him.

He handed it over. He obviously wasn't finished with it yet. The bird had one wing and just the beginning of a head and beak. It looked like it was trying to escape the wood and was halfway between capture and release.

"Where did you learn how to do that?" I asked.

"Boy Scout camp."

I looked up at him. His mouth was twisted in a mocking way. There was something about the stubborn set of his jaw and the way he'd hidden in the shadows that made me think he had a hard time playing by someone else's rules. "You don't really seem the Boy Scout type."

He raised his eyebrows. "Oh really? And how do Boy Scouts look?"

I thought about it for a minute. "Clean-cut."

"And I don't?"

His hair was dark and disheveled and made his eyes even bluer. But there were shadows underneath them, and his shoulders were stooped, like he was bracing himself for a blow. He looked cut, but not cleanly.

I handed the bird back to him. "I plead the fifth."

The wind tangled my hair, and I pushed it out of my face and shivered. I'd forgotten to bring a jacket.

Ian stood up. "Let me buy you coffee," he said, jerking his head toward the diner across the street. "Since you didn't give me away earlier."

"I don't know." Leaving the hospital grounds was probably a bad idea. I should have been keeping the peace between Mom and Mops. I needed to check on Pops, but I didn't want to see him hooked up to all those machines. He was supposed to be in his shop, fixing an old chair, or sitting on the bank of the pond with a beer and a pole. I didn't want to see him any other way. I was such a coward.

Ian put his hands in his pockets and looked at me from underneath thick lashes. "I'm infinitely better company than that notebook."

"Are you sure about that?" I had to admit, he was much less intimidating than the blank page.

He laughed. "What? You don't trust me?"

"I don't know you," I said.

He gave me a crooked grin. "But you want to."

Maybe. Wasn't October all about possibility?

"Is that the best you got?" I asked.

"It usually works on most girls."

"Probably not as much as you think it does." But I was lying, because he was almost as charming as he thought he was. His grin was arrogant, but his eyes were sad. I was intrigued. Besides, I was cold and not yet ready to go back inside the hospital. I stood up. "I'm buying my own coffee."

"My kind of girl."

We trekked through the trees to the busy highway that ran next to the hospital. I stopped, but Ian stepped off the curb. When he saw I wasn't following, he stepped back at the same time I started to walk. He laughed and grabbed my hand, pulling me forward as we ran across the street. I wanted to be shocked that I was holding hands with a guy I barely knew, but the connection was nice.

Ian dropped my hand as soon as we made it to the other side, but the warmth remained. We each bought coffee before sitting at one of the few open tables at the back of the crowded diner.

"Where are you from?" I asked, dumping in three packets of sugar. Ian drank his black.

He ran his hand through his hair and leaned back. "What makes you think I'm not from here?"

I grinned. "Your accent." Ian finished his words instead of dropping the endings. And his one-syllable words stayed that way.

He laughed. "You're one to talk."

"Oh please," I said, wrapping my hands around my cup to warm them. "You should hear my Pops." His thick Southern drawl was one of the things I loved about him. It added depth to his already colorful stories. He'd be better tomorrow. Maybe they'd even let him go home.

"Are you okay?" Ian asked. His voice was soft and full of concern.

"Sure," I said, taking a sip of my coffee. "Why?"

"You looked sad for a minute."

I didn't want to be. I sighed. "My grandpa's over there." I jerked my head toward the hospital.

There was something about the way his eyes found mine that made me think he knew what it was like to lose someone "I'm sorry."

I looked away. I wasn't ready to accept sympathy for something that hadn't happened yet, something that might not happen for a very long time. "He'll be fine." I hoped saying the words out loud would make them true.

"Are you hungry?" he asked.

I glanced at my phone and realized it was well past lunch and I still hadn't eaten. I never missed a meal. "A little."

"Be right back."

He walked over to the counter with his hands in his pockets. I could just see his eyes as he leaned over to study the pastry case, a tiny crease between his brows. He was taking his selection seriously.

His phone buzzed, bouncing around on the table where he'd left it. I couldn't help but glance at the screen. *Dr. Benson is waiting. Where are you?*

Ian returned with four different pieces of pie. "I couldn't decide," he said,, "so I thought we'd better try them all."

"Best idea I've ever heard." I took two of the plates from him. "I love pie."

"Better than cake?"

"Much better. I actually don't like icing."

He froze, holding one of his plates in mid-air. "I'm sad for you."

I laughed. "Don't be. For my birthday my grandma always makes me apple pies. They're my favorite." And Mom's. Our birthdays were three days apart, and we celebrated every year by eating apple pie and ice cream for dinner for an entire week. We also had matching birthday tiaras, but I'd stopped wearing mine when I was nine. Mom hadn't outgrown hers yet.

"Perfect." His phone buzzed again, but he ignored it, pointing instead at each of the desserts in turn. "I have apple, coconut cream, pumpkin, and pecan."

"We need more coffee." I picked my way across the diner, which was cozy and warm and filled with students and those trying to escape the October chill. Those of us trying to escape reality, too.

I returned with the refills. "You never answered my question," I said, setting the coffee on the table.

"Which one?" He took a bite of the pumpkin pie before sliding the plate toward me.

"Where you're from."

He shrugged. "Who knows? My dad's in the Army, so we move around all the time."

"Really?" I couldn't imagine. I'd been born in the Middleton hospital and lived in Solitude all my life. "Where else have you lived?"

"Colorado. Florida. Germany." He rattled these off like they were no big deal, but I envied people who'd actually seen the world instead of just imagining it. "Right now we live in Massachusetts."

"You're kidding." I wanted to go everywhere, only I'd never really been anywhere—a fact I was planning on changing as soon as I graduated. "Why in the world would you come here?"

"My mom's a nurse," he said, "and she's visiting a doctor friend."

"She made you tag along?"

"Long story. But we're leaving tomorrow." His mouth turned down at the corners, and I couldn't tell if he was relieved or disappointed.

"Where was your favorite place to live?" I asked.

"Colorado," he answered without hesitation.

"Not Germany?" I'd always wanted to go to Europe, and I imagined Germany was something out of a fairy tale, all dark forests and twisting castles. Florida would have been a cool place to live too. I'd only seen the ocean once, when I'd gone with my best friend Becca's family to the beach two years ago, but I'd fallen in love with it—the way it smelled, the way it whispered, the fact that it reached out and touched the other side of the world. I loved that the ocean stretched from exotic places to wash against my feet, and I couldn't even begin to imagine all the stories it carried.

"I was pretty young when we lived in Germany," he said. "I only remember pieces of it."

"Why Colorado?"

"It's open and clean," he said. "There's so much to do there, and there's not a whole bunch of people right on top of you. You can spread out in Colorado."

It sounded amazing. I could see him there, framed by mountains, his eyes the color of the open sky. I couldn't help being fascinated by this boy who had been to all the places I'd only ever dreamed about. I realized I was staring—and that he was staring back.

His phone buzzed again.

"I think someone is looking for you," I said. I was surprised my mom hadn't called yet. Hopefully Pops was better. Mom was probably too busy resenting Mops to realize I was even gone.

He picked the phone up and turned it off. "Maybe I don't want to be found."

I knew exactly what he meant.

We talked ourselves through all four pieces of pie. Ian let me have the last bite of apple. It wasn't until a siren wailed around us that I realized it was getting darker. Time seemed to have raced past me instead of plodding along like it normally did.

"I'd better get back," I said. I didn't want to go, but Mom and Mops had probably started another war in my absence. Ian's hand hovered over the small of my back as we left the coffee shop, and I felt warm even though he wasn't touching me. We crossed the street and strolled through the pines that covered the hospital grounds. There was a tension, a drawing out of the conversation as we realized we were soon going to have to go our separate ways. Tomorrow, he would be going back to Massachusetts, and I would be back in Solitude.

"Have you ever felt like you were standing on the edge of something?" I asked.

He leaned closer to me, his hair falling in his eyes. "I feel like that right now."

My face flushed under his scrutiny, and I wondered if Ian and I could talk so honestly because we knew we'd never see each other again. "I just feel like I'm waiting for something great to happen. I don't know what it is yet, but sometimes I wake up and I'm excited for no reason." I smiled. "You know how you felt on Christmas morning when you were a kid?"

He nodded.

"You ever feel that now?"

"Sometimes," he said. "And sometimes I feel like I've already stepped off the edge and hit bottom."

His face was full of regret, and he sounded so much older than he was.

My phone rang. Mom. I didn't answer it, but I knew my time with Ian was up. "I've got to go."

Ian's smile was sad. "Thanks for the company," he said. "I needed it."

And until he said it, I hadn't realized how much I'd needed it too.

He reached out and grabbed my hand. His was warm and calloused, and a flush fanned across my cheeks. He turned my palm up and gently opened my fingers.

He dropped the whittled wood into my hand. It was still warm from his pocket, and I ran my thumb over the smoothed edge. He pushed my fingers closed until they were tight around the half-finished seagull.

"So you'll remember me," he said. And then he was gone.

ONE

JENNA

Mom dragged Pops's memory behind her like an overpacked bag. It was late May, seven months after his death, and she still wore her grief like a shroud. It changed everything about her. Sometimes, when I was alone, I forgot he was gone. I forgot that he wasn't at home, puttering around in his shop, or sitting on his back porch, complaining about the heat. It was weird how someone so alive could suddenly cease to exist. But when I looked at Mom, I couldn't forget. His death was etched in the stoop of her shoulders and the lines at the corners of her mouth. Her eyes, which used to be full of laughter, were empty.

It wasn't that I didn't love Pops, or that I didn't miss him. I loved him to the moon and back, which was what we always said when I was little and would crawl up in his lap. And I missed the hell out of him. I'd always thought that those I loved were invincible, immune. I took his life for granted, thinking we had all this time, but I was wrong. Which was why I wasn't planning on wasting any more of it.

While Pops's body was in the Solitude Cemetery, his spirit was very much in our house. I didn't believe in the kind of ghosts that rattled chains and appeared out of thin air, but I knew that memories could haunt. Pops wasn't ever really going to be gone because he'd left so much of himself behind.

I was being hard on my mom, mostly because I didn't know what else to do. And maybe I felt a little guilty. I wasn't with Pops when he'd taken his last breath. I didn't get to say good-bye. It was a decision I couldn't take back, a mistake that would haunt me for the rest of my life. But I couldn't change it; I could only try to move on. Surely that wouldn't be so impossible.

It was late when Mom came home from work, but I'd come to expect that. She had her back to me as I walked into the kitchen—heels, pencil skirt, responsible blazer. Mom had mastered camouflage. But she was chugging something out of her plastic glass, and I knew it wasn't milk.

"Hey," I said.

She jumped at my voice, then set her cup in the sink and turned around, throwing me a forced smile. She tried to pretend she wasn't falling apart, but by the time she got home, the paint was beginning to peel. "Hey!"

"You hungry?" I asked. I opened the fridge and started pulling out leftovers.

"I grabbed something on the way home," she told me. I wasn't sure if she was telling the truth or not, but I shoved everything back in the fridge. "Becca got off okay?" she asked.

"As far as I know." Becca was off touring Europe with some rogue aunt. She'd left this morning, the first day of summer vacation. I was trying not to be bitter about the fact that I was stuck in Solitude.

Mom made a small noise, like a wounded animal in a trap, and I closed the refrigerator door and looked at her. She was crying. Again.

I hated myself for being aggravated with her. What kind of horrible person was I? But I couldn't stand it when Mom cried, and she had cried every single day for the past seven months. I missed Pops more than anything, but crying every day wasn't ever going to bring him back, and I didn't see the point. She needed to pull herself together.

"What's wrong?" I asked, although I didn't have to.

"I sold the house."

"Pops's house?" I asked. Mom flinched. "When?"

"Last week."

She'd sold the house. I didn't think she was ever going to. If we hadn't needed the money, I guess she wouldn't have. It would've just sat out there, lonely and empty, until it rotted to the ground. I tried sketching out a possible tenant, but it was weird imagining someone else in Pops's house.

"Why didn't you tell me?"

"I didn't feel like talking about it. But they're moving in this week, so…" Her voice trailed off as she turned her back to me and stared out the window into the dark. "I'm an orphan," she said.

I stepped closer and put my hand on her shoulder. It was shaking. "Mom, you're thirty-five years old. And you still have Mops. You're not an orphan."

"But it feels like I am," she argued.

"I'm sorry." I didn't know what else to say.

"Ignore me," she said, but she didn't really mean it. "I'm just tired. I'm going to bed."

She slunk into the shadowed living room, and I listened for the click of her bedroom door.

I needed out of the house. I put on my running shoes and slipped into the dark.

I ran out to the train yard. I couldn't see more than a couple of steps in front of me, and I had to be careful not to trip over the abandoned tracks. Chains clanked somewhere in the distance, the ghost of a memory, of a time when Solitude was a place people came to instead of one they tried to leave. Back when the trains ran. Nothing ran here anymore. Just me, fueled by escape. I'd always wanted to ride on a train. Pops had been full of stories about the railroad, and when he'd told them, I'd heard the metal heartbeat and shrill whistle, sounds that promised adventure or, at the very least, a change in scenery. But now the only thing that blew across the open space was emptiness, trailed by a stifling breeze that couldn't even dry the sweat covering my skin.

God, I loved running at night. I loved the quietness of it, loved the cocoon it wrapped around me, loved that it was a two-way mirror, a way for me to view the world without being seen. That was one reason I always waited until dark to go running. That, and to escape the heat. To escape my mother. Sometimes I thought if I ran fast enough, I could escape everything, could step out of my own skin as easily as shrugging off a sweater. It hadn't happened yet, but it might. I was getting faster.

I let my legs lead. That was another thing I loved about running--autopilot. There were several glorious minutes whenI wasn't thinking at all before I realized I was running a well-worn path out toward Pops's. I hadn't used the trail in a while. The paved road was the long way around. I had blazed a shortcut long ago, cutting the ten-mile drive to three on foot.

I stepped out of the trees at the back edge of the property and was surprised to see a single light on in an upstairs window. A shadow crossed briefly in front, and there was an odd tug in my chest. I wondered how long it would take me to get used to someone else living in Pops's house, strangers eating meals in the kitchen and working in his shop. I couldn't believe a person could build an entire life, so completely inhabit a place like Pops had, and then just disappear. Did the house remember him at all?

I stopped at the edge of the pond. Pops had all sorts of stories about this pond, like the catfish that swallowed his best hunting dog. He'd scared me with that one for years, until I was finally old enough to figure out he was pulling my leg. But the stories I liked best were the ones we'd written ourselves. Like the time Mops had fallen in headfirst trying to reel in a fish. She'd lost her balance and tumbled over into the water. She'd jumped up, sputtering and fussing, and Pops had laughed until tears rolled down his cheeks. She was as mad as an old wet hen, and Pops had called her that for several weeks.

But mostly I remembered the quiet of the water lapping against the shore and the sweet smell of Pops's pipe. I'd always liked it out here. It was a shame I hadn't really appreciated it until it was no longer mine to enjoy.

The light in the window cut off, leaving me with nothing else to focus on other than memories and a small rock on the edge of the pond. There was a tiny silver-colored vein running through it, and if I eyed it at just the right angle, it looked like a heart. I scooped it up and held it tightly in my fist as I turned around and headed home. I didn't want to get caught trespassing. It made me sad knowing I was no longer welcome on the land where I'd grown up. Such an inconsequential thing, but in a small town, the slightest disruption from normalcy could seem like a cataclysmic shift.

Mom was asleep on the couch when I got home, her knees curled to her chest, her hands tucked underneath her chin. Her red tumbler sat next to an empty bottle of wine, and she had washed away her ruined mascara. She looked like a kid. I pulled the blanket off the recliner and covered her up, kissing her on the forehead like she had when she'd put me to bed when I was small. It was much easier to love my mother when she was asleep.

I awoke the next morning to Shakespeare: *Bid me run, and I will strive with things impossible.* I stretched and let my eyes trace the words over and over again. I had sixty-seven quotes painted on my ceiling, all intended to inspire me to greatness in every aspect of my life. But mostly I waded around in mediocrity, thinking I'd found my way forward only to discover I'd circled back to where I'd started.

Mom was in the kitchen when I got there, still nursing her coffee. She was usually at work by now. "Get dressed," she said.

"Good morning to you, too." I looked down at my shorts and T-shirt. "I *am* dressed."

"In something that doesn't look like you fished it out of the trash."

"Why?"

"Because you're taking this to Mrs. McAlister." She pointed to a huge basket that was taking up most of the counter. There was a bottle of wine in it, as well as fruit and nuts. I couldn't see everything because there was an enormous pink and black polka-dotted bow covering most of it.

"Who?"

"Ruth McAlister." Mom took a deep breath. "She's the one who bought the house."

"So why do we have to go over there?" I asked.

"You. *You're* going over there. I can't."

I glared at her. I was not volunteering for the mission. I really didn't want to see other people's things in Pops's house. "No."

Mom sighed. She'd never had much patience. "It's the polite thing to do. To welcome them to town and thank them for doing business with me." Mom was a real estate agent. She gave me a guilty look. "And to pick up the rest of the boxes. We need to get them out of their way."

"Shouldn't we have done that before they moved in?" I asked.

"They were sort of in a hurry. And I wasn't ready."

She still wasn't.

I poured myself a bowl of cereal and curled up in the overstuffed chair in the corner. It was my favorite place in the house, aside from my room. Sunlight streamed over my shoulders. "Well I can't," I told her around a mouthful of cereal. "I'm working today. Besides, that's your job, not mine."

Mom had perfected the eye of judgment. "You're going," she said, "because I said so. Besides, I already called Mops and told her you'd be late." Mom's voice was tight. It always was when she talked about her mother. "She was fine with it."

Sometimes having my grandma as my boss sucked.

"Anyway," Mom was still talking, "I think Mrs. McAlister has a son just your age."

As if that was going to make everything about this okay. I rolled my eyes. I couldn't understand why Mom wanted me all fixed up with a boyfriend. When she was my age, she'd dated the hottest guy in school, and that hadn't worked out so well for her. I was focused on getting an academic scholarship out of here, shaving a minute off my 5K time, and finally seeing all the places I'd only ever read about.

"He's going to be a senior," Mom said, "and he's new in town and doesn't know anyone. You're going, and you're going to be nice."

"Fine." But I wasn't changing clothes.

* * *

I had to admit, I was a little curious as to just who in the world had decided that Solitude would be a good place to live. It was too small to be on a map. But Solitude was safe. People rarely locked their doors. The most dangerous thing that ever happened here was when ancient Mrs. Pettigo decided to drive herself to the store instead of waiting on her elderly son. And since old Mrs. Pettigo couldn't see a damn thing, anyone within a quarter mile of her and her moving vehicle was likely to lose a limb.

Pops's place was between Solitude and Middleton and in the middle of exactly nowhere; I had to turn off the paved road long before I wanted to. There was nothing but woods that far out, the houses spaced apart enough that they couldn't be considered neighbors. The stretches between them were filled with trees, broken occasionally by open fields. I knew every tree, every curve in the road. And even though it had been seven months since I'd driven out that way, it was like returning home after a long trip—not that I would know anything about that. But I imagined it was something like this, a tugging on the heart in two different directions, and I couldn't blame my mom for refusing to come. She had way more memories tied up in this place than I ever could.

The driveway was overgrown, testifying to Pops's absence, but I couldn't have passed it if I tried—the Bronco slowed automatically. It had been Pops's before it became mine, his fishing rig that usually sat underneath the metal canopy attached to the side of the workshop. The shiny truck parked there instead was an imposter.

The house gave me a reproachful look as I pulled up in front and hopped out, the yard full of tangled bushes and brown spots. I grabbed the welcome basket, which had gained at least five pounds on the ride over. I labored up the steps and tried to shuffle it a bit, but there was no way I was going to be able to hold that thing with one arm. I kicked the door instead of knocking.

Footsteps echoed through the house, and for a split second, I half-expected Pops to answer, grumbling about having to get up to get the door. I turned sideways just as the door opened. It wasn't Pops, but I would be lying if I said those blue eyes weren't familiar.

TWO

IAN

Legs. That's all I saw when I wrenched open the old door. Long, lean, muscled legs. Beautiful. Then the girl turned. I pried my eyes away from her tanned legs. Her eyes were green with gold flecks. I hadn't ever seen anything like them. Her hair was brown, but with red that somehow managed to catch the sunlight even though she was standing in the shade of the porch. She gave me a blinding smile that I somehow felt I didn't deserve.

"Ian, who is it?" Mom shouted from somewhere inside.

"Um." I hadn't even asked.

The girl's smile faded and then disappeared completely. "Jenna," she said, her voice hoarse.

Mom walked up behind me then, wiping her hands on her shorts. Her smile was plastered on like some overdone Halloween mask. Jenna didn't seem to notice.

"My mom, Vivian Oliver, sent this over. To welcome you to Solitude."

"Please, come in," Mom said, stepping out of the way. She pinched my arm hard.

21

"Oh, sorry," I said, feeling stupid. "Let me." I grabbed the basket from her—it was ridiculously heavy—and followed Mom into the kitchen.

"Excuse the mess," Mom said, "we're still unpacking."

I set the basket on the counter. Jenna looked around the kitchen, her eyes a little sad. She smiled politely at my mom. It was hard to get my brain to focus. I just kept staring like an idiot.

"I also need to get the boxes my mom left," Jenna said.

Mom nodded. "They're in the dining room. Ian will help you carry them out to your car. I should finish unpacking." Mom threw me a warning look out of the corner of her eye, which was unnecessary. I knew the rules—she reminded me often enough.

"So what's in the boxes?" I asked, picking one up and carrying it out to her car.

She opened the back. "My grandpa's stuff. He died in October." I couldn't read the look she gave me.

"I'm sorry," I said.

We grabbed more boxes from the house, piling them into her Bronco. There weren't many, but my shirt soon stuck to my back.

"So," I asked, "how long have you lived in Solitude?"

"All my life." She sighed.

I couldn't imagine staying in one place for so long.

After we filled her backseat, we headed back inside to double-check that we'd gotten everything.

"You really don't remember me?" Jenna asked.

"Should I?" I spoke before I thought. Of course I should. She was just going to be one of the many things I was supposed to remember but didn't. But I couldn't understand how this beautiful girl could tumble into the dark holes of my memory.

"No," she said, squaring her shoulders. "I don't guess you should."

I heard Luke rattling around in his room. Typical. He'd holed up in there as soon as we got here, but let a pretty girl stop by, and he was suddenly ready to make an appearance. He was always ruining things. But Mom had made it very clear that I was supposed to try to keep him out of trouble. It was going to be a full-time job.

"Um, I'd better get back to work. I have a lot left to unpack," I said.

"Of course." Jenna's voice was hard. "I'm sorry I just showed up. My mom," she said, as if that were all the explanation I needed.

"It was nice to meet you." I hurried out of the room. Mom eyed me as I passed by—she must have heard Luke too.

Jenna said something in return, but I was already halfway up the stairs. Not a good impression at all. It was all Luke's fault. Most things were.

JENNA

He really didn't remember me. It bothered me, mostly because I felt guilty. I didn't want to admit that I'd been with a boy I hardly knew when Pops died. I'd said good-bye to Ian instead of my own grandfather. I'd carried that guilt around for the past seven months. Obviously, he hadn't been worth it. I didn't even warrant a footnote in his life.

I walked back into the kitchen, which, despite how achingly familiar it was, had undergone its own metamorphosis. The wallpaper was peeling and the kitchen cabinets were warped and stained. The refrigerator was too big for the opening, so it was sitting in the middle of the room. The familiar gingham curtains were gone, leaving the window naked. The house had been shut up for a long time, and it smelled musty; it used to smell like cinnamon and pipe tobacco. I walked to the laundry room. Pops had marked my mom's height on the doorjamb with black marker, then mine with red. I reached over and ran my fingers along the wood. My red lines were always just above Mom's. Her lines stopped at twelve, when she reached five feet. Mine stopped at thirteen—I'd hit five feet six inches that year. I'd shot up over the summer, showing up to seventh grade taller than any of the boys. They'd teased me about my skinny legs, and I'd cried when they weren't looking.

God, this was like being seven all over again. I'd sat on the counters and helped Mops cook. She'd let me make all kinds of messes. We dyed Easter eggs there, and carved pumpkins, and made really ugly Christmas cookies. The past seemed to hover somewhere just out of sight, waiting for me to look the other way so it could slide into place. I remembered where every dish was supposed to go. The nail where Mops's apron used to hang was empty.

Even after Mops had moved out, she would come over here on Sundays and bring Pops dinner. We would all sit at the table and listen to his stories. He was always full of them—and full of bull too. After dinner, Mops would clean up the kitchen while Pops would lean back in his chair and smoke his pipe. In the summers we might go down to the pond before dark; sometimes we'd throw a line in, and sometimes I'd look for turtles and catch tadpoles.

The house didn't smell the way I remembered   didn't sound the same, didn't feel the same. Standing in the kitchen, I was slapped in the face with Pops's death. I couldn't forget, couldn't pretend he was just out of sight. The house screamed his absence.

"Looking for something?"

I whirled around at Mrs. McAlister's voice. She couldn't have been much older than forty, but she looked tired. There were lines around her eyes and ones that pulled down at the corners of her mouth. Her dark hair was streaked with gray. She looked wary. I got the feeling she wanted me to leave.

"Sorry," I said. "My grandpa used to live here."

Mrs. McAlister gave me a small smile. "Thank you so much for stopping by." She didn't really look like she meant it. "And for the basket."

"Sure." I stepped around her and out into the hall. She followed me to the door and shut it behind me before I'd even gotten off the porch.

I opened the Bronco door, then looked up at the house before I slid in. Ian's face peered out of an upstairs window—the room I'd once slept in. I climbed in and started the car. When I looked back at the window, he was gone.

THREE

IAN

I woke up late, and it took me a minute to remember where I was. I'd dreamt about the tree house again. For just a moment, caught in that strip between waking and sleeping, I could smell the cut wood and hear the buzz of a lawn mower. But then I was fully awake, and the feeling shattered.

It was quiet upstairs. Luke wasn't around—hadn't been much in the week since we'd moved in. There were unpacked boxes still stacked outside his bedroom door. He'd always been irresponsible; it was one of the reasons he and Dad couldn't get along. They'd walked away from their last argument bloody and bruised—literally. Fistfights had a tendency to do that. Some mistakes just couldn't be forgiven. We left because our family refused to look our problems directly in the eye. Better to neglect them completely and hope they starved to death. Then Dad could hide the bones in the basement, and Mom could plant roses in front so our neighbors could go on admiring our perfect yard while all the time there were piles of problems decomposing underneath us. The divorce was a shitstorm that had threatened to unearth everything we'd been trying to keep buried. Mom was going to make sure that didn't happen again—because the McAlisters were perfect.

Even though Luke and I had once been inseparable, we mostly avoided each other these days. He was the reason my parents divorced. If he'd just been able to control his temper then Dad would have been able to control his. I blamed Luke for having to leave the familiar behind. I didn't know who I was here. I wasn't an athlete or an honor student. I wasn't anything everyone kept telling me I was supposed to be but couldn't really remember. And God, I wanted to. Because if I could just remember, maybe we would be normal again. But at least there weren't any bones in this basement. Yet. Mom was determined to keep it that way, which meant I was stuck reining in my brother. And he was being moodier than usual.

"Ian?" My mom's voice came from the living room.

"Yeah, it's me." I walked across the hall. There were dents in the old wooden floor, a paint splatter here and there. Our house in Massachusetts had been new and pristine, still smelling like paint and wood—the perfect museum for the perfect family of the perfect soldier. This house smelled a little musty, and the wallpaper was peeling in places. This was a better setting for the family we were now—broken and scattered.

This house had a lot of windows, and Mom had tacked thick blankets over them until we could get curtains. The only things close enough to see in our windows were bugs and coyotes, but Mom was used to neighborhoods—or maybe she was just protecting our secrets. The blankets made the living room feel like a cave. Or a tomb.

Mom was sitting on the floor, a busted cardboard box next to her, the floor strewn with photo albums. The pictures were scattered.

"What happened in here?" I asked.

She'd been crying. She tried to play it off, but I could tell. I always could. "I was trying to put these away, and the box broke." I sat next to her and helped her sort the pictures, our lives reduced to ink on paper, every single moment of the past seventeen years frozen in time.

"Remember that trip?" she asked. She sounded hopeful as she showed me a picture of our whole family in front of the Yellowstone sign.

I did. "Gophers," I said.

Mom laughed. "I'd forgotten that part."

Luke had begged Dad for a slingshot when we'd stopped at an old-fashioned general store on the drive west. Dad had gotten us each one, but Luke was the only one who could use his. When we'd stopped at some cabins to spend a few days, Luke and I had hidden behind a bush, lying on our bellies and being as still as eight-year-old boys can be. I was surprised when the first gopher popped up out of his hole. I was even more surprised when Luke nailed it in the side of the head with a rock. I'd tried hitting a couple but never even got close. I'd watched him instead. He'd also hit a bird and a passing car. That was what got us in trouble. The driver slammed on his brakes and Luke and I took off sprinting for our cabin, but the guy followed and told on us. Dad made us apologize and went to see the damage—there was none, somehow—but when he'd gotten back, instead of punishing Luke, he'd congratulated him on his aim. That was back before the cracks appeared.

Funny how my memory worked, that I could remember that so easily but couldn't recall a year ago. And while I was grateful that the black hole in my brain hadn't gobbled up everything, I was desperate to find the pieces it had.

The years were jumbled together on the floor, and I picked up a photo of me with a girl I should have recognized but didn't. Mom snatched it out of my hand and stuck it in the middle of her pile. I'd only gotten the briefest of glimpses, but the girl had been looking at me and laughing. I couldn't remember if I'd been happy. There were a few of me in my football jersey and one in my baseball uniform, but none of them felt real because I couldn't remember them for myself. I couldn't hold them in my head and examine them from all angles.

I picked up another picture, this one showing Luke and me outfitted for Cub Scouts. We had our little shirts with patches – Luke had a Craftsman for woodworking and I had one for Citizenship. Luke never did earn that one. We had our arms slung around each other. I had this big goofy grin, but Luke had already perfected his crooked smirk. It made him look like trouble, even at ten.

"Remember Luke getting us kicked out of camp?" I asked Mom, showing her the picture.

Dallas Caruthers had dared Luke to sneak over to the girls' church camp on the other side of the lake. It was a good three-mile hike, and Luke had wanted me to go with him, but I wouldn't. I didn't want to get in trouble. Luke never backed out of a dare, so he'd marched through the woods alone, circling around the lake and whispering at an open window until Mary Catherine Johnson had come out in her nightgown and agreed to go canoeing with him. I had no idea how he pulled that one off, but they were busted trying to launch the canoe. Poor Mary Catherine. Her dad had been the lead pastor at that camp. They'd probably sent her to a convent.

"I can't believe they kicked me out too. I didn't even do anything." I was always paying for Luke's mistakes.

"They didn't kick you out," Mom said. "Don't you remember?"

I didn't. I shook my head.

Her smile was sad. "Your dad was in the car, reaming Luke out, and I came to your cabin to say bye. Your face got all red when you realized Luke wasn't staying. I'd never seen you so mad. You said if Luke was leaving, you were too. Then you ripped the Citizenship patch off your shirt, threw it at the camp counselor, and stormed out to the car. Your dad was furious."

I remembered *that* part. We'd been grounded for the rest of the summer. "Has he called?"

Mom concentrated on getting the pictures back in the album. "He's been really busy."

"Yeah," I said, getting to my feet. "I'm sure that's it." Mom opened her mouth to say something, but I interrupted. "I'm hungry."

I rummaged around in the fridge, piling everything I could find on the counter, and fixed myself a couple of sandwiches. I hadn't talked to Dad since the day we'd left—which had been almost three weeks ago. No one was *that* busy. He didn't forgive or forget, but I was surprised that he could cut us out of his life so completely, like we were some parasitic tumor he was glad to finally be rid of. How was I supposed to piece the family back together when no one else was even trying?

"I have to work tonight," Mom said as she stepped into the kitchen. She rummaged through one of the remaining boxes. "Late," she added.

She was always working late. She'd thrown herself into her new job at the Middleton hospital, and I was pretty sure it was the only thing holding her together. She had to focus on what everyone else needed instead of what was happening here. She had to take care of other people instead of taking care of herself. If she stood still for just a moment, the world might come crashing in, a wave on the beach. I was doing everything I could to help keep the waves out at sea, but I was afraid that, eventually, they were going to knock us all down. And I wouldn't be able to stop them.

Mom stacked a few pans in the bottom cupboard and tried to shut the door. It swung open slowly, the hinges creaking. She tried again, but the door refused to stay closed. I leaned against the counter, watching her get more and more frustrated, knowing that her anger had nothing to do with the cabinet. She slammed it shut, and it held until she stood up and opened another box. Then it swung open again.

She swore at the cabinets and glared at the fridge. "We'll need to have some work done in here," she said.

"Luke can do it." He'd spent the last couple of summers working with Mom's brother in his cabinet shop.

Mom pressed her mouth into a tight, thin line and nodded once. Her eyes were hard. She was mad at Luke too. "Your first appointment with Dr. Benson is next Thursday."

"I don't understand why I have to talk to him." I'd been seeing a doctor in Massachusetts, but he'd been useless. Just like I was pretty sure this one would be. I couldn't count on someone else to find my memories or get rid of the headaches. I was going to have to do that myself.

"He's one of the reasons we moved here. He thinks he can help you." Mom refused to look at me.

"Help me with what, Mom? There's nothing wrong with me!" The waves sounded closer. "What about Luke?" Mom flinched. "He should be the one going, not me." He was supposed to go in Massachusetts, but he'd always refused to show up. "The divorce, the bags under your eyes—they're all his fault!" I tossed my plate, sandwiches uneaten, into the sink. The plate snapped in two. "I'm not Luke," I said, gripping the edge of the sink, "so stop punishing me for his screwups."

Mom looked at me then, her eyes full of tears. I was the one who had to look away. I couldn't stand to see my mother cry.

"Of course there's nothing wrong with you. I never said there was. But, under the circumstances..." She stopped, like she'd said too much. But she hadn't said anything at all. She never did. No one ever did. Something had happened to cause my memory to gum up, but no one was saying what. Everyone thought it would be better for me to figure it out on my own. I was trying as hard as I could, but nothing seemed to be working.

I sighed. I didn't know where that sudden anger had come from—that wasn't me—but it was just as suddenly gone, leaving me raw and worn-out. "Wait." I crossed the small space and put my arms around her. She was so fragile and tiny, and I had no idea when that had happened. "I'm sorry."

She patted my shoulder and stepped away. "This is hard on all of us." She wouldn't look at me. She went to her room, leaving me in the kitchen with my guilt. I leaned over the sink and stared at the broken plate. It had cracked cleanly down the middle.

"That was elegant."

I looked up and saw Luke's reflection in the window.

"Haven't seen much of you lately," I said.

"Thought you didn't want to."

He was right. "Can we not do this right now? I'm really not in the mood to deal with your bullshit."

"Fine." He shrugged, but there was hurt in his voice. If I was going to piece us back together, I was going to have to forgive him. Just not today.

Luke stared out the window, refusing to look at me as I turned and headed back to my room. When he spoke, there was something like fear in his voice. "Maybe he *can* help you remember," he said.

But the way everyone was acting, I wondered if I really wanted to.

FOUR

JENNA

"Mops?" The little bell above the door jingled as I stepped into the store, the smell of old paper and dust welcoming me home.

"Back here!" Her disembodied voice floated across the stacks of books. I followed it to the back corner, where Mops was digging through an old shopping bag. She looked like she'd already put in a full day's work. It didn't matter what time Mops went to bed; she was always up at dawn, and before most people had even had their coffee, Mops had done a load of laundry, cooked breakfast, read the paper, and straightened her apartment.

Reclaimed was her store. It was cozy, full of books and chairs too ugly to keep in someone's house and too comfortable to throw away. There were rusted washing machines and clothes no one would dare wear in public, as well as old rugs and anything else no one wanted but couldn't stand to toss in the trash. Mops hated waste, and since she never threw anything away, she pretty much had to open a secondhand store. "Old Miss Harris dropped this off over the weekend," she told me, elbow-deep in the torn bag.

I loved the way Mops called other people "old," people who were only slightly older than she was. Or sometimes who were younger. But Mops didn't age. She was the youngest sixty-year-old on the planet.

Mops stood up, grimacing pleasantly as her back cracked, and swiped her freckled arm across her freckled forehead. Her hair was swept up in a nub of a ponytail, but several graying strands had escaped and were sticking to her neck. She dusted her hands on her overalls and grinned at me. "I put these aside for you."

She pulled a plastic shopping bag out from behind one of the shelves. It was full of books Mops thought I might like—travel books on Bali, Canada, and New Zealand. It was hard to believe that anyone from Solitude had actually been to those places. There were several old classics, too. *Frankenstein* was missing a cover, and *The Strange Case of Dr. Jekyll and Mr. Hyde* had been taped back together. There was also some book called *The Hounds of the Morrigan*, which I'd never heard of but looked pretty good. The last book in the bag was a good-condition hardback on writing.

"Thanks." I grinned.

Mops shrugged, not even looking at me. "Just thought they sounded interesting."

"How much do I owe you?"

"I'll take it out of your check," she lied. Mops had been supplying me with books since I was born. She'd taught me to read and love words, then Pops had taught me how to weave them into a story. Or in his case, a tall tale.

At noon we locked the front door and headed upstairs to eat. She'd moved into the apartment upstairs when I was seven, but she'd gone by Pops's house on Sundays. Sometimes, if Pops was "showing out," as Mops called it, she would let him fend for himself until he could straighten up, but that never lasted for long. She loved Pops—she just hadn't been able to live with him anymore. They didn't divorce, just lived apart. I was pretty sure she missed Pops even more than Mom did. She just didn't show it the same way. Mops pulled several large containers of leftovers out of the fridge; she still hadn't figured out how to cook for one. It worked in my favor, since Mops had to be the best cook in the county.

"You working tonight?" Mops asked.

"No. Right now he has me on the schedule for Wednesdays, Thursdays, and every other Saturday, but I'm sure I'll be filling in a lot." This summer I'd added a job at the pizza place. College was going to be expensive—and my only ticket out.

"Heard from Becca lately?" Mops asked.

"Got an email yesterday." She was forbidden to text me from Europe. "She's somewhere in France." Becca didn't even know how lucky she was, since she wasn't the least bit interested in looking at "paintings of dead people" or "eating in a crappy pub where some writer dropped dead." (Her words, not mine.) But she was enjoying the scenery— she'd already flirted with a half-dozen guys and managed to kiss one who didn't speak a word of English. She'd barely been there a week.

"I would have loved to see the Eiffel Tower," Mops said, "although, to be honest, the one place I really wanted to go was Rome. In high school, our English teacher took a group there one summer. I didn't get to go."

"You regret it?"

Mops poured us each a glass of tea while I set the plates on the table. "At my age, one has a lot of regrets. But I'd be afraid to go back and change a one of them." She set the glasses on the table and took the leftovers out of the microwave. Mops was good at taking the past and making it work—leftovers, secondhand clothes. But I didn't want a life of recycled regrets. I wanted something new.

"If I changed one thing," she said, "it might change everything. And while there's a lot I would have done differently, there's things that came out of my mistakes that were worth it. That's what life is—a whole bunch of good and bad strung together, and without the bad, the good wouldn't be as good."

I knew she was probably right, but I wanted her to have something new, too. "You could still go, you know," I said.

"Nah, you can go for me. You know, when you get right down to it, a place is just a place. You can be unhappy drinking champagne in Paris, or you can be happy in Solitude, digging through other people's junk."

I didn't agree with her there. I was getting out.

My mom had spent her childhood envisioning herself becoming something. Instead, she'd gotten pregnant her senior year, a mistake that had followed her around her entire life. People in Solitude didn't forget, especially when that mistake lived and breathed and ran cross-country for Solitude High School. It hadn't mattered that Mom had been a cheerleader, honor student, and president of the drama club. And I hadn't figured out how to step out of the shade cast by my mother's mistakes. How did Peter Pan separate himself from his own shadow? My only option was to escape to a place where no one knew who Vivian Oliver was. That way, I could finally have the space to be who I was—and make my own mistakes instead of being someone else's.

"I don't want to get stuck here," I told Mops.

"Like me?" she asked.

"No. Like Mom. You chose to stay here. That's different." More than anything, I wanted my life to be a result of my *choices*, not chance.

"She had a choice too. We all do. And you should probably ease up on your mom a bit."

That surprised me. "Why? She's never eased up on you." If anything, she'd gotten more critical in the months since Pops died. Pops had been the seam that had tacked those two very different materials together—Mom's silk to Mops's denim—and when the seam unraveled, the cloth tore. And while denim was strong and easily patched, silk was delicate and irreparable. I didn't even know where to begin.

Mops sighed, and in that moment, she looked every bit of sixty. "You shouldn't make the same mistakes as your mother."

I wasn't planning on it.

We spent most of the afternoon combing through several tubs of junk that had been stacked in a back corner and forgotten. So far, the most interesting thing I'd found was a container of used leg wax. I was relieved when Mops sent me to the post office. Mr. Anderson waved at me as I passed the pharmacy. He'd been standing at the same counter for as long as I could remember, and he looked exactly the same as he had when I was a kid. He'd given me a sucker every time Mops and I had gone in, and if he thought Mops wasn't looking, he'd given me two.

The sun glared off the glass in the windows of the insurance company, and my shirt was damp before I'd even gone half a block. There was a "For Lease" sign hanging crooked in the old Marshall's Cleaners building, and Tommy's Shoes still had a "Going out of Business" sign plastered to the front window, even though they'd been out of business for at least five years. Solitude began trickling away years ago when the railroad left, but it didn't get really bad until five years ago when the appliance factory shut its doors for good. Now the only people who remained were either the ones who had nowhere else to go or those who were too stubborn to let go. And for all my complaining, it made me sad to imagine what this place would look like in twenty years.

The heat radiated off the cracked sidewalk, which had been put down in more prosperous times, and I was grateful for the cold air as I stepped into the tiny post office.

"Jenna Oliver!" Mrs. Bridges exclaimed. I saw her at least once a week, but each time she still acted as if she hadn't seen me in a year. "Heard your mom finally sold the house."

"Yes, ma'am." I stuck the key in the lock and turned. Not much mail today.

"It was about time." She sniffed. "I hope they aren't Communists," she added in her mock whisper.

I had to bite my cheek to keep from laughing. "Now, Mrs. Bridges," I teased, "you know Mom wouldn't sell Pops's house to Communists."

"I would hope not," she said. "Now you tell your grandma I said hello."

"Sure will." I pushed through the door and back out into the oppressive heat. And right into Ian McAlister.

"Oh!" I exclaimed. And then that was it. I didn't know what else to say.

Mrs. Bridges was right behind me, and since I'd frozen where I stood, she nearly ran me over. "Jenna Oliver, you know better than to block doorways."

"Sorry, Mrs. Bridges." I stepped out of her way.

She glared at Ian. "I don't know you."

"This is Ian McAlister," I told her. "He just moved into Pops's place."

Her eyes narrowed. "You aren't a Communist, are you?"

Ian looked at me for help, but he was on his own with that one. "Um, no?" he said.

I tried not to laugh as she got into her car and backed out of the space. She barely avoided clipping the light pole.

"Who was that?" Ian asked.

"Helen Bridges. She's been protecting Solitude from Communists since 1952."

"Oh." And then he said my name. I didn't know why that caused my heart to pound so hard. I'd heard my name thousands of times in my life. And it wasn't anything special—just the mixing of ordinary letters in an ordinary way. But there was something about his voice and my name that seemed too intimate for the post office.

"I'm really glad I ran into you," Ian said. "I wanted to apologize for the other day."

"Forget it." I was trying to. I was also trying to ignore how sincere he looked and how, somehow, with him standing right in front of me, it was easier to pretend life was as solid as it had been seven months ago. Before Pops died. Before Mom started drinking.

"But see, forgetting is the easy part," he said. "Probably the only thing I'm really good at these days. Well, besides being rude. But can you blame me? Just moved to town and a beautiful girl shows up on my porch."

"Spare me."

"At least let me take you out to make up for the way I acted." He did look remorseful.

"So a date with me is penance?"

He grinned. "Are you always this difficult?"

I shrugged. "Depends on who you ask."

"Please," he said, and I swear his cool blue eyes dropped the air temperature by two degrees. "I'm new to town. The least you could do is show me around."

"So now you want to guilt me into a date?" I asked.

He looked hopeful. "Is it working?"

More than he knew. Way more than I wanted it to. I had no idea what it was about this boy. I'd told myself I wasn't going to waste my time. But my resolve was slipping.

I sighed and tried to sound as if I were doing him a favor. "Fine."

"Great. Friday?"

"Okay. Are you going to guilt me into paying, too?"

"Might. You will have to pick the place. I don't really know my way around yet."

"You'll learn in five minutes. It's a small town. Well, if you want something edible, it'll have to be Repete's." I didn't really want to spend my night off in there, but there wasn't much else. "Hope you like pizza."

"Sounds great. Should I pick you up?"

"I get off at five. I'll meet you there at six," I told him.

"I'm looking forward to it," he said. When he smiled, it was October all over again.

FIVE

LUKE

I was alone in the kitchen when Mom came home. Ian had gone to bed hours earlier. I suspected it was one of his headaches, though he wouldn't admit it. Mom's footsteps were tired and heavy as she climbed the steps and crossed the porch. The door groaned as she came in. She tossed her keys on the hall table and stepped into the kitchen.

She narrowed her eyes when she saw me. "Ian?"

"Luke," I corrected. What kind of mother couldn't tell her own children apart? Identical didn't mean we were the same. After seventeen years, I'd have thought she'd be better at it than she was.

She nodded, a quick jerk of the head that could have meant anything, then went to the cabinet and took down a glass.

"My day was good, thanks for asking," I said. "How about yours?" She didn't answer. She sure wasn't making this easy. "Sorry. Look, have you heard from Dad?"

Her shoulders stiffened, so I knew she heard me, but she didn't even acknowledge I was there. I understood her anger—hell, I deserved it—but she was my mother. She couldn't possibly punish me forever. Could she?

She'd cared more once. Mom was the one who had always run interference with Dad and, on occasion, had kept me from getting in even worse trouble. When I was thirteen, she'd let me practice driving by myself. I was backing the car out of the garage, so focused on getting the back end around a lawn chair that I'd let the front end swing too wide and smash into the side of the garage. She'd told Dad she'd done it so I wouldn't get in trouble.

Or sometimes, if Dad was out in the field and Ian was at practice, we'd watch a movie and order pizza—just the two of us. Mom had the greatest laugh. But now she kept it locked up somewhere so tight that I hadn't heard it try to escape even once. In those moments, when it had been just my mom and me, sometimes I'd forgotten I was the disappointment, that I was always one step, one point, one score behind Ian. That I caused trouble. In those moments, it had been okay to be Luke.

Then the fight with Dad happened. I should've controlled my temper. I shouldn't have hit him, but it felt good. I'd put all the anger and frustration I felt about never having been perfect enough for him. I had enough resentment in there to break his nose. Maybe we could have gotten past that eventually. But then he'd punched me in the face, and Mom pulled us out of there before the blood dried. She would never forgive Dad for that. I was pretty sure Mom would never forgive me either, which made me seriously doubt the existence of unconditional love. There were always conditions.

Mom took leftovers out of the fridge and stuck them in the microwave. I leaned against the sink, watching her, willing her to look at me. How could two people standing in the same room be so far apart? How could two people, who had once been physically connected, have no connection at all?

She kept her back to me while she warmed her food, the outline of her shoulder blades pushing against the thin cloth of her scrubs. Her hair, which was pulled back in a ponytail, was streaked with gray. That was probably my fault, too.

She still hadn't looked at me. I gripped the edge of the counter, trying to keep my temper under control. I watched the numbers on the microwave count down. Ten. Nine. Eight. Seven.

"I'm sorry," I said. "I really am." She had to believe me. Even I could hear the remorse in my voice.

Three. Two.

"Stop ignoring me!" My voice filled the tiny kitchen, and Mom jumped. The microwave beeped. Mom moved to open the door, like I hadn't just spoken, like my words had no weight at all. As if they didn't matter. As if *I* didn't matter.

I grabbed a kitchen chair and slammed it into the cabinets. The wood splintered with a loud crack. Mom whipped around, her eyes wide, finally looking at me. She was pale, and I knew I should stop, except I was glad to finally have her attention. I didn't want to lose it.

"I'm right here!" I shouted, smashing the chair into a cabinet door and cracking it down the middle. "You can't ignore me forever!" Destruction felt good—satisfying. I was like a teakettle, the pressure building until I screamed. So I released a little pressure.

"Why are you doing this?" Mom asked.

Her ragged voice took all the fight out of me. I dropped the chair and crossed the space between us. She put her hands up to stop me. "Don't," she said, tears running down her face. She left me standing there. I heard her bedroom door slam several seconds later.

I slumped down in a kitchen chair, one I hadn't destroyed. Ian emerged from his room. He always hid when there was trouble. Maybe that was why he always avoided it, and I always managed to rake it up like a pile of dead leaves and dive in headfirst.

"I thought you had a headache."

"Damn," Ian said when he saw what I'd done to the kitchen.

I laughed blackly. "I destroy everything I touch."

He looked toward Mom's room. "Even people," he whispered.

"Maybe especially people."

SIX

IAN

My headaches, and the dreams that came after, were getting worse. I'd just wanted to lie down for a minute, and the next thing I knew, it was late afternoon. Friday. I jumped out of bed and threw on a clean shirt. I couldn't be late—I wasn't going to make any more mistakes with Jenna. I was surprised she'd agreed to go out with me at all, considering.

My truck kicked up a cloud of dust as I tore down the dirt road, bouncing over ruts. The grass in the ditches was brown and brittle, the ditches themselves baked dry by the unrelenting sun. It was a hell of a lot hotter than Massachusetts. I cranked the air up to high.

The woods became pasture, which slowly became the town of Solitude. I drove past a subdivision and a sprawling trailer park. A bunch of kids were playing with a water hose, their feet covered in mud.

The town itself was small but neat. A sprinkler arced water across an oval patch of grass. Several cars were lined up outside Jimmy's Dairy Bar, and red-faced kids sat at outdoor tables and tried to eat their ice cream before it melted.

Repete's was on the east side of town, curving around both sides of a long brick building. A maroon and white awning covered the corner door. I pulled down a narrow side street and into the back. There were two rows of cars, and I parked at the end, next to Jenna's rust-colored Bronco. She was leaning against the driver's door.

She looked amazing. Her hair glinted copper in the sun, and I couldn't stop staring at her legs. I threw the truck in park and climbed out.

"Punctual," she said. "Add that to the list of things I like about you."

"What else is on the list?" I asked.

She grinned. "Not much."

We walked across the gravel parking lot and stepped into the dim restaurant. The walls were brick and lined with sports paraphernalia, most of it maroon and white—the Solitude Warriors. Signs proclaiming victories dated back to the 1920s, and a large wooden plaque had a picture of a spear with the dates of more recent football state championships. They'd won two years in a row, but that had been ten years ago. My old high school had won state almost three years ago, when I was a freshman. I hadn't been the starting quarterback then, but I'd gotten a lot of playing time. I knew it was going to be hard to waltz into a new town and get on the team. Another thing I should resent my brother for. My dad sure did.

I followed Jenna toward the counter. We threaded our way through tables, the restaurant about half-full, everyone staring as we passed.

"Get quiet and stay alert," Jenna said. "They've scented you."

But I got the distinct feeling that they were more interested in Jenna than me. She smiled and waved at a family sitting against the far wall, then was stopped by a table of old men. The man who grabbed her arm was wearing a short-sleeved plaid shirt and had more hair in his ears than on his head.

"Heard your mom sold the house," he said, barely glancing at me before looking back to Jenna. "What are they like?"

"You're looking at one of them." She grinned and jerked her head in my direction. "Mrs. Bridges thinks he might be a Commie," she whispered conspiratorially. The old men roared with laughter. "I'm going to ply him with pizza and see if he talks."

The men looked me up and down, although I had no idea what they thought they might be looking for. "Ian McAlister," I said, sticking out my hand.

"Jimmy Dempsey," the man replied, gripping my hand firmly. "And the peanut gallery," he added, letting go and jerking a thumb at the two other guys at the table. "Now, you tell your grandma I said hi," he told Jenna.

"Sure," she promised. We had started back to the counter when he added, "And watch out for Commies." He threw her a wink and she laughed.

"They went to school with my grandparents," she explained. "Mr. Dempsey's almost as full of shit as Pops was."

The girl behind the register smiled as we walked up. "Hey, Jenna." Her eyes slid over me, and her grin became suggestive.

Jenna ignored her and turned to me. "I always get the number seven. It's the best thing on the menu."

I glanced up at the large board on the opposite wall. Number seven—shrimp pizza. Nope.

"I'm allergic to shellfish," I told her. "Sorry."

"Really? That sucks." She looked like I'd just admitted to having the clap or something.

"I manage."

"Okay, you pick," she told me. "I eat anything."

The girl behind the counter snorted, and Jenna grinned. I ordered something with lots of sausage. The girl handed me a number.

"I'm Amber," she said.

"Oh, sorry about that," said Jenna. "Amber, this is Ian. He just moved to town. Ian, Amber. She's a junior."

"Nice to meet you," I said.

"Definitely," she answered.

We took our drinks and sat in the back corner. Photos covered the wooden tables. Under thick layers of shellac were old black and white pictures of guys in basketball uniforms, showing way too much leg, surrounded by cheerleaders who weren't showing enough. There were colored pictures where everyone had huge hair, and several yellowed newspaper articles. Almost all of them had something to do with sports.

"Hey," I told Jenna, "this girl kind of looks like you." I pointed to a cheerleader in one of the older color pictures. She was laughing, her head thrown back in a squeal, as a football player lifted her up in the air. She had Jenna's nose and freckles.

Jenna didn't even look over. "That's my mom."

"No way." I leaned in closer. Jenna didn't seem the least bit interested in the picture, but I couldn't imagine being so familiar with a place—or having one that was so familiar with me. The longest we'd ever stayed somewhere was five years. "Is this the only picture of her here?"

"She's on tables thirteen, seven, and twenty." She pointed around the room. "She was Solitude's sweetheart," she added, rolling her eyes.

"Who's the guy?"

"My dad." Jenna's voice was steel. "They'd just won the state championship."

"You don't get along with your dad?" I asked.

"I've never met my dad," she said. "He left when my mom was pregnant."

I was such an idiot. "My parents just got divorced," I told her, hoping to make her feel better. Like my family's dysfunction plus her family's dysfunction equaled no dysfunction at all.

"That must be hard," she said. "Do you miss him?"

"Sometimes." That was as close to the truth as I could get. "My dad is complicated."

Jenna's expression changed from pity to understanding. "'Complicated' is the exact word I would use to describe my mother."

But she seemed unwilling to say anything else.

"Look, about the other day," I began.

Jenna held up her hand. "You already apologized. Besides," she said, her voice dropping, "a lot can happen in seven months."

Seven months. So I met her just after my three-month blackout period. For some reason, I was afraid to ask about it.

"Let's just start over." She stuck her hand out. "Jenna Oliver."

Starting over was all I had. "Ian McAlister." I shook her hand, holding it a bit longer than necessary. "Nice to meet you."

She smiled, which made me feel lighter than I had in months. Talking with her gave me this feeling of the sun coming up—like my memories might come out of the dark. I could just see a vague outline, but at least there was something there. It was enough.

JENNA

Kyle Couty and his crew pushed through the doors. I tried to disappear inside the shadows, but in Solitude there was no place to hide. Mr. Hoffman stopped the boys and asked about the upcoming season. Kyle went on and on about shotgun formation and a bunch of other things—football was a language I didn't speak. Then it was our turn.

"Looking good, Oliver." Kyle only used last names.

Steven and Chris were with Kyle, along with Amy, Steph, and a bunch of juniors. They all pulled up chairs to the table.

"Do you need something?" I asked.

Kyle feigned innocence. "I just wanted to see how your summer was going. You haven't been around," he said. "And I wanted to introduce myself to our new student." Gossip broke speed limits in Solitude. Kyle turned to Ian and smiled. He didn't look very welcoming—it was more like he was showing his teeth in some kind of juvenile display of dominance. Ian didn't seem to notice.

"Ian McAlister," he said.

"Kyle." He sounded friendly enough, but I wasn't fooled. I was sure Kyle wanted something. He turned back to me. "We're going to the lake on Sunday. You coming?"

"No," I said. I'd made the mistake of dating Kyle when we were sophomores, and even though we were all friends, I avoided hanging out with him—and his ego—as much as possible.

"I guess you could bring him," he said, jerking his thumb at Ian.

"Generous, but still no."

"Relax," Kyle said, reaching over to rub my shoulders, "you might surprise everyone and have a good time."

"If you are even remotely interested in continuing to play football, I suggest you stop touching me." I hoped my smile suggested violence.

Dani Peters looked at me like I was out of my mind for talking like that to Kyle, much less objecting to him having his hands on me. She didn't strike me as the type to complain about Kyle Couty's hands.

"Jenna, your order's ready." Amber's voice cut through the chatter.

I got up, leaving Ian to defend himself against the wolves. He was going to have to deal with them sooner or later anyway.

I watched the boys. They kept eyeing Ian, like he'd just trespassed on their property, probably because all the girls were cutting glances at him. I half-expected the guys to pee on the wall to mark their territory. It would have been easier.

"Okay," I said, sliding the pizza on the table. I slapped Chris's hand out of the way when he reached for a piece, and he grinned at me. "Find your own table."

"Aw, did we interrupt your date?" Kyle asked.

"Actually, yes. And you have to be taken in small doses."

"Whatever. If you change your mind about the lake, we're meeting at ten o'clock." Kyle slung an arm around Dani Peters and left. She was obviously his flavor of the week.

"They seemed nice enough," Ian said.

"They are." I slid a large slice of pizza onto my plate, burning my fingers. Cheese strung back to the pan. "Kyle just gets on my nerves sometimes."

"I'd like it if you went to the lake with me," Ian said.

"You're going?" That was fast. But I could tell just by looking at Ian that he was going to get major attention when school started. Which was probably why Kyle was trying to act human.

"It sounds like fun. He said they'd have a couple of boats and some Jet Skis. Plus," he added, grinning, "my status would be elevated from new guy to stud if I showed up with you."

"When you put it that way," I told him, "it's so much easier to say no."

He laughed. "Cut me some slack, all right? You're the only person I know around here. It's your responsibility as a loyal citizen of Solitude to acquaint me with the town and all of its amenities."

"That won't take long," I assured him, grabbing another piece of pizza. Ian was on his third. He'd piled so much Parmesan cheese onto it that I couldn't even see the toppings.

"Then you'll only be rid of me sooner," he said.

"You promise?"

"Yes." There always seemed to be a smile behind his eyes. "But I should warn you," he added, "I'm a compulsive liar."

"I'll keep that in mind."

It was surprisingly easy to be with Ian. He wanted to be an architect, and I had to appreciate the way he had it all planned out. It was so hard for me to settle on any one thing, since I wanted to do so many. I only knew one thing for sure--whatever I did, I wasn't going to be doing it in Solitude. I was dying to know about all the different places he'd lived, but Ian was much more interested in hearing about me—and Solitude.

"There's not much to tell," I said. "I've lived here my whole life. My family has lived their entire lives here."

"But that's so cool," he insisted. "I can't imagine that. Everything here must have a memory for you."

Sometimes that was the problem. "There are some good things about small towns," I said. "But it can get boring. I see the same people every day. They're even starting to look alike."

He raised his eyebrows. "It's because they're all married to their cousins, isn't it?"

"Probably." Almost everyone else in the restaurant had filtered out, but we hadn't moved. We were both leaning forward, our hands resting on the table. If I moved my pinkie a little to the left, I could've touched him. I wanted to. I remembered the way he'd held my hand in October. I never dreamed I'd see him again. I kept staring at the line of his jaw, and the curve of his lips, and the way his hair curled against his collar.

He looked around the empty room. "We'd better go before they make us help clean up."

"I was thinking about it," Pete yelled from the back. He and I were going to have a little talk about eavesdropping.

Ian took my hand on the way out the door, like it was the most natural thing in the world. My cheeks flushed, and I was glad it was dark.

He walked me to my car. "I had a really nice time," he said.

"Me too."

"Do you want me to pick you up Sunday?"

"That's fine," I told him. "Here." I wrote down my address on the back of a receipt I found in my car. "Think you can find it?"

"It's Solitude, right? How hard can it be?"

He opened my car door, but he didn't try to kiss me. He pulled out of the lot ahead of me, and I watched his taillights disappear into the dark.

SEVEN

JENNA

On Saturday morning, I was in the shop ringing up Mr. Dempsey when the bell over the door jingled. Two customers in the store at the same time was practically a rush. My face grew warm when Ian walked in, but he didn't return my smile.

I handed Mr. Dempsey his change. "Don't spend it all in one place."

He winked at me. "Now you tell your Mops I stopped by."

"Will do," I promised, although she already knew. It was why she was hiding in the back. We were both pretty sure Mr. Dempsey was after her, but Mops said that taking care of Pops had been enough and she wasn't about to sign up for that again. Plus, Mr. Dempsey had a lot of ear hair. He couldn't have handled Mops anyway. She would have eaten him alive.

I stared at Ian's back, at the width of his shoulders and the way his muscles pushed against his T-shirt. The way he seemed to be pointedly ignoring me.

"Do you need help finding something?" I asked. I sure wasn't going to stand there while he pretended I was invisible.

"How much for the lathe?" He didn't even turn around. What was with him?

"Two hundred dollars," Mops said, slinking out of the back room. "But I might be able to cut you a deal."

Ian nodded and moved into the back of the store. He continued to ignore me and I pretended it didn't bother me as much as it did.

"Is Jimmy gone?" Mops whispered.

"All clear," I told her.

"Good." She wiped her hand dramatically across her forehead. "It's hard being this good-looking." She giggled, a laugh that should have been out of place on anyone older than twelve. But it worked for Mops.

I rolled my eyes and pointed at Ian, who was now holding a couple of books. Mops brushed her hand through the air, like she was dismissing a fly. Mops didn't get embarrassed.

Ian dumped his books on the counter, finally forced to look at me. There were dark half-moons under his eyes, which today resembled gray storm clouds rather than blue sky. "Is everything okay?" I asked. He really didn't look like himself. "Did something happen last night after you left?"

His face darkened. "I'm fine," he grumbled, handing me a five. Then he was gone.

I was aggravated at myself for letting the rejection hurt. I had way too many things to deal with already without adding in moody boys. But what had happened to the guy I'd gone out with the night before? The one who was funny and sweet and always seemed to be smiling? This Ian didn't seem to have smiled in a long time.

"Piss poor personal skills, but I bet he's got abs that would put my grandmama's washboard to shame," said Mops, leaning against the counter.

"Mops!" Not that anything she said ever really shocked me.

She winked. "Just calling it like I see it. Pops had a pretty nice butt when he was that age."

I did not want to be having this conversation.

Mops laughed at the trapped look on my face. "You want to help me go through that box?"

"As long as we don't have to talk." I was surprised my ears hadn't started bleeding already.

LUKE

I kept having the same dream. I was in my room, sitting on the bed. Sometimes I was reading, sometimes I was staring at the picture of Ian and me that was on my bedside table. I heard a grinding noise, like rusty gears, and at first I couldn't be sure where it was coming from. Then I noticed the walls of my room getting closer. It was subtle at first, but then the books started to move toward the center of the room, followed by the bed. I jumped up and ran to the door, but I couldn't open it. I stood in the middle of the room—sweating, breathing hard. I wasn't sure what to do. The walls just got closer and closer. I put my hands out to try to stop them, but I couldn't. I started to imagine how bad it was going to hurt when I was smashed between the walls—except when they finally pressed together, I didn't feel a thing. Because I wasn't there. That was when I woke up, sweating and thrashing. Maybe I was just trying to remind myself that I did exist.

That was why I had to go to town. I wasn't supposed to, but I'd stayed inside about as long as I could stand it, and I felt as faded as the ugly wallpaper in the dining room. Besides, I had some remodeling to do, which meant I needed to go to the hardware store. Surely I would be safe in a hardware store.

Except there was a junk store across the street with a really cool old lathe in the window, and I couldn't resist. If I was going to have to stay out of sight indefinitely, then I needed something to keep me busy. Otherwise I was going to cause some trouble, and nobody wanted that. Even I didn't want that.

Reclaimed was a tiny store squashed between an insurance company and the pharmacy. A bell jingled loudly as I pushed open the glass door. I was greeted by gloriously cold air and the dry scent of books.

And her. She was standing at the counter helping some old man, but when I walked in, she looked up and smiled.

Funny how a simple smile could destroy a person. Like a small storm that turned into a tornado. Or a tiny ripple that became a wave. Her smile washed over me, blew through me so completely that I was surprised to find myself still on my feet. Still staring at the freckles scattered across her nose. Still staring at her auburn hair. Trying to avoid the confusion in her eyes, confusion I put there because I didn't smile back. Because that would have been my undoing.

Somehow I managed to ask about the lathe, but I didn't hear the answer, and I didn't see the titles on the books I was pretending to look at. This had been a bad idea. I wasn't supposed to leave the house, and I wasn't really supposed to talk to anybody. Besides, I didn't deserve to talk to her. I didn't deserve to be here at all, but Fate was a bitch who enjoyed tormenting me.

I grabbed a couple of books without even looking at them. I should have left without them. I didn't know why I couldn't. At the counter, I had to look at her. I had to stand close enough that I could smell her shampoo.

She asked me if I was okay. A familiar tone, like I knew her. Like I knew her well.

Damn. She'd already been out with Ian. Fantasy shattered. I had to respond. I owed him that much at least.

"I'm fine." It was the best I could do. I got the hell out of there.

EIGHT

IAN

Mom and Luke were both still asleep when I left for the lake on Sunday morning. I wrote a note explaining where I was. Mom was going to be upset when she got up, but that was standard operating procedure these days. I was pretty sure it would be worth it.

Jenna and her friends were just the kind of normal I needed. They hadn't met Luke. They didn't worry about my headaches or memory loss, which meant I could relax. Take it easy. Smile. I'd wanted to kiss Jenna Friday night, but I was being careful instead. Doing everything right. Maybe doing things right with Jenna would balance out everything else that was wrong.

Jenna lived in an older subdivision outside of town, and she was waiting on her front porch when I pulled up. She had on a ratty pair of cutoffs and an old T-shirt, but damn she looked amazing. Her hair was pulled up in a messy ponytail, and even though she wasn't wearing any makeup at all, she looked more beautiful than most girls do when they spend hours in front of the mirror. I doubted Jenna knew her effect on people—I wondered if she even cared.

She didn't look happy to see me. "I'm surprised you showed up."

"I'm sorry?" I couldn't have done something wrong already.

Jenna folded her arms across her chest. "I don't get your mood swings. One minute you're practically begging me for a date, and the next, you don't even speak when you see me."

I hated this feeling. The frustration of someone remembering something I didn't, something I couldn't. It was *my* life, and I was sick of having my memories repeated to me instead of being able to recall them myself. I had to work harder with Dr. Benson. Maybe if I could keep my memories from falling away, I could keep my family from slipping away. Maybe I could even quit screwing up with the one person I was interested in getting to know.

Jenna must have realized I had no idea what she was talking about. "At the shop. You bought a couple of books and asked about an old lathe, then you couldn't get away fast enough. It's like you're two completely different people."

Moody and interested in a lathe? Only Luke would be asking about woodworking equipment. Damn it. This had nothing to do with my memory and everything to do with my brother. We were going to have a talk when I got home. "House arrest" meant he was not supposed to be running around town. He knew the rules as well as I did, but I was the only one who seemed to give a damn about them.

I debated telling Jenna about Luke right then, but I didn't want her to know about him at all. I couldn't tell her that my twin brother was—what? Even I wasn't sure. He was hiding something, even from me, or especially from me, but I got the feeling it was the reason for everything—the fight with Dad, Mom's disintegration, our slinking out of the state in the night. Luke couldn't be trusted. So where did that leave me? We were two pieces of a whole—at least, we had been. Once.

"I'm sorry," I said. "Migraines."

"That keep you from speaking?"

"That keep me from remembering," I skimmed the top off the truth, leaving the heavier parts to settle to the bottom. "I'm sorry if I was rude."

"You know, that excuse is getting pretty thin."

She had no idea. "One more chance. If I screw up again today, you can drown me."

"Jenna?" A woman's voice called out from inside the house, and Jenna turned.

"I'm going to the lake, Mom," she hollered. "I'll be home later." Jenna grabbed her bag from behind the door, then shut it before her mom could answer.

I didn't know if Jenna had agreed to go with me because she was giving me another chance or because she wanted away from her house. Whatever the reason, I'd take it.

JENNA

I wanted to stay mad at Ian, but my need to get away from my mother was stronger. She'd had several glasses of wine last night. Every time she'd thought my back was turned, she'd tipped her head back and drained her glass. I wasn't very worldly, but I knew normal people didn't drink like that. And then she'd forced me to look at old yearbooks while she told me overinflated stories of her glory. Spending time with her when she was like that always made my skin feel too small. Last night I couldn't go anywhere. Today, escape won out.

Ian headed to his truck, while I walked to the Bronco. "I'm driving," I called after him. "You can either follow in your truck or ride along." I didn't wait to see which one he chose.

I tossed my bag in the back of the Bronco and climbed into the driver's seat just as he opened the passenger side door. "I won't come if you don't want me to," he said.

I stuck the key in the ignition and started the truck. "You can come if you want. You promised I could drown you, remember?"

He grinned, climbing inside and slamming the door. "I have a feeling I might regret that later."

"I have a feeling you're right."

There were a pair of muddy running shoes on the floorboard, and Ian tossed them into the backseat as I pulled out of my driveway.

"I run cross-country," I explained.

"Really?" He seemed surprised. "Running was always my punishment. What made you pick that?"

I shrugged. "Why do you play football?" Why does anyone do anything?

"I'm not sure," Ian said. "I don't actually remember why I even started. I have a picture in my room of me right after a game. I'm covered in sweat and blood and grinning like hell. But I don't remember playing that game. I remember that we won, that I was interviewed and everything, but I can't remember actually playing the game."

He shook his head in frustration, and I felt bad for him. While there were a few things in my life I wouldn't mind forgetting, I couldn't imagine what it would be like to lose those that meant something. Who would I be if I couldn't remember Pops? If I didn't remember my mom before his death?

"Are you a good runner?" he asked.

I was getting pretty good at running away. "I'm all right." I wasn't breaking any records, but if I could shave a minute off my time, I might qualify for at least a partial scholarship. "I like running because I can set goals and reach them if I work hard enough. Life isn't always like that."

"I know exactly what you mean," he said, and I was surprised to find that he sounded like he actually did. Most of the time Becca just rolled her eyes and told me to lighten up. It was nice that Ian actually heard and understood what I was saying.

"There are some things that, no matter how hard you try, no matter how much work you put into, don't ever happen," Ian said. "I can't stand it when I can't change things. When it's out of my hands."

Staying mad at him made more sense than the way I actually felt. His face was honest and open when he spoke, his words a truth I could almost hold in my hands.

"I run the drills and I get better at football. I study for a test and I get an A. But no matter how hard or how bad I want it, I can't find my memories or get rid of my headaches. I can't fix my…" He stopped short and turned in his seat, his voice lower. "I can't make the right impression on this really great girl, because no matter how hard I try, I keep screwing it up. Wouldn't it be great if willpower made things happen?"

My thoughts, someone else's voice. Because if everything worked like that, I could fix my family before I graduated high school. I wouldn't have to worry about them crumbling when I was no longer here to hold them together. I wouldn't have to fear failure—or escape.

"Okay," I said, slowing down as we rolled through town. "If that were true, what would you make happen?" I waited for the single stoplight in town to turn green while Ian thought of an answer.

"Well, besides the obvious one…" he began. He leaned over the console, his arm brushing against mine. His mouth twitched as he tried to hold back a smile. He failed. It was so easy to smile back.

"Which obvious one?" I asked.

"Willing myself not to forget beautiful girls."

I was relieved when the light finally turned green and I had to focus on the road instead of the way Ian was looking at me. There was just something about him that kept me from being able to stay mad. Maybe it was the easy way he smiled or the laughter that seemed to be just behind his eyes. Or maybe it was simply because we felt the same need to work toward what we wanted. It shouldn't have been that simple, but it was.

"How many beautiful girls have you forgotten?" I asked.

"I've forgotten them, haven't I?"

I had to laugh. The fact that Ian could joke about something that wasn't really funny helped me forgive him. Losing memories had to be one of the worst things in the world. Being mad because he couldn't remember a couple minutes with me was selfish. It wasn't his fault. I knew all about dealing with the crap life dealt. It felt like that was all I was doing these days.

"What about you?" he asked. "What would you make happen?"

Even though I wasn't mad anymore, he hadn't earned the right to be let in yet. I noticed he hadn't answered my question either. "What, besides the obvious one?"

"What obvious one?" There was laughter in his voice.

"Willing myself not to be chased by forgetful boys."

"Is that what I'm doing? Chasing you?" He leaned forward to catch my eye before placing his hand over the top of mine. "You must not be as quick as you thought."

I pulled my hand away and placed it on the steering wheel. "You haven't caught me yet," I said.

IAN

Jenna turned onto a dirt road lined with trees, and the forest swallowed us. When we finally pulled into a large open area, I was surprised to see it full of people. It had seemed like we were so far away from everything else. Jenna parked and climbed out of the Bronco. Everyone smiled and called to her. Maybe that was what finding my memories would be like--wandering alone in the wilderness would become a gathering of childhood friends.

Jenna introduced me around, but I immediately forgot everyone's name. It was hard enough for my brain to hold onto whole days; names slipped through like smoke. I wanted to remember enough to know at least a few people before school started. I hoped getting my memory back would solve this problem. I didn't want to spend the rest of my life desperately trying to hold on to details.

"Oliver and the new guy!" Kyle shouted from a nearby boat. He waved us over, and we'd barely gotten in and away from the shore before Kyle punched it. Several kids on Jet Skis passed us up, and Kyle pushed the throttle forward. Water splashed over the sides of the boat and onto a couple of squealing girls. Jenna glared fiercely into the wind, her hair streaming behind her like flames.

We sat in the back of the boat, and Jenna tethered me to Solitude with her stories. I could've spent the entire day just listening to her talk. Her words created images vivid enough that I could almost steal her memories for my own. I liked her stories. I liked her.

"My grandpa used to take me fishing here," she said. We had to lean in close to hear each other over the growl of the engine and the roar of the wind. I didn't mind. "He used to get so mad because I wouldn't leave my line in the water." She smiled. "I just liked to reel it in."

Kyle was standing at the wheel, and he turned halfway. "Did you ever jump off the Point?" he asked Jenna. He pointed toward a cliff on the left side of the boat.

"People jump off that?" I asked. It had to be at least thirty feet high.

"Not anymore," Kyle said. "Some kid broke his neck a few years back."

"His name was Peter," Jenna said.

"Oh yeah." Kyle started telling the story. But when Jenna turned back to me, I forgot to listen.

We rode to the other side of the lake, slowing once we neared a tiny island in the middle of a large cove. Cliffs jutted out at odd angles from either bank, and the island itself was covered in large trees that gave way to a rocky shore. Kyle eased the boat onto the island, then started tossing everything onto the dirt.

I sat at the edge of their group and tried to remember what it had been like when I belonged. They talked about people I didn't know and places I'd never been. They had inside jokes that I would never understand. But I'd been a part of a group once. I'd had my own friends and inside jokes. Even though I no longer remembered the specific details, being with Jenna helped me see the shadows still cast by those moments. When Jenna threw her head back and laughed, I wanted to memorize every single note and gesture before I lost it completely. If I couldn't have those old moments back, I would fill myself with new ones.

JENNA

After lunch, Ian and the guys threw a football around. He made fitting in look so much easier than it must have been. Moving to Solitude had to be rough, especially since our groups had been formed in the sandbox when we were five.

Steph came and sat by me. We were best friends in second grade when we'd both had Mrs. Campbell. We weren't that close anymore, but I still liked her, although the fact that she was hanging out with Dani Peters caused me to worry a little about her sanity. "He seems nice," Steph said.

I turned and glanced at Ian. He kicked up the sandy dirt as he ran for the ball Kyle threw. He caught it just before falling into a scraggly bush, but came up grinning. There wasn't even a hint that he was bothered by anything other than making sure he didn't drop the ball. Maybe this was one of the reasons I liked Ian. He was so present in the moment. All his baggage must have been tucked neatly out of sight, because he sure wasn't hauling it around for the world to see. And he only knew me in this moment as well. He didn't remember me throwing up on Mrs. Kitchener the first day of kindergarten. He didn't recall every single stupid thing I'd ever regretted. Because he was a clean slate, so was I. He was easy to be with, and without even trying, he managed to loosen the knot that formed whenever I was at home. But I wasn't going to lose my head over any boy, no matter how handsome he was or how much my heart beat against my chest and demanded I change my mind.

I knew Ian was coming before I saw him walk up because Steph sat up straighter and grinned.

"Steven said we could use his Jet Skis," Ian told me. "You up for it?"

"Sure," I said, standing up and brushing the dirt off my legs.

I tried not to stare as Ian pulled off his shirt and tossed it on his towel. I wasn't the type to be easily swayed by broad shoulders and defined abs. And Ian had both. I focused instead on fastening my life jacket and getting the Jet Ski turned around. We eased out of the shallows, then I roared off, spraying Ian.

The wind tore at my hair and made my eyes water. Ian and I cut around each other and jumped the wakes. We rode out toward the spillway, the green banks and cliffs a blur as we raced faster and faster. I found myself laughing out loud, a sound that was snatched away instantly. I wondered if, somewhere, someone was standing on the porch and heard my laughter carried on the wind.

We circled around to the Point. It was the quietest part of the lake, secluded in a tiny cove accessible by a small road that twisted through the woods. A narrow inlet led from the lake to the cove. We eased through, parking the Jet Skis and climbing off. We sat on our life jackets and dried off in the sun.

I'd never seen someone absorb a place like Ian. He looked at everything and wanted to know the intricacies of Solitude.

"Places like this have long memories," he said. He didn't have to tell me. Small towns weren't subtle and they didn't have secrets.

"Yeah, no one ever forgets," I said.

"Forgetting isn't always a good thing," said Ian, and I regretted my choice of words. "Familiarity isn't always bad. You want those you love to know you so well they don't have to ask you what you want on your burger or what movie you want to see. They just know."

"What does that have to do with Solitude?" But I knew exactly what he was getting at. I just didn't know how he managed to voice the fears I couldn't.

"Because when you walk down the street, everyone knows who you are. You don't have to impress anyone or try to get noticed."

"I don't want to be noticed."

"Not all the time," he said. "But you don't want to be forgotten either. When no one knows you, you have to prove yourself every single day. It's exhausting."

I understood what he meant. Having to reinvent myself was something I both looked forward to and feared. I didn't know who I would be when I no longer lived in Solitude.

"It's not that difficult to fit in around here," I told him. "Get on the football team and complain about the heat, and you'll be a local in no time."

He smiled and leaned back. The hum of insects made me drowsy.

"So why Solitude?" I asked.

"Mom found a doctor in Middleton who thinks he can help me with my headaches."

"So that's why you were here in October? To meet with the doctor?"

He shrugged. "I don't remember being here before." His face was so full of remorse that he didn't have to say the words. "I'm really sorry."

"Me too." Because October was part of the reason I was lying in the sun with Ian right then. I hated that he didn't have the same memories of me that I had of him. "Why don't you remember?" I turned my head to look at him, but he was staring off into the trees. He looked like he was searching for the words, but I knew he wouldn't find them there. I never did.

"I don't know," he finally said. "I really don't."

I didn't push it. Not knowing the cause had to be the worst part about the whole thing.

We listened to the water and the wind. There was the occasional sound of a boat passing, but mostly it was quiet. The silence was one of the most beautiful parts of the Point.

"I thought I was going to hate it here," Ian admitted after a minute.

"And now?" I opened my eyes, turning my head to look at him. I wondered how long he'd been watching me; the thought made my insides squirm.

The corners of his mouth curved up in an endearing grin. "It's looking pretty good so far."

I smiled back. "So you don't miss Massachusetts?"

"Right now I can't think of one good thing about it."

His eyes drifted to my lips, but he didn't try to kiss me.

NINE

IAN

We built a fire as the evening wore on, needing light rather than warmth. The party really started as the stars, and two more boats full of football players and alcohol, showed up. Laughter echoed over the lake.

"I'm serious!" a guy said as I stepped out of the shadows and sat near the flickering light. "She was home from college to watch her little brother compete."

"The only action you got was poison ivy." Steven laughed.

"Keep it up," the guy warned, "and I won't let you have any melon bomb."

Steven shut up.

"Melon bomb?" I asked.

Steven grinned. "Drunk watermelon. Chris here fills it with vodka."

Chris lifted the lid of the cooler, revealing a huge watermelon surrounded by ice.

"How much did you put in?" Steven asked.

"More than enough," Chris promised. "It'll knock you on your ass."

I passed on the watermelon, but took the beer Steven offered me even though I didn't drink it. The smell gnawed at the back of my mind, a finger that seemed to probe my memory, sending up images I couldn't hang on to, like wisps of smoke.

Kyle loped up, his girlfriend trotting alongside. "New Guy!" he hollered. He was already drunk. I wondered if he even knew my name.

"Drunk Guy!" I hollered back.

Kyle laughed and slammed a large hand on my shoulder. "Where's Oliver?" he asked. His girlfriend scowled.

I shrugged, though I was pretty sure I'd seen her helping one of the girls who'd already had too much to drink. Jenna seemed to make taking care of people her responsibility.

A scrawny boy walked up and tossed Kyle some tubing. "You're up." The circle moved around Kyle.

I stood just outside it. I was used to being new, but this was different. They had a familiarity with each other that resembled family rather than friends, like cousins at a reunion. Most of these kids had been hanging together since kindergarten, and I couldn't even begin to imagine all the memories they shared. It made me miss mine even more.

The air was heavy and humid, and the fire just made it hotter. The flames glowed brighter and brighter until my eyes hurt. Pain blossomed in the center of my forehead, a pinprick of agony that grew until the edges of my vision went dark.

Luke hooked the tube to a funnel. I blinked. It wasn't possible—Luke wasn't here. I closed my eyes, then opened them, the light stinging. Kyle was hooking the tube to the funnel. Of course. But there was an overwhelming sense of déjà vu, like I'd lived this life before. Like I'd failed the first test and was having to retake it.

Beer spilled down the front of Kyle's shirt, and Steven turned to say something, except I was hollow, and his words went straight through me. A blonde girl stood underneath the tree where the keg sat, but she wasn't watching Kyle like everyone else was. She was watching me. She didn't smile or scowl or move at all. Her feet were bare. She kept staring at me, and I knew I was supposed to know her. But I didn't. She held something in her hand, and I had the craziest idea that it was for me, that if I could just reach out and take it, I would know her.

And then the feeling was gone. Steven shouted again, and night sped back up, filling with sounds and those damn bright lights. When I looked back at the tree, the girl was gone, taking whatever she had with her.

"You okay?" Jenna walked up behind me.

"Of course." It was almost the truth. I did feel better being near her. I could pretend that my life was normal, that my family wasn't falling apart. I wanted to say something witty and intelligent. Instead, I just stood there.

Jenna looked at Kyle with disgust. "Let's get out of here."

I would have followed her anywhere.

JENNA

We wandered away from the party, leaving behind the noise and ritual, finding silence and stars on the other side of the island.

"Crunchy or creamy?" Ian asked.

I laughed. "What kind of question is that?"

"I can tell everything about a person based on their choice of peanut butter," he said.

"Well, in that case," I said, "both." Ian tried to argue, but I interrupted him. "I'm sorry, but you can't expect me to pick between the two. They each have their own distinct roles. Now analyze me."

"You didn't answer fairly. Another question," he argued.

"Fine."

"Vanilla or chocolate?"

"Vanilla. Why do all of your questions have only two answers? There's more to life than either/or," I insisted. At least, I was hoping there was. I didn't want two roads. I wanted an interchange with endless possibilities.

"You're very hard to please," he said. "Okay. Let me think."

A line of trees rose tall and dark in the center of the island, and cicadas interrupted the quiet.

"One thing you really want to do before you die," Ian finally said.

"That's not a peanut butter question." I reached up and pulled my hair off the back of my neck, tying it into a knot. The air was sticky, with barely any breeze to stir it. I wasn't sure how to answer his question. There was so much I wanted to do before I died. Hell, there were a million things I wanted to do before I was thirty.

"Right now, I'd say swimming in Switzerland," I told him. I walked to the edge of the water, taking off my shoes and letting the lake lap over my toes. "But I guess I'll have to settle for tepid lake water for now."

Ian stepped closer and blew lightly on the back of my neck. Chills immediately erupted across my damp skin. "Better?" he asked.

"Um, yeah," I said, clearing my throat. "Thanks." I waded in past my ankles.

"So what's one thing *you* want to do before you die?" I asked him. It wasn't fair that I was the one getting grilled. Nor was it fair that he could make my brain misfire like that. I was having a hard time focusing.

"Graduate high school. Go to college. Become immortal."

I laughed. "How are you going to do that?"

Ian walked closer and stood right behind me. "By building something that stands forever."

His words were pronouncements, and I could hear the conviction in his voice. He was going to do exactly what he said. I wanted that kind of certainty in my life.

I didn't want to speak my dreams out loud. Putting weight to my words might destroy their magic. I was such a coward. As much as I wanted to see the world and re-create it on the page, I was even more afraid of failure. I was terrified I wasn't good enough to do all that I dreamed of doing. I couldn't be sure I was strong enough to deal with the kind of disappointment that came from watching everything I ever wanted sail out of my reach. Having an audience for that would make it worse.

I turned to look at Ian. It was hard to see him in the dark. He was a shadow, a line here, an angle there. He reached up and ran a finger along my cheek, and I shivered despite the heat. He leaned down, stopping just before his lips touched mine. Was he trying to kill me? I didn't move, not even to breathe.

"Do you think it would be okay if I kissed you?" he whispered. His breath tickled my face.

I didn't bother answering with words.

TEN

LUKE

Mondays were my worst days. In the past, I'd nursed hangovers and struggled to recall all the trouble I'd gotten into, and out of, over the weekend. And while I didn't have a hangover, I was going to spend this Monday trying to atone for my sins.

I measured the kitchen wall again just to make sure, then rechecked the numbers I'd written down. They had to be exact—there was no room for screwing up in building. Even a quarter of an inch difference could throw everything horribly out of whack. I stuck the tip of the pencil underneath my hat, clipped the tape onto the waistband of my shorts, and grabbed my drawings. Rough sketches, actually. I wasn't really artistic, but I was pretty good with lines and angles, and I could draft out the picture in my head. I took everything out back.

The shop was a little eerie, like someone had walked away to answer the phone and never come back. There were piles of rusted junk in the corners, but there were also fishing poles propped against the back wall and jars of nails and screws organized by size. An old hat sat on a bench, its bill thick with dust. I also found some decent tools; once I'd cleaned the rust off, they worked pretty well.

I was thrilled the day we'd moved in and I'd found the workshop. Being on house arrest sounded like certain death, but the tools promised an outlet for my energy. I'd always been good with my hands, and Uncle Danny had taught me how to build cabinets. I'd never done a job this big by myself before. But I didn't have a choice—I'd put holes in the existing kitchen cabinets. Guilt was a great motivator.

Working in the shop was relaxing. I had to focus on what I was doing so that I didn't screw up by cutting the boards the wrong length or taking off my thumb. When I was building, everything else became background noise. I didn't have to worry about my parents or probation. I didn't have to think about the girl in the thrift store, the one I couldn't stop thinking about, the one I shouldn't have been thinking about. She'd already met Ian, which put me at a severe disadvantage. Besides, I was supposed to be hiding out and pretending I didn't exist. So if I didn't *have* to think about all of this, why was I? I just needed to focus on one thing and get it right. That I could do.

I began building the boxes for the cabinets. Nothing fancy, just a frame for the shelves and around the dishwasher. Another one to go around the stove. There wasn't all that much room. I was going to have to install some of the boxes before I built the others. Systematic steps. Order always made me feel better. More in control.

Which was ironic, since most people who thought they knew me would disagree if I told them I liked order. Chaos usually reigned in my world, but that wasn't the way I wanted it. I didn't know why I kept making choices I knew were bad, as if I had no choice at all. Maybe there was something fundamentally wrong with me. Like Ian got all the good genes, and I got the junk left over. We'd been so similar when we were young, but at some point I quit being able to keep up. I was always just behind him, in grades and sports and my dad's eyes, and while what I was accomplishing was pretty good on its own, when compared to Ian's achievements, it looked like moldy leftovers. So I quit trying to compete. I found my own sport, one I excelled in—deviance. And sometimes it just felt really good to piss off my dad. But sometimes even that fell flat. And it didn't take some catastrophe to make me realize my mistakes. I'd known them all along. But I was only just paying for them.

I laid out my tools like a surgeon, setting my nail gun, wood glue, and drawings in a neat row on the shelf. I fastened the nail pouch around my waist and began sweating out my frustration. Just me and the work. I focused on what I was doing, soon finding a rhythm, cutting boards, fitting them together, driving the nails. I measured. Adjusted. Created. It was better than destroying, and my mind found that quiet place of contentment.

And then she was there.

JENNA

I was on my way home from work Monday afternoon when the Bronco just steered its way over to Ian's house. I wanted to turn around; I tried to focus on Ian's strange behavior and my plans, which didn't include him, but all I could think about was how easy it was to forget everything else when he smiled.

I parked in front of the house, but I didn't see his truck. I was starting to climb the steps to the porch when I heard hammering from around the back, in the direction of the shop.

I stopped in the middle of the yard, not sure if I wanted to go in. I'd spent many afternoons watching Pops fix things in his shop. I'd smashed my finger with his hammer after he'd told me not to touch it. I'd found his stash of whiskey and kept it a secret, even from Mops. When Pops died, we'd simply shut the shop doors and left everything the way he had. It would be strange seeing Ian using his tools, but I wouldn't be like Mom, afraid to move on.

Both doors were propped open. Ian had his shirt off, his back to me. His shoulders were broad, and the muscles in his back moved as he cut a piece of wood. He couldn't hear me over the whine of the blade and the roar of the fan. I watched him fit the pieces together, eye them, then pull the trigger on the nail gun. He eyed the wood again and nodded that it was right. He was graceful and fluid, skin on muscle on bone, his movements a dance. He was talented, and it wasn't odd at all, seeing how easily Pops's shop fit around him; he belonged there.

Ian turned to grab another board and saw me. He froze and I blushed. I couldn't help it—he'd caught me staring. The fact that he looked so amazing without a shirt made me blush even harder, as if he could read my mind.

He wiped his hands and face with a towel, but didn't say anything, just gave me a mysterious smile. What was that all about?

"I was headed home from work and thought I'd stop by," I told him. "But you look busy."

"No, it's okay. I could use a break."

I followed him to the back porch. He leaned against the railing and took a deep drink from a water jug. I tried not to stare at his chest, which was nice and defined, or his abs. His shorts were slung low on his hips, revealing a long pink scar on his right side that I hadn't noticed at the lake. I sat on the top step and tried looking back at his face.

He smiled wickedly at me. "Ian's not here."

I decided to play along. "Do you know when he might be back?"

Ian shrugged. "I have no idea. Not for a while, I hope. He might get angry if he thought I was trying to seduce his girlfriend."

I didn't have a response to that. I wasn't sure which part I was supposed to be concerned about—the seducing, or the fact he'd called me his girlfriend. I didn't know what to do with either.

He must have seen how uncomfortable I was. "Sorry." He raked a hand through his hair. "He's really not here." He did look serious. "Ah," Ian said, his face changing to understanding. "He hasn't mentioned me, has he?"

I had absolutely no idea what he was talking about.

"I'm Luke," he said. "Ian's brother. Twin brother, obviously."

Obviously. And I was staring. With my mouth open a little. "Sorry," I mumbled. I shut my mouth with a snap. There were two of them?

"No problem," Luke said. "It happens all the time."

There were two of them. "I'm Jenna. But I…why wouldn't Ian…" I still couldn't make any sense of this. The fact that Ian had a brother he'd never mentioned was kind of hard to take in.

Luke's face darkened. "We aren't exactly getting along right now. He blames me for the move."

"Why?"

"Because it's my fault. Ian is perfect. I'm the outlaw. You picked the right brother." Despite his crooked smile, Luke's voice was black.

"I didn't pick anybody." I wasn't sure why I was protesting.

He raised his eyebrows. "Oh? Still browsing? Maybe you'd like to try me on for size."

I narrowed my eyes. "You know, you could get dressed," I said. His skin was making me uncomfortable.

His smirk was pure arrogance. "Am I bothering you?" His tone suggested that was exactly what he hoped he was doing.

"No, it's just rude."

"Yeah, well, my brother got the manners. I got the looks."

"That's really too bad," I told him. "Seems like you got the short end of that stick."

"There's nothing short about my—sorry." He looked abashed. "Reflex."

"So how do people tell you two apart?" I asked, trying to change the subject. They couldn't. I hadn't. Right then I was having a hard time believing that Ian wasn't playing some elaborate joke on me. They were beyond identical.

"Easy," Luke said. "I'm the one with all the girls following me."

"It doesn't seem so in this case."

His grin was appreciative. "Touché. But you were not aware of my existence until ten minutes ago. Now that you've met me, you won't be able to think of anything else."

"I'm sure I'll manage." Although I did find myself staring at his abs. It wouldn't have killed him to put on a shirt.

I jerked my chin in the direction of the shop, giving my eyes something else to do. "What are you working on?"

His grin made his arrogance fall away, unmasking a big kid. "Wanna see?"

"Sure."

I followed him into the shop. Almost everything was exactly where Pops had left it—even one of his hats. There were several piles of old wood on the floor, along with scraps and wood shavings. An outline of a box was sitting on the worktable.

"What kind of wood is that?" I asked. It was full of nails and covered in old paint, chipped and peeling in places.

"Old cypress. Some people call it reclaimed cypress. It's just really old wood that's worth a lot. It looks way better when it's all cleaned up."

"Why would you use old wood?"

"Because it's pretty—and rare. It's not like they're making more of it. Imagine where this stuff has been. What it saw. Once I get all the nails out and plane it down, it'll look really good. And it's worth more because of the nail holes and everything. I like taking something that's all beaten up and making it better."

"Like redemption," I said.

Luke looked at me then, really looked at me, his eyes intense. "Exactly."

I broke his gaze, which made me feel like I was standing naked in church, by walking around and looking at all the memories piled in the back corner. The fishing poles and tackle box were as familiar to me as the Bronco. Pops used to take me fishing in the little pond down the hill. We threw most of the fish back, but every once in a while we'd keep the big ones and fry them up right there by the pond. Sometimes, Mops and Mom would come too, and we'd have fried potatoes and hush puppies. On those long afternoons, no one was drinking. On those days, we didn't have to pretend everything was perfect.

My little red wagon was propped in the corner, the bottom rusted out. Sometimes I had carted a stuffed animal or two, but usually I was wheeling around a frog or some lizards or, even once, a harmless grass snake. Mops had nearly fainted over that one. The rusted Coca-Cola sign was still there, as was the scar on my calf where it had sliced into me. I'd had to get a tetanus shot. There were so many other things, which, while I had no tale on them, probably had plenty of stories of their own.

"I know, it's a lot of junk," said Luke. "I need to go through it and throw most of it out when I get a chance."

That comment, that people's lives could be tossed aside so easily, made my heart hurt, even if we *had* left all of this stuff to rot. "It's not junk," I told him. "My grandpa owned this once, and it wouldn't have been here if it hadn't been important."

"Your grandfather?" he asked.

"You didn't know he used to live here? Your mom bought the house from my mom."

"Really?" He sounded interested—and surprised.

"I guess Ian has been keeping us both a secret," I said. "See that fishing pole back there?" I pointed to the one with the pink handle. "I've caught more fish with that pole than I can remember. And two snapping turtles. It's not junk."

"So why'd you leave it here?" he asked.

"Because sometimes there are too many memories and not enough rooms." There was a softening in Luke's face that made me think he knew exactly what I was talking about. He handed me a pair of goggles.

"What are these for?" I asked.

"I thought you might like to help me clean up the wood."

"I don't know how," I told him.

"There's nothing to it. Just turn this on," he pointed to a switch on the side of a monstrous piece of equipment, "and run the board through. The planer does all the work—it peels off the old layers of paint and stuff. You'll probably need this, too." He handed me a dust mask.

"You want me to do your work for you?" I asked. He had to be kidding.

He nodded. "You're probably right. I mean, you're pretty small, and a girl at that. You probably couldn't do it even if you wanted to."

And even though I knew he was manipulating me, it totally worked. "Give me that."

He grinned and handed over the mask. He showed me how to feed the wood into the machine, then stepped back and watched.

He corrected me a couple of times, but after a while I didn't even notice he was standing there. It was hot, even with the fan on, but it was nice working up a sweat and getting my hands dirty. It was even better when I finished with a plank of wood. I stepped back and looked at the grimy, dented board that was now smooth and golden. Beautiful. The nail holes left black streaks in the honey-colored wood, a smudge of character that proved the board had history.

The cut wood smelled so clean. I had shavings all over me—they coated the front of my shirt, settled into my hair, and filled the edges of my tennis shoes.

"That's really good," Luke said, startling me as he came up behind me.

I smiled. "I know. It looks amazing."

"If you came over here every day, I could have this job knocked out in no time." Luke reached up and touched my shoulder.

"You couldn't afford me," I said, surprised at how nonchalant I sounded. My stomach was knotted in a million different places, and I found myself wishing we were standing closer together. And farther apart at the same time.

"I should go," I said.

Luke gave me a dark look. "That's probably a good idea."

What the hell did he mean by that? "Tell Ian I stopped by."

"Sure," he said. But he didn't sound like he would.

ELEVEN

IAN

There were seven pencils in the ceramic mug on Dr. Benson's desk. All of the erasers were still new. There were also a picture of a smiling family at Disneyland and a bronze clock. I tried not to notice how slow the hands on the clock were moving.

"I'm glad you're getting settled in," Dr. Benson said. "Meeting new people. Tell me about them."

I tried, but their names and faces blended together. They were shadows in the light. Her light. I only remembered them because she'd been there.

"Jenna." My voice surprised me. I hadn't meant to say her name out loud.

Dr. Benson looked at me over the top of his glasses. "You met a girl?"

I gave him a faint smile. "They do make up half the population. It was bound to happen eventually."

"Of course," Dr. Benson said, writing something down. "She's just a girl."

"There's nothing *just* about Jenna. She—" I leaned forward, my elbows on my knees, and stared at the floor. "She makes me believe it's possible to be normal again."

"How so?"

There was a small burn at the corner of the rug, a mar in its pattern. "When she talks, it's like I can see again. Like I've been sitting alone in the dark and she stepped in to turn on the light."

"Could you explain what you mean by that?"

I tried. "She has all these stories. These memories. And I envy that. It makes me want to find mine even more." I needed those memories to mend all the cracks. Spending time with Jenna helped. "At the lake…"

The clock ticked loudly in the silence.

"Yes?" Dr. Benson finally asked.

"I think I had a memory." Except I didn't know if that's what it had been at all.

"Tell me about it."

I sat up, leaning back in my chair. Dr. Benson seemed so interested, so concerned. I looked out the window. "I guess it was more a feeling than an actual memory. Like déjà vu. Just a feeling of someone I might have known before."

I tried to picture what had happened at the lake, but concentrating on the hazy image brought a stabbing pain in my head. I grimaced.

"Ian? What is it?"

I rubbed at the tension in my neck. "Headache."

"They're not getting any better."

"No." If anything, they were getting worse.

Dr. Benson scribbled something in his notes. "I'll alter your meds a bit, see if that helps." He finished writing and glanced at his watch. It must have been moving just as slowly as his clock. "Now last week you mentioned Luke had damaged the kitchen. How did that make you feel?"

Like I was watching someone drown and I couldn't do a thing about it because I didn't know how to swim.

"Tired, Doc," I said instead. "It made me feel tired."

JENNA

Repete's was packed on Thursday night. The kitchen was hot, and tiny little hairs escaped my ponytail and curled around my face. I burned myself trying to hurry to get pizzas out of the oven, and twice some kid dumped his drink in the middle of his table. By eight-thirty, I was ready to get off my feet.

"Hey!" I said, grinning as Mike Sanderson and Robert Bolds ambled up to the counter. They were both on the cross-country team.

"Where you been hiding?" Mike asked, sitting next to the register. I reached up and pushed him off the counter.

"Working," I answered. It felt like that was all I was doing. I'd gotten an email from Becca early this morning; she'd just finished her stay in France and was heading to Italy for a couple of weeks. I had to work hard to keep from being resentful.

"I hear you," Robert said. "I've been hauling hay for my dad. Sucks."

They each ordered a large pizza. They were both tall and wiry, but they could put away some food. All of the cross-country team could. I'd won plenty of bets that way.

"I saw Coach last week," Mike was saying. "He wants us to run the Miles by the Moon 5K in Centerville. It's the weekend school starts."

I tossed his order to the kitchen. "Cool."

"You going to break eighteen?" Robert asked.

I shrugged. "Guess we'll find out."

I'd been trying to break eighteen minutes in the 5K for the past year, and I doubted I would do it at the Moon. August was too hot and humid for a Personal Record, even if the race did start at eight o'clock at night.

Robert leaned in and lowered his voice. "You'll do it this time."

Maybe not this time, but soon. I nodded and handed him his plastic number.

"See you around," he said, straightening up and giving me a sympathetic smile.

An hour later, I was bussing one of the tables when Chuck Scott, who tended bar next door, came in to talk with Pete. They looked over at me, their faces tight, and my stomach twisted itself into painful knots. I carried the dirty dishes to the back and tried to convince myself their conversation had nothing to do with me. I was wrong.

Pete met me in the kitchen. He took the bin full of dishes from me and dumped it in the sink. "Look, Chuck said your mom is over there." He grimaced. He didn't have to say another word.

My face ignited, my skin flushing cold then hot at the humiliation of my mother showing out in the bar. By morning, most of the town would know.

This had gone beyond a few drinks at home. It had started when Pops died, but it had gotten much worse in the last three months. I was trying to keep it quiet and under control. But everything I'd been doing to keep the drinking a secret crumbled the minute my mother got drunk in public. I took off my apron, dried my hands, and glanced at the table where Robert and Mike had been sitting. They were gone. Luckily, the restaurant was mostly empty. I didn't want an audience.

Pete followed me into the dim bar, which was really just a small den at the end of a dark hallway connecting it with the restaurant. There were only about ten people in there, but that was enough to pack the place. There was a baseball game on the TV perched in the corner, but no one was watching it.

My mother was sitting in a small booth against the back wall, mascara running down her face. "Jenna!" she shouted, her fake smile plastered on. I flinched. I resented her for giving me a reason to be ashamed.

"Let's go." I leaned in and took hold of her arm, but she jerked away from me.

"I'm not ready to go yet," she said.

I was tempted to turn my back and leave her there. But I couldn't.

"You're drunk," I growled. "Let's go."

"I am not drunk," she said. "I had a bad day. I just needed one drink."

But it was obvious she'd had way more than one.

Pete came to my rescue. "Come on, Vivian. It's late. Let Jenna take you home."

"Pete Orcino," Mom slurred, smiling. "You were in my homeroom."

He smiled, his eyes warm and understanding. "You were the prettiest girl in there," he said. He was talking to her like she was a child, trying to appease her. It worked.

She took his arm, standing and smiling up at him. "Well, aren't you sweet? I was homecoming queen too, remember?"

Pete nodded as he led her outside, and I rolled my eyes. She was clinging to a past that no longer existed. She didn't realize she'd stopped being the homecoming queen as soon as she'd gotten pregnant; now, most people remembered her as the girl who'd gotten knocked up.

I followed behind them, trying to keep my temper under control. Mom looked small next to Pete, who was tall and broad. She clung to his oversized forearm, and I was pretty sure that, if she let go, she'd fall over. I wasn't sure what I felt more—humiliation or gratitude.

I unlocked the passenger door of the Bronco, and Pete picked Mom up and sat her in the seat. Her head lolled to the side. I prayed she wouldn't pass out.

"I'll get her car in the morning," I told Pete.

He looked worried. "You be careful getting home."

"I will." I climbed in and cranked the engine. Mom sat up a little as I pulled out of the parking lot and onto the road.

"It's Pops's birthday," she said. "He would've been sixty-four."

I gripped the steering wheel. I'd forgotten. Completely.

Mops hadn't said a word about it at work today. I hadn't even noticed if she seemed sad. God, I was turning out to be just as selfish and self-absorbed as I blamed Mom for being. I should have remembered. I should've at least noticed if Mops was taking it hard. I felt very alone, despite the fact that Mom was drunk and crying next to me—or because of it.

I pulled into the driveway, parking in Mom's spot instead of mine, and left Mom in the car with her head propped on the dash while I unlocked the door and turned on the lights.

I opened the passenger door and Mom slid out of her seat; I just barely had a chance to catch her before she fell. I wanted to throw her in a heap and leave her to sleep it off in the driveway. I wanted to trade her in for a sober mom with a smidge of self-control. Instead, I wrapped my arm around her waist and maneuvered her inside. We had a little trouble navigating the steps, and I was afraid we were both going to tumble backward, but then I managed to shift our momentum forward and into the house.

I took Mom straight to her room and sat her on the stool in front of her bathroom vanity, then ran warm water in the sink and washed her face.

"You could be so pretty," Mom slurred, reaching up to tuck a strand of hair behind my ear, "if you tried a little."

I gritted my teeth to keep from saying something hateful. I sure didn't need her to point out my shortcomings—I stared at them every day. They ate away at my spine and whispered to me in the dark. They slunk in the shadows in between runs. They told me I wasn't creative enough to ever write anything worth reading. They told me I was too small-town to survive anywhere else. The world acknowledged my shortcomings, but my mother shone a spotlight on them. And it was always brighter when she'd been drinking. *In vino veritas.*

Mom tried to hold still, but her body swayed slightly as I took the washcloth and gently removed her makeup. I wondered what I might uncover if I could just scrub hard enough. Her tears spilled over, and I washed those away too.

"I just miss him so much," Mom said.

"I know," I soothed, wiping the warm cloth underneath her eyes. "I do, too."

Mom brushed her teeth while I grabbed a gown out of her drawer. I changed her, helped her to bed, and tucked her in, just like she had me, at least until I was eight. Except I had to make sure she was on her side in case she threw up. She mumbled something incoherent, then her breathing deepened. She was asleep within minutes.

I brought in a glass of water and a bottle of aspirin. I hoped she had a killer headache in the morning.

I dragged myself up the stairs to my room. I sat on the edge of my bed, slipped off my shoes, and dropped my head into my hands.

I wanted to feel sorry for myself and hate my mother, but both were too bitter for my taste. What I did know was that I'd spent the last two years making plans, and while other kids were enjoying their last summer of high school, while Becca was off playing in Europe, I was in Solitude with my head down and my hands busy. But none of that was going to matter if I couldn't get my mom under control. Because of her piss-poor coping skills, it looked like I just might get stuck going to Middleton Community College and taking care of my drunken mother. And who was I to believe it could have been any other way?

I bit down on the inside of my cheek to keep myself from screaming. I wanted to throw something. I flopped over backward on the bed instead, searching for answers in the words on my ceiling. I found them. *Stuff your eyes with wonder, live as if you'd drop dead in ten seconds. See the world. It's more fantastic than any dream made or paid for in factories.*

I needed out. I put on my running shoes, slipped down the stairs, and headed out into the dark. Within minutes, I was pounding out my frustration. I eased into a rhythm, the sound of the cicadas loud in my ears. My feet were soft on the path, and I reveled in the way my body moved. Science says bodies in motion will stay in motion. I was counting on it.

TWELVE

LUKE

I spent all day Saturday out in the workshop, and it was late when I finally went inside. I didn't know why I was having so much trouble sleeping, but I was up at night more and more often. Probably because I felt the most freedom then—Ian was usually asleep and Mom was at work. Nobody was watching me. Nobody was waiting for me to screw up or lose my temper. At night, I could be myself, which was sometimes both a relief and a burden. My family found it hard to live with me. My dad couldn't even be in the same state. But they had no idea what hard was. It was even harder to have to live with myself. Destroying an innocent girl did that to a person.

I couldn't believe the amount of damage I'd done to the kitchen. I wanted to be ashamed, but instead felt a sliver of satisfaction at getting Mom to drop the silent treatment, even if she had spoken less than ten words. At least she'd finally looked at me. And it wasn't that I wanted to hurt her—I didn't. I was just so damn tired of her stepping around me like I was some ugly family heirloom she didn't want but wasn't willing to throw out yet. Besides, she wouldn't ever be able to punish me any worse than I'd already punished myself.

The bulb on the back stoop cast weak light through the kitchen window. I'd removed all the cabinet doors, and the shelves were bare, jutting out like the ribs of a carcass that had been picked clean. I ran my fingers along the dents my anger had left. At least I would be able to fix those. The ones I left everywhere else? Not so much.

I'd gotten into building when I was ten, at Boy Scout camp. That had been before they kicked me out for corrupting a pastor's daughter. I grinned into the dark. That had been kind of interesting. After camp, I'd spent all my time out in the garage nailing together every board I could find. Most of my stuff had started out crooked or gapped, but eventually I got better. The summer Ian and I were twelve, I'd built us a tree house.

We were living in Colorado then, and that summer was the last time I remembered our family completely intact and happy. That was before Dad had figured out I wasn't as talented as Ian, before my teachers realized we weren't exactly the same. Before I quit trying to keep up. That summer, Ian and I were still inseparable. I'd let him design the tree house, since he was always drawing—at least when Dad wasn't around. Dad didn't really approve of his boys pursuing feminine hobbies like art. But he'd pretty much left us alone that summer, so Ian had drawn the tree house and I'd built it. By myself. With my own hands.

It had been slow at first, trying to get the boards fitted and level in the big oak tree in the backyard. But then it had started taking shape—the floor, the skeleton walls that finally filled in, a roof to keep out the rain. It was the most beautiful thing I'd ever seen, and the last time I remembered my dad being proud of me. Ian and I had spent the rest of the summer in that tree, eyeing the teenage girls next door, staying out of the house. Mom had even let us sleep in it, once I'd convinced her we wouldn't roll out in the middle of the night. The summer I was twelve had been perfect. Back when Ian and I were just *we*.

I walked into the laundry room, stripping off my sweaty shirt and throwing it in the hamper. There was a growth chart on the molding around the door. I'd passed it several times, but now one of the names had a face, one I hadn't been able to get out of my head all week. I flipped on the light.

"Jenna" was written in red on the right side, along with her ages. I ran my fingers along her name. "Vivian" was written on the left side in black ink, also with hash marks and ages. "Billy" was written in faded blue, but his marks stopped at age five.

I ran out to the shop and got the crowbar. I stuck the metal bar where molding and wall met, then pushed. The molding moved with a loud squeal, the nails protesting as they were pulled out of the wood. I was careful not to splinter it. I pushed a couple more times and finally pulled the entire piece free.

I took it out to the shop, putting it somewhere safe, out of reach of my temper. I ran my finger along her name one more time. Something like hope kindled in the space behind my ribs. It was a strange feeling, like breathing again on my own after being on life support.

IAN

Luke was walking up the stairs as I came out of my room. "Hey," he said.

"Hey." I stopped. He looked uncomfortable, which meant he wanted to talk.

"Look," Luke said finally, "do you think you could tell Mom I'm sorry? I guess I got a little out of hand."

"Tell her yourself." I was tired of being the only one trying to piece everything together.

He glowered at me. "She still won't talk to me." He ran his fingers through his hair, a sign of his frustration that made him look just like Dad.

"Do you blame her?" I asked. He *had* demolished the kitchen.

His head drooped, like it was simply too heavy for him to hold up anymore, and he clenched his fists. "I don't know how to fix it." His voice was rough and low, and I was pretty sure we weren't still talking about the kitchen.

"I don't think you can," I said.

He raised his head and gave me a quizzical smile. "Wait." He disappeared into his room. I heard him banging around, but I didn't go in. Luke was very particular about his room— he didn't let anyone in. He reemerged after a minute or so, holding a blue birdhouse. The paint was chipping off at the corners.

"Do you remember this?" he asked.

Vaguely. "You built that, didn't you?" It was hazy, like seeing trees through thick fog. I could make out an outline, but not many details.

"In Mr. Shot's woodshop. Remember?" He was grinning at me.

"I was failing woodshop," I said, the edges becoming clearer, "and Dad was mad. He wanted to know what boy failed woodshop." I remembered his anger, which was more shame than anything. He couldn't imagine that I wouldn't be good at something as simple as using tools. "You pretended to be me every day that week, until you'd finished the birdhouse. I got an A. But what was I doing that week you were me?" I asked. That part of the memory was in shadows.

"You were me, of course. You brought my C in math up to a B. And had to do one of my detentions." His laugh burst out of him, like he had been trying to keep it in and failed miserably.

"So what happened?" I asked. His smile disappeared; he knew what I was referring to. When did we go from spending every waking moment together to hardly being able to be in the same room? Sometimes I almost had it. But it was like trying to hold on to a dream right after I'd woken up. I could feel the tone and mood, but I couldn't remember the details. And then the feeling was gone, and I couldn't even be sure I'd remembered that right.

"I don't know," he admitted, and the strain in his voice convinced me he was telling the truth.

I didn't remember the math class. I remembered the birdhouse, but I didn't remember pretending to be Luke. I could remember playing in our tree house, but I couldn't remember when we'd been dismantled. The holes in my brain were infuriating, and there didn't seem to be any logic to the gaps. I'd been to four sessions with Dr. Benson in the three weeks since we'd been here, but things weren't any clearer. Not that I'd expected them to be. This was something I had to do on my own. "*What* can't I remember?" That was probably the most important question.

His eyes were sad. "I don't know, Ian. I really don't."

I was pretty sure he was lying. I just didn't know why.

THIRTEEN

JENNA

It was the third week of June already. Work kept me busy, while Becca's emails kept me deflated. She'd been in Europe almost a month, her days brimming over with famous places and picturesque kisses. My summer was a waiting room. I was stuck between when and then, and I wondered if it was ever going to be my time. I prepared for college and races, and I dreamed of a day when I could live by my own words instead of someone else's. But when was I supposed to stop preparing and start experiencing? How was I supposed to know when I'd reached that point?

The fact that my senior year loomed on the threshold made me a little afraid. And exhilarated. But mostly afraid.

Because that meant I had less than a year to polish my ACT score and shine up my GPA so that I wouldn't be stuck at Middleton Community College. And money—I needed way more of that than I had now.

Mom refused to talk about what happened. I'd tried the next morning when I drove her to her car. But the silence had filled the Bronco like a balloon, our exhales expanding it until it pushed me against the steering wheel. She'd informed me, her perfectly plucked eyebrow raised, that she was allowed to have a bad day. I just wished she'd quit stringing those bad days together.

On Tuesday afternoon, I was in the back of the shop sorting through several boxes of clothes that had been dropped off that morning. All of the clothes were at least twenty years old, which, according to Mops, meant they were back in style, but I was pretty doubtful as I pulled out pants that seemed to be made out of plastic shopping bags.

The bell over the door jingled, and Mops spoke. The answering voice was high-pitched enough to break glass, a nasal voice with a hint of a whine. Sandy Smith. I dropped the clothes I was holding and stood up, feeling like I'd just flown by a police car at a hundred miles an hour. Busted. Four days. It took four days for Mops to find out what I'd been trying to keep quiet for seven months.

"Looking for anything in particular?" Mops asked. I eased out of the back room and hid behind a shelf of cracked kitchen gadgets.

"Not really," Sandy said.

But I knew she was lying. She was looking for dirt, the kind that I'd been sweeping under the rug.

Mops went back to the counter, and Sandy shuffled over to look at some dishes. She was like a lioness slowly stalking her prey, waiting until just the right time to bound out of hiding. I measured time by the beats of my heart—after forty-seven thuds, Sandy Smith pounced.

"How's Vivian?" she asked, her voice turning into a whine at the end of her question.

"Fine." Mops looked up from her ledger, suspicious.

Sandy clucked her tongue. "I've been so worried about her," she said. "Tommy told me what happened at Pete's. She's taking her dad's death hard, isn't she?"

Mops flinched. "It's not easy losing someone." I could tell she wasn't sure where this conversation was going.

"But to be that drunk, and in front of Jenna." Sandy shook her head. "You must be so worried, considering..." Her voice trailed off, leaving Mops to finish the sentence. As if any of us needed reminding that being drunk was an inherited trait in the Oliver family. Sandy wrinkled her nose like she smelled something rotten. "How bad is it?"

Understanding crossed Mops's face, and she straightened up, shoulders rigid. "She's perfectly fine, thank you." Mops's smile was forced and looked more like a snarl than an actual smile; her voice was sugarcoated glass. "But I'll pass along your concern. And while we're at it, please remind Tommy that AA meetings are at the Methodist church every Thursday night. From what I hear, he's been drunk at Pete's more than once."

Sandy's eyes flew wide and indignation colored her cheeks. Her mouth twitched, like it was desperate to fire back and couldn't quite figure out how. Sandy spun around and headed for the door, her back so straight it looked like her spine was fused together.

"Now be sure to tell everyone down at the beauty shop I said hello," Mops added. The only answer she got was the angry jingle of the bell and the silence of a closing door.

Mops sighed and flipped the ledger shut. "Come on out," she said. I stepped from my hiding place.

"That one was always jealous of your mother," said Mops. "She had the biggest crush on Jake, and she made your mom's life miserable after she got pregnant." Mops slid the ledger into the drawer under the cash register, then grabbed a couple of shopping bags and carried them over to the reading area. "Sandy acted like Vivian was the first girl around here who'd ever gotten pregnant in high school. She flounced around like a saint, all wide-eyed and innocent, but the way I heard it, she was doing half the football team." Mops dumped the bags out on the rug and started sorting through the clothes, categorizing in a way only she could. "I was so mad when your mom announced she was pregnant, and I sure don't condone what she did. But she got caught doing what most of the other girls were doing. And they trashed her anyway. At least she loved Jake. Not that it mattered to him. He'd already gotten what he wanted."

I stood there like a deer in headlights. Mops and I had never had this conversation; I wasn't so sure I wanted to now.

"I'm very proud of your mom," Mops continued, "the way she held her head up despite the abuse. That sorry excuse of a boyfriend slunk out of town with his tail between his legs. Coward. But your mom didn't run."

I'd never looked at it that way before. I'd never seen Mom as brave—I always thought she'd been too scared to leave. I still wasn't so sure that hadn't been the case. But the way Mops put it, I could see where it would take a lot of guts for Mom to stay put and face her critics every day.

"Have you told her that?" I asked, even though I was pretty sure I already knew the answer. Open communication was not a hobby those two shared.

She shook her head. "I tried. Probably not hard enough. Your mom thinks she has me all figured out, and I don't reckon she's about to change her mind anytime soon."

Mom and Mops were a lot more alike than either would admit. Mules, both of them.

"So, your mom is drinking." It wasn't a question. "Why the hell haven't you said anything?"

Because I was trying to protect everyone. Myself. Mom. Mops. I was trying to plug the leaks in the boat before it went down, only every time I thought I had one leak taken care of, two more appeared. But I was starting to believe that some things couldn't be fixed. The past was never really past, and every choice, mistake or not, had consequences.

Mops sighed when I didn't answer. "Did your mother ever tell you why I stopped drinking?"

"No." I knew what had caused Mops and Pops to start. Mom's little brother died of diabetes when he was just five. They hadn't known he had it, and one day, he just slipped into a coma and never woke up. But I'd never asked why Mops stopped—or why Pops couldn't.

I grabbed a box that hadn't been unpacked yet and joined Mops. This seemed like the kind of conversation that needed busy hands. I sat next to Mops on the carpet, just like I had almost every day of my childhood. But I figured this story wasn't going to be anything like the fairy tales she used to tell me.

"I was a bad drunk," Mops said matter-of-factly. "I got angry. I yelled and threw things and hit Pops."

That didn't sound like the Mops I knew. My Mops was patient and kind, always cooking for other people or visiting them in the hospital. I didn't know the woman she was talking about.

"Pops was a melancholy drunk. He would get sad and just sit and stare out into space. Or cry. Sometimes I hated him for that."

He sounded like Mom. I hadn't known that Pops either, not really, because they'd always tried to keep me away from him when he was drunk.

"I was angry at the world. I started drinking to numb the pain of losing Billy, but it didn't work. It just made everything worse, and by the time I realized it, it was too late. I couldn't stop. So I would get drunk and blame everyone else for my problems. I blamed God for taking Billy. He could have taken anyone. He could have taken me, even. But Billy didn't deserve to die."

I wondered why people always said that. No one really *deserved* to die—it just happened. Besides, death was only a punishment for those of us left behind.

Mops didn't look at me as she continued, just kept picking through the clothes and putting them in piles. "One night, when your mother was sixteen or so, I got really drunk and decided I wanted to go out to the cemetery and see Billy. Pops was asleep on the couch, and your mother was out. She didn't spend a lot of time at home. Not that I blamed her." Mops stopped for a minute and stared at a pair of jeans that were so ripped up they seemed to be pleading to be put out of their misery. She didn't seem to know what to do with them. I took them from her and tossed them in my trash pile. Mops was never willing to give up on things.

She sighed. "Anyway, I have no idea how it happened. One minute I was driving along fine, and the next minute my car was sitting in a house over on Azalea Street. There were bricks and dust all over my car. I'd hit my head pretty hard, and there was blood pouring down my face, but other than that, I was okay. I climbed out of the car, really shaky, and there, pinned in the headlights, was a crib."

The lines on Mops's forehead looked deeper than usual, her freckles darker on her pale face. She clasped her hands tightly in her lap, like she was trying to hold herself together. I listened to her voice, ripples through the air, as it strung letters into words, words into sentences, sentences into story. But the meaning flowed straight through me, swift and cold, leaving me numb. Because this story couldn't have been about Mops. I was afraid to hear more; I was too afraid not to.

"The crib was mangled and crushed, bent around the hood of my car and pushed against the opposite wall. I sobered up fast. I thought I was going to throw up, and I remember begging God that I hadn't killed that baby. I don't know how I managed to get over to that crib. I was numb from the waist down, and shaking so badly it was a wonder I could walk at all." Her hands were unsteady as she tried several times to fold a sweater. She finally gave up, squeezing it into a ball instead.

"I thought my heart would stop as I reached out to look under a tumbled pile of blankets. But there was a teddy bear in the crib. No baby."

Mops took a deep breath at the same time I let mine out. Inhale—regret. Exhale—relief. I wondered how many times she'd dreamt it, woken up in a panic, wet with sweat. Something like that gnaws at a person, devouring from the inside out. It was a memory that clung to each day, unwilling to let go.

"The cops came shortly after that and took me in. They ticketed me, and my driver's license was suspended for a while. We had to pay for the damage to the house. But I didn't care about any of that. I knew I deserved worse. That baby had been in the kitchen with its mother, getting a bottle. If it hadn't been, I would have killed someone else's child."

Mops started helping me sort through my box. Somewhere in the middle of her story, I'd forgotten what I was supposed to be doing.

"I hated myself," she said. "I hated that I could have been the reason someone lost their baby, just like I lost mine. I quit drinking cold turkey. Not that it was easy. I went to meetings. I almost caved several times. Pops kept right on drinking, no matter how much I tried to help him. It wasn't easy having it in the house. And your mom never forgave me. Sometimes I think she got pregnant just to punish me.

"But you were the best gift ever," she added, reaching over and cupping my face. "After you came, I had a better reason to stay sober."

Another reason I was going to feel guilty if I could manage to make it out of here. If I left, what would happen to Mom and Mops? I was the only family they had.

"Why are you telling me this now?" I asked.

"You should know." Her face darkened. "And your mom needs to remember. She hasn't ever forgiven me for being a drunk. She doesn't need to make the same mistake I did."

"She's not a drunk," I said, "not yet." She hadn't really started drinking until Pops died. She couldn't become an alcoholic in seven months, could she? "It won't get that bad." But I'd learned that saying the words didn't make them true.

"Let's hope not."

We closed the shop early, and I was home by four-thirty. It was too hot to run, but I needed to fly. The air was heavy and oppressive, and storm clouds built on the horizon. Maybe they'd be empty when they reached me. Maybe I'd be.

LUKE

Solitude—what a perfect name. Our house was miles from town, which was miles from anywhere. Circles upon circles of nothing, with my room in the center. I'd never spent this much time alone before. It had always been *we*, not *me*. I was starting to get on my nerves. I needed out.

The air was thick and strained to hold up the clouds. I walked down the hill and past the small pond. Two weathered chairs guarded the marshy bank, their paint warped and peeling. A lazy drizzle scattered the pond's stillness. I followed a small path into the woods. It was quiet. Even the birds and bugs waited to see what was going to happen.

I walked.

The drizzle turned to rain.

I kept walking.

Thunder began somewhere on the horizon and rumbled its way closer. I continued putting one foot in front of the other. It poured, soaking me, but I didn't mind. It separated me from the rest of the world, a curtain of water that tucked me away. So I wasn't at all prepared when she ran into view.

Jenna. She colored my thoughts, turning gray into Technicolor. Which was a bad thing. Just one of many. I couldn't stop thinking about her, maybe because I shouldn't have wanted her. Couldn't have her. She was gorgeous—a risk I shouldn't take. But I knew it was more than that. *She* was more than that. Like the way she held her head or the expression on her face when she thought I wasn't looking. She was even more intriguing than she was beautiful.

Jenna wore gray cotton shorts and a gray tank top with maroon lettering. SHS Warriors. She was drenched, and I envied the rain. But despite the lightning, and the mud that was splattered on her shins, she was grinning. Watching her, I fell in love with storms.

She was pure movement. Powerful. Graceful. Moments after she appeared, she vanished into the trees, only to reappear much closer to me.

She didn't see me until she was almost on top of me. Her smile disappeared as she jumped, startled, and darted away from me. I scared her. Not surprising. I sort of had that effect on people. Then she smiled at me, and my heart felt too big for my chest.

"Ian! You scared the hell out of me!"

Of course she thought I was Ian. Again. I was willing to bet he had no intention of telling her about me. I couldn't blame him. I'd made a mess out of everything. And he didn't even remember what happened to the last girlfriend of his I kissed. So the fact that I wanted to touch this beautiful girl standing in front of me threatened to ruin me. I'd always been a little self-destructive.

Jenna's brow furrowed, and I knew she was wondering why I hadn't said anything. Why *hadn't* I said anything?

"Or not," she said. "You're Luke, aren't you?"

"Guilty." In all ways possible.

"Sorry."

And then we stood there, staring at one another while the rain fell through the trees. Lightning struck somewhere nearby, the resulting boom shaking the earth.

"You'd better get home," I told her. Better for everyone. Safer.

Her eyes narrowed. She didn't like me telling her what to do. "You'd better get home too," she said. She looked behind her. "Look, I live right over there. You should come in and wait out the storm. You're a good three miles from your house."

I should have said no, but I didn't want to. And I usually did what I wanted, even though it almost always got me in trouble. Ian was going to be pissed. Jenna just might cause way more damage than any storm.

Jenna jogged ahead, and it wasn't as easy to keep up with her as I thought it would be. I stared at the space in between her shoulders blades, pointedly keeping myself from staring at her butt. Or her legs. Both were pretty nice.

Her gray shirt melded into the sheet of rain. We sprinted behind a row of houses. With no trees to slow its fall, the rain pounded down on us, making sure I was thoroughly drenched. More lightning, louder thunder.

I followed Jenna into her garage and through the back door, both of us dripping water all over the tile. She handed me a towel, but I was too wet for it to do much good.

"I'll be right back," she told me, and she disappeared.

I felt really stupid just standing there. I tried to squeeze some of the wet out of my clothes, but that just made an even larger puddle on the floor. I was trying to clean it up when Jenna came back.

"Here." She handed me a stack of clothes. "It's the best I could do." She pointed to the laundry room. "Change in there and toss your clothes in the dryer."

"Already trying to get me out of my clothes."

She laughed, and I felt the world stop. Her laugh was deep and loud and so full of possibility that it made me sad. Sad because I wanted to know her better. Sad because I couldn't.

"Just do what I said," she ordered.

I did as I was told, like a good boy. If she only knew. I winced at that. I would rather she didn't. I had lost count of the lives I'd managed to destroy. That right there should've made me leave this girl alone. It didn't.

I threw my clothes in the dryer, shoes too, which banged loudly once I turned the thing on. I put on the clothes she'd given me.

"You're joking, right?" I shouted through the closed door, and over the thump of the dryer, I heard her giggle.

"Best I could do, remember?"

She'd brought me some of *her* clothes. The sweatpants were about four inches too short, and the T-shirt was really tight across my chest and arms. It was going to be all stretched out when I was through with it. I looked ridiculous. Not really the way I'd played it all out in my head. It was going to be hard to come off cool when I was dressed this way.

"This is pretty cruel," I said as I came into the kitchen. Her face turned red as she tried not to laugh. "I mean, first you arrange for this storm so you can get me naked. Then you force me to wear girls' clothes."

"I didn't force you to do anything."

"So you wouldn't mind if I just went *au naturel* while I waited for my clothes to dry?" I asked.

She eyed me, daring me. "Be my guest."

She had no idea who she was talking to. I started to take off the shirt.

"No!" she hollered. She sounded a little afraid.

I laughed. "You're right. The full effect can be a bit overwhelming."

She filled a kettle and set it on the stove. "We don't have any men around here," she explained, "so it was that or one of my mom's dresses."

"Then this is perfect." I sat down in one of the large chairs over by the window. It was a really comfortable room, and Jenna looked at home here, almost as much as she had in the woods. Almost. Stacked books sat on the small table between the two chairs, all of them worn and weathered, their covers creased and torn, their pages ruffled. An old lamp warmed the room as the rain continued to splash against the windows.

Jenna stood in the kitchen, barefoot and wearing sweatpants and a T-shirt that matched mine. A winged shoe was stamped at her hip and across the front of the shirt. Her hair hung in a braid down her back and left a wet spot between her shoulder blades, and I discovered that I had never wanted to kiss someone as much as I wanted to kiss her.

"You run cross-country?" I asked, trying to get the image of her lips out of my head.

"Yep. I'm one of two girls on the team." She twisted her mouth down, but her voice gave her away—she was proud of that. She took two mugs out of the cabinet, and I tried not to look at the flat planes of her stomach as her T-shirt rode up. The kettle began to scream, and I looked away.

I picked up the book on the top of the stack and flipped through it. India.

"I like to read about different places," she explained, pouring the boiling water over the tea bags. "Sugar?"

"Sure."

She finished with the tea and handed me the steaming mug before folding herself into the other chair.

"So. Twins. That's really cool."

"It used to be," I admitted. Now it was just awkward.

"Which one of you is the oldest?"

"I am, by seven minutes." The room wrapped itself around Jenna. "You have any brothers or sisters?"

"Nope. Only child," she said. "Just me, my mom, and Mops."

"Who's Mops?"

"My grandmother. She owns the secondhand store where I work." She paused, her mouth forming a perfect "o." Then she smiled. "That was you in there that day."

I had to look away; her eyes were making me nervous. They kept me from thinking straight. "Sorry about that. I wasn't supposed to go to town."

"Why not?"

Shit. "Let's just say I got into a little trouble back home. It's a long story." She had no idea how long. And she wasn't going to know, not if I could help it.

JENNA

At first it was weird, looking at Ian who wasn't Ian. But after a while, I saw Luke. Even though he looked exactly like Ian, Luke was different. Darker. Funnier. His eyes had questions behind them rather than laughter, his jaw harsher than his brother's.

I hardly noticed the storm. Hardly noticed the banging coming from the dryer or the fact that my tea had gotten cold. I really didn't notice anything but Luke.

"God, can your mother even tell you two apart?" I joked. I'd been staring at Luke for the past half-hour and I was just noticing the subtle differences.

It was obviously the wrong question to ask. Luke's eyes got very dark and there was something dangerous in his face. For a moment, I was afraid of him. For a moment, I realized that I'd invited a complete stranger into the house. And that my mom wouldn't be home for hours.

But then he grinned, and my fears melted away in the warmth of that smile. "We used to play tricks on her all the time when we were little. But tell me about Solitude," Luke said. He looked genuinely interested—poor thing. It wouldn't take long.

"Solitude sucks."

He smiled. "Surely there are some good things about it."

Not really. "Everybody is in everybody else's business and I just want to go somewhere where no one knows me or my mom or my grandmother, where I can start fresh and do all sorts of unpredictable things I can't do here."

"Like what?" he asked. I could have drowned in the blue of his eyes.

"I don't know. Anything. Everything. Just last week my best friend Becca was drinking coffee at a sidewalk café in the shadow of the Eiffel Tower and in the Louvre looking at paintings she didn't appreciate." I hated how bitter I sounded, but I'd been working and taking care of my mom and being responsible. "Hell, I'd settle for running naked through a subway station or something."

"*That* I would like to see," he said.

"There are some good things about Solitude." I tried not to sound so cranky. "I love the store and the old train yard. I run in the woods all the time without ever seeing anyone."

Luke smiled at me.

"Well, rarely seeing anyone," I amended. "And the lake. Solitude Point is pretty cool."

"Solitude Point—sounds lonely."

"Yeah, everything around here is pretty lonely, but it's a nice place to go if you want quiet. There's this bluff, the Point, which juts out over the water. We used to jump off, before they outlawed it."

"I'd love to see it," he said, and his voice sent ripples through my stomach.

"We'll go sometime, take a picnic or something," I promised. I shouldn't have. I should have been thinking about Ian. Not that he was my boyfriend. But it felt a little like cheating. But for once, I was doing something that wasn't completely responsible. And that felt a little like freedom.

"I should probably get going," Luke said.

I turned around and looked out the window. It was still pouring. "I'll give you a ride."

"No, really, that's okay. I can walk. I'd rather walk."

"Not in this. That's stupid."

He looked out the window, then back at me. "Okay. I do need to get back before my mom gets home. She doesn't like me being out."

I couldn't imagine what he'd done that was so bad. I didn't really want to.

Luke disappeared into the laundry room, and I laid my head back against the chair. I was more than a little bit confused. Unsettled.

"Not completely dry, but it'll do," he said, coming back into the kitchen. "I just left yours in there."

"That's fine. Let me grab my shoes."

We sprinted out to the Bronco, but it didn't matter—we were both soaked by the time we climbed inside.

"Cool ride," Luke said.

It was. I'd loved that Bronco since I was eight years old. "Yeah, although she doesn't have air, and she burns through oil really fast."

"Those are the best kinds. They have personality. I miss my truck."

"Where is it?" I asked. The wipers were on high, but the rain was coming down too fast for them to be much use. I drove slowly.

Luke stared out the windshield. "I got in trouble last summer and Dad made me get rid of it. He also took my phone and anything else useful he didn't think I deserved." When he looked at me, his eyes were hard. "The silver truck is Ian's. Dad bought it for him because he's the perfect twin. I'm the disappointment, so I had to buy my own." He shrugged, then grinned at me. "I liked it better that way. I helped my uncle build cabinets all summer to buy that truck. I earned it."

The windows fogged up, making it hard to see where I was going. We couldn't roll them down, so it was stuffy and sticky inside the Bronco. I didn't know what to say, so we didn't say anything, just listened to the rain loud on the roof and the back and forth of the wipers.

The dirt road was muddy and slippery, and I had to concentrate to keep out of the ditch. I wondered how I was going to act if Ian was home.

I didn't see his truck when we pulled up, but then again, I couldn't really see anything at all. "Thanks for the ride," Luke said.

"No problem." But it was. The fact that I was hoping to see him again was a big problem.

Luke pulled the handle, but the door didn't budge. He smiled and pushed against it with his shoulder. Nothing.

"Yeah, sometimes it gets stuck. You have to pull it up, out, and slightly to the left," I told him.

He tried and failed. I laughed. "It's an art, really. Here."

I put the car in park and leaned across Luke. My arm pressed against his chest as I jimmied the handle. The door popped open, and rain poured in. Luke's hand brushed mine as he pulled the door partway closed, blocking some of the rain. I was embarrassed at how hard my heart was pounding. Surely it was loud enough to be heard over the rain. I slid over into my seat.

"You're going to get me in trouble," he murmured.

Funny, I thought as he disappeared into the rain. *I was thinking the exact same thing.*

FOURTEEN

JENNA

It was late, that ambiguous place where time was suspended and yesterday kissed tomorrow before putting on today. When my phone rang, I wasn't sure if the call was coming from Tuesday night or Wednesday morning. I groaned and groped for the phone on the nightstand, knocking my glass of water to the floor.

I swore and tumbled out of bed, stepping in the water on the floor, cussed some more, then stumbled around the room and tried to locate the wailing phone. I stubbed my toe on the corner of the bed, which woke me up quickly. When I finally found the phone in the pocket of my shorts, it had stopped ringing.

I glared at the screen. I'd missed a call from Ian. We'd texted a few times since the lake party, but we kept missing each other's calls. Work, and my mother, took up most of my time these days. I jumped when it started ringing again.

"What?" I snapped, trying to keep my voice down so I wouldn't wake my mom. If she'd been able to sleep through all that in the first place.

"Hey, it's Luke."

"You want me to hate you, don't you?"

He chuckled softly. "I thought we could find some trouble together."

My stomach tightened. "How about telling me what you want without delivering some over-rehearsed line."

"You promised to take me on a picnic at the Point," he reminded me.

"It's the middle of the night!" What was he thinking? And sneaking out with Ian's brother seemed like a very bad idea. "Some other time."

"But I'm awake now." He was pleading. It might have been cute if it wasn't so annoying.

But now I was awake. Responsible Jenna would have said no, especially after recently kissing Ian. But then I thought of Becca, and some of my guilt turned into a desire for adventure. For once I was going to do something simply because I wanted to. And maybe partly because I shouldn't.

"All right." I sighed, a little too dramatically. He laughed; he knew I wanted to go.

"When can you be here?"

"I'm here now."

I rushed to the window and looked out, trying to see anything in the dark. The moon peered down, but it wasn't much help. There might have been a darker shadow underneath the tree, but I couldn't be sure. "Prove it."

A flashlight came on. Luke held it underneath his chin like kids do when they're telling ghost stories. I grinned.

"Give me five minutes."

I managed to make it out the back door without waking Mom. Only the morning would reveal whether this had been worth it or not. Luke stood underneath the tree, his grin devilish. I didn't know if my racing pulse had more to do with him or the possibility of getting busted.

"I'm not so sure about this," I said.

"Which is exactly why you should do it," he argued. "You'll never get another chance. You'll never get a do-over, because you'll never be at this exact same moment again."

Well, when he put it *that* way. "So who's driving?" I asked.

"Me." He took off across the yard. "I parked down the street."

We didn't say anything as we walked to the truck. The air tasted different, and it felt like the entire neighborhood was stuffed with cotton. Nothing moved except us.

I climbed in the truck, careful not to slam the door too loudly or think too much about what I was doing. There were two large bags in the backseat. "What's that?" I asked as Luke slid into the driver's seat.

"The picnic, of course."

"How did you know I'd come?"

It was too dark in the truck to read the look he gave me. But I felt his eyes on mine. "Girls have a hard time telling me no."

"I'm sure I won't find it too difficult."

He grinned. "You already did."

The engine roared as Luke started the truck, saving me from having to come up with some appropriate retort. I was sure we'd just woken up the entire neighborhood, but everything stayed dark as we pulled away from the curb and down the deserted street. It felt like we were the only two people left on an abandoned planet. We rolled through the center of town. The streets were dark, the streetlights like tiny fairies suspended in the night. Even the lawn in front of the courthouse looked charming, the flowers bursts of color in the headlights, fading to gray as we passed. It was as if the whole world had pulled out its magnificence just for us—like we were seeing the secret splendor that only appeared when everyone was sleeping. We were silent, and I held my breath, afraid to shatter the spell.

Each road grew smaller and wilder as we drove into the country, the layers of civilization peeling away until we eased down a tiny dirt road through the center of the woods, finally taking an even smaller one to the cove. We pulled out of the trees and into a tiny clearing. The moon turned the lake silver, and the Point protruded like a bony finger. Luke parked and turned off the engine; the hush of night rushed in. "Wait here," he said.

The dark was different out here, like maybe how dark was supposed to be before man tamed it. The moon kept my secret, giving me just enough light to see Luke's outline but not enough to let him see the conflict that must have been on my face.

Luke took my hand and helped me out of the truck. It was the first time we'd consciously touched, and I couldn't ignore the way his skin melted into mine. A blanket lay underneath a pine tree growing close to the water. Luke had set a small lantern in the center of the blanket, and I folded down next to a pizza box from Repete's. I laughed and opened the box. Cold shrimp pizza. My favorite.

"You're not allergic?" I asked.

"Nope. Just Ian."

"Weird," I said, grabbing a slice and putting it on the paper plate Luke had set out. "I thought twins were exactly alike." But I knew better. Luke was nothing like Ian. And I hadn't yet figured out how I felt about that.

"Hardly." His voice was low and rough, his jaw a sharp line.

"Sorry."

"Don't be. Honest mistake." He loaded his plate with pizza. "We are identical, literally split in half. But allergies aren't in our DNA, so he got them and I didn't."

The water slapped softly against the shore, a gentle percussion backed up by the hum of insects. The night made us whisper. The pizza sat uneaten. I forgot food when I was talking to Luke. I forgot to envy Becca and resent my mom. I forgot escape, because when Luke spoke, there was nowhere else to go. I made him describe all the places he'd lived. I felt small when he talked about the Rockies and indescribably young when he talked about one of the castles he remembered visiting in Germany. After a while, some of Luke's black arrogance fell away and I saw the boy underneath.

We took off our shoes and stuck our feet in the warm water. Solitude Point's jagged edge jutted out to our left and seemed to cut the sky in half. We lay on our backs and looked up at the stars. Luke and I weren't touching, but I could feel the heat rolling off his skin.

"What do you miss most about home?" I asked him.

"Which one?"

"Any of them," I said. "All of them."

I turned my head to look at him. He was looking up, his profile dark and angular in the shadows.

"I knew exactly who I was back there," he whispered. "Here, I could be anyone."

"Isn't that a good thing?" I asked. That was one of the reasons I wanted to leave here. Go somewhere where no one knew me, so I could be exactly whoever I wanted to be, instead of trying to play the part I was given back before I was even born.

"Not always." He rolled his head toward me, our faces almost touching in the dark. "Sometimes when you lose yourself, you never find your way back."

It got harder and harder to breathe with him looking at me like that. He was so sad.

He sat up abruptly. "Let's go for a swim." I could tell it took some effort for him to make his voice light.

"I don't have my suit," I said.

His laugh was loud in the quiet night. "No suits necessary." He stood up and pulled off his shirt in one swift movement.

I blushed and was glad it was dark. "Already trying to get me out of my clothes," I said.

He laughed again. "You coming or not?"

And before I had a chance to change my mind, I waded in, clothes and all. "I'm not that easy."

The water was warm, although the farther we swam, the more cold pockets we found. I tried not to think about what was swimming underneath me in the dark.

"I'm feeling a little reckless," I admitted. There was something about being here with Luke that made me want to see what it would be like to make choices based on this moment, rather than future ones.

"Oh really?" His voice taunted me in the dark. "Because I have all sorts of ideas."

"Don't get too excited," I explained, jerking my head toward the cliff. "I'm talking about jumping off the Point."

"You've jumped before?" he asked.

"It's been awhile," I told him. "It's illegal now." For good reason. But tonight I wasn't going to think about then. I was only going to think about now.

"I take it you don't break the law," Luke said, treading water until I caught up.

I kicked harder and swam past him. "I take it you do."

He chuckled. "Only the stupid ones."

We pulled through the black water, everything quiet but our splashes and the sound of our breathing. Tiny goose bumps appeared on my arms as I put my feet down and waded onto shore.

"How do we get up there?" Luke asked, staring up at the towering cliff.

"We climb."

I gripped the sharp rock and positioned my feet, pushing up with my legs, then balancing and placing my hands. It wasn't an easy climb, especially in the dark, and I didn't look down. Luke was halfway up when I reached the top, and I waited for him.

He was out of breath. "How far down is it?"

"Twenty or thirty feet. I'm not sure exactly."

I peered over the cliff, my toes grabbing the edge. I couldn't see the water. The rock was solid and safe, but I couldn't wait to leap into the unknown. It could end badly, or it could be glorious. All I knew was that I wanted to have a chance to fly.

Life held so much possibility—failure or wild success, poverty or wealth, love or heartache. And with the varying shades in between each of those, I had no idea what would happen. There would be pain, and eventually death, but oh God, the possibility. If I stayed put, I was fairly certain how my life would turn out. But out there, there was no way of knowing. Absolutely none. And that was the rush—the chance that absolutely anything could happen. Here, nothing ever would. Not really.

I leaned out, letting my body pull me forward into nothing. At the very last moment, I pulled my hands above my head and pushed away from the cliff, diving headfirst into the dark.

It was several glorious, completely uncontrollable seconds before I hit the water. I let myself dive farther and farther toward the bottom, then curved toward the surface in a huge arc, kicking hard with my legs. Just when

I thought I wasn't going to be able to hold my breath any longer, I broke the surface and pulled in a deep breath.

"Jenna? You okay?" Luke's voice floated somewhere above me.

"I'm great! Your turn," I shouted back, sending my voice out toward his.

Luke ran and leapt from the edge, throwing himself off the cliff in a sudden burst of momentum. He hit the water hard, spray flying back up almost to the cliff's edge. He came up grinning.

"You made that look too easy," he said.

We swam back toward the cliff. Luke reached the Point first and wrapped his hand around my wrist, pulling me through the water and into his chest. I stopped breathing.

He was standing on a ledge at the base of the Point, and I put my feet down as he turned my back to the rock and leaned in toward me. Water lapped at my waist, the rock rough through my wet clothes. I wondered if Luke could hear my heart beating against my skin. I could—it was so loud in my ears that it drowned out every other sound.

He reached up and traced his fingers down the side of my face, and I shivered as they trailed across my throat.

"Aren't you going to ask if you can kiss me?" I whispered. I couldn't help remembering that Ian had.

His answer had no words but said everything. I couldn't think about Ian when Luke's lips moved against mine. I put my arms around his neck and pulled him closer, feeling more reckless than I had when I'd thrown myself off the Point. When he ran his fingers down the side of my neck, I couldn't think at all.

Luke pulled away, and I felt his whisper on my skin. "I never ask permission."

LUKE

The world was a different place when Jenna spoke. Her words revealed the box where I'd hidden pieces of myself. Her kiss broke the lock. Her voice coaxed the ragged shards out of the dark. I started to come back together, finding what I thought had been lost forever. We talked, and the water sighed against the shore. We talked, and the sky changed from black to purple. Blue hinted at the horizon. We were going to have to get back. My mom would be home from work soon. We needed to slink back under cover of darkness. If I wasn't there when she got in, there would be hell to pay. But it would be worth it.

I reached out and brushed the hair away from Jenna's face. She looked up at me, her eyes wide and trusting, and in that moment, I didn't care what happened. I would risk everything just to stay there. I wanted to tether the sun to the earth, keep it from coming up and ending the perfect night. Instead, I sat up and reached for my shirt.

"Where did you get that scar?" Jenna asked. She reached across the space between us, her fingers trembling just a little bit, like she was afraid to touch me. To be honest, I was afraid of her touching me, like it was some line we were about to cross. It was ridiculous. I'd crossed that line when I'd shown up at her house. And that kiss had been more like running across a bridge and setting it ablaze. I knew now that, no matter what happened, we couldn't go back. And I hated myself for it. Because if she got hurt, it would be all my fault. And there was no way she wouldn't get hurt at this point. No matter what happened, it was going to be painful.

I caught my breath as her fingers lightly stroked the scar that ran along my right side. Her fingers were cool, and I brought her hand to my lips and kissed her palm. I wanted to bury my hands in her hair and forget everything else, but I answered her question instead.

"When Ian and I were twelve, he had appendicitis. Emergency, so they had to cut him open to take it out. He has a scar too, except his isn't as rough." I was the one with all the jagged edges. "I hated that he had a mark I didn't, something to tell us apart. We were really close when we were little, and it felt like that scar had separated us." I'd been so young then. Naïve. That scar hadn't separated us. I had. "One night, I got out of bed and snuck down to the kitchen. I took a kitchen knife and sliced into my stomach."

Jenna flinched and pulled away. "You must have been out of your mind. You could have died."

"I didn't cut that deep," I told her. "Just a few stitches, good as new, and Ian and I were identical again."

She shook her head. It was a pretty gruesome story. "What happened?" she asked.

I knew what she was talking about. And I wasn't ready to tell her everything just yet. I wanted a little more time with her. I'd always been a selfish bastard.

"We grew up." I slid on my shirt. "We'd better go."

She nodded and helped me carry the stuff back to the truck.

"You probably shouldn't mention this to Ian," I said. I had enough problems already.

"I wasn't planning on it."

I grinned. "I believe I've been a bad influence on you."

"Don't flatter yourself." She climbed in the passenger side of the truck and slammed the door.

I knew I should feel bad about wanting to see her again. Ian was the better brother, the one more deserving of Jenna, but I couldn't help but hope she would pick me, as impossible and improbable as I knew that was.

I started the truck. "You know, I really don't mind a little competition." Hell, I'd been competing with my brother my whole life. In school, in sports, for our parents' attention. He always won.

"Who said it would be a competition?" she asked, arching her eyebrow.

Ouch.

FIFTEEN

JENNA

I didn't know what to do, so I avoided them both. I worked. I took down and dusted all the books, making sure they were organized correctly and that none had fallen to the back of the shelves. I went through numerous boxes from the back, pricing and displaying whatever was inside. I filled my mind with stories, creating lives for the remnants I found—a single chopstick with mother-of-pearl inlay, a Scooby Doo lunchbox, two handfuls of costume jewelry. When my stories gained characters similar to either Ian or Luke, I found something else to do.

At night I ran, trying to outdistance the demons. But sometimes the absurdity of the whole thing caught up with me, overtook me on the trails and shouldered its way next to me, matching me stride for stride. Who was I to think I even got to choose? They weren't outfits—I couldn't just put Ian on one day and Luke the next. And who said either one of them was interested in me anyway? They sure hadn't called.

Becca sent me an email from Italy with a picture of her sitting on the edge of a fountain, laughing. She had her arms around two dark-haired boys. She ended her note with "sorry your summer sucks." And even though I knew she hadn't meant anything by it, I was even more determined to prove her wrong.

And while working at Repete's wasn't the kind of adventure I was looking for, at least taking orders and making pizzas kept my mind occupied enough that it didn't wander to Ian or Luke. I prayed they wouldn't come in, and they didn't, and then I hated myself for wanting them to—and for not knowing which one I wanted to see.

"Everything okay at home?" Pete asked. It was Monday afternoon and we were both in the kitchen working on a to-go order for a birthday party.

I shrugged. Nothing was okay, but Pete didn't need the gory details.

"I lost both my parents before I was twenty-five," Pete told me, "and I drank to try and get through some of the worst of it, especially after I lost my football scholarship. It didn't help."

I hadn't heard this story—I didn't even know he'd gone to college.

He nodded, answering my unasked question, and continued layering pepperoni. "My dad died in the spring of my freshman year at the university. I came home to help my mom settle a few things, and when a few things turned into way more than we could handle and I couldn't get back for summer workouts, they cut me loose."

"That's awful," I said. I couldn't imagine anything worse than finally making it out only to be pulled back in again, like drowning, getting a gulp of air, then being pulled farther and farther under until that lungful of air was replaced by a mouthful of water.

Pete turned and slid the pizza in the oven. "I couldn't control it. Mom died a few years later, but it was too late for me to go back. But your mom," he said, bringing the conversation back around, "she'll pull through." But that wasn't something he could promise. No one could.

A familiar truck was parked against the curb when I pulled into my driveway after work, and a dark figure was sitting on my top step. I analyzed his clothes and hair and the way he was looking at me, but I wasn't sure until he stood up and smiled. He stood straight, not slouched, and there was nothing mocking or taunting in that smile. Ian. My heart pulled in opposite directions, equally split between relief and disappointment. And guilt for feeling both.

Ian waited for me on the porch, his back against the railing. He gave me a half-wave and a sheepish grin.

"Hey," I said, slamming the car door.

"I'm sorry," he blurted out. "For not calling."

"Which time?" I asked. It had been almost a week since his last text or missed call. Two weeks since the party. But I hadn't exactly been sitting by the phone either.

He rubbed the back of his neck. "All of them," he said.

"Don't worry about it." I unlocked the front door.

He stood just outside, looking guilty and uncertain. "I hope I haven't messed things up." He said what I should have been saying.

"You want to stay for dinner?" I asked.

His answering smile was so honest and unmasked that it nearly took my breath away.

Mom came home an hour later. Ian and I were facing one another on the couch playing a made-up trivia game; he was winning.

"Jenna! You didn't tell me you had a date." Mom smiled at Ian and batted her eyelashes, a move she'd probably perfected by the time she was five. "I'm Vivian Oliver," she said.

Ian stood up. "Ian McAlister." He shook her hand.

Mom's eyebrows went up about three inches. "Ah," she said, as if she had solved some great mystery. "You just moved in." Her voice caught, and she smiled wider, playing it off. "Nice to meet you."

"I invited him for dinner."

"Great!" Mom was practically floating. "Hope you like frozen lasagna."

"Well, I prefer it cooked, but whatever," he said.

A woman who looked like my mother threw back her head and laughed. "If you insist."

We sat in the kitchen while the lasagna was in the oven, Mom at the bar, Ian and I in the chairs underneath the window. Mom recycled some of Pops's old jokes, and I couldn't tell if she was pretending or if she was finding pieces of her old self. A flash of a smile, eyes that were alert—memories of who she'd been surfaced in her face, but I wasn't sure I trusted them. She was drinking out of her tumbler, and when she stepped out of the room, I sniffed it. It smelled like Diet Coke, but I couldn't be sure, so I took a sip. Diet Coke. Usually it was more vodka than anything else, but tonight, she was just herself. Mom without the high-octane. I was more comfortable with her that way— when she was just my mom. When she was someone I had to babysit—protect from herself—then I was tensed muscles and nausea. Drinking Mom said hurtful things and made me ashamed of who she was and who I wasn't. I couldn't settle when she was like that.

But Ian settled us both. He wasn't barbs and nettles; his edges were water, not rock. He helped me make the salad and set the table. He reminded me what normal felt like. For the first time in months, it felt like home rather than rehab.

I knew she was behaving because we had company. Tomorrow, or even after Ian left, she'd probably be right back where she'd been for the past several months. But it was nice, being reminded of what it had been like before.

"Has Jenna given you the grand tour of Solitude?" Mom asked. She had actually eaten her lasagna rather than deconstructing it and pushing it around her plate.

I rolled my eyes. "Ian has seen all Solitude has to offer— the lake and Repete's. There's not much else."

"So what did you think?" Mom pressed. "You like it here?"

"It's nice," Ian said.

"You don't have to lie," I told him.

He smiled at me, his expression transparent. He looked incapable of lying at all. "Really," he assured me. "It's different from any other place I've ever lived."

That I believed.

"I saw your picture on the table at Repete's," Ian told Mom. "It's like you're a celebrity."

It was all I could do not to groan out loud. She smiled so wide I was afraid she was going to dislocate her cheek. And then I had to hear the story about the championship game and her cheerleading fame. I'd heard it all I needed to.

What I didn't understand about the story was the way she talked about my father. I'd never once heard her say anything bad about him. It didn't make any sense. He'd left her, pregnant and scared, and gone off to fulfill his dreams. He didn't call. He didn't send money. His parents moved off when he got married so that they could be closer to their real grandchildren. The ones they claimed. I never knew them, either. And Mom didn't seem the least bit resentful. I knew she'd loved him—anyone could hear it in her voice. But she never once blamed him. She was way more forgiving than I ever would have been. Then again, I would never have been in that position. I would never let a guy destroy my future.

Mom offered to clean the kitchen and sent Ian and me outside. We wandered out to the back porch and sat on the swing. The shadows grew longer as the sun fell, and the tiniest of breezes kicked up, enough to keep the mosquitos from landing for too long. I leaned my head against the back of the swing, closed my eyes, and listened to myself breathe.

"Tell me a memory," Ian said.

I turned my head and opened my eyes. He was leaning against the back of the swing, staring at me, a lazy smile on his face. I couldn't help smiling back.

"What kind of memory?" I asked.

"Something happy."

"Why?"

His smile was sad and a bit hopeful. "I'm collecting memories."

I closed my eyes again and told him about Pops. Since Ian was living in Pops's house, I wanted him to have those memories. That way, a piece of Pops was still in the house. I only told Ian the good parts. I skipped over the time that Mops and I were in the kitchen cooking dinner when Pops stumbled in drunk. He'd sat down to take off his boots and just slid into the middle of the floor, out cold. I stuck to the happy memories—like when Pops took me fishing or picking strawberries. I told him about all the meals we'd had in the kitchen that was now his. I told him about the time Pops and I had sat on the back porch and watched a storm roll in, staying outside until the rain blew across the boards and stung our faces. I gave him more than one memory, because I just couldn't pick the best one.

Ian didn't say anything, not even when I ran out of words. I turned my head to look at him. He was studying my face.

"What are you looking at?" I asked, self-conscious. I never knew if my reflection was the real me or not. Maybe the person everyone else saw wasn't the one I really thought I was.

"You," he answered, and I wondered what he saw.

A tiny glow of light flickered out in the yard, the first of the lightning bugs making their nightly appearance. I cupped Ian's chin in my hand and turned his head away from me. At first there was just the one. I traced its path as it darted at the edge of the woods. Then more joined in, creating an entire blanket of lights bobbing at the edge of the yard.

"I caught one once," I told him. "When I was seven or so. I put it in a jar and set it on the table next to my bed. It made the tiniest of lights in my bedroom that night, and I fell asleep staring at it. The next morning, it was dead." I hadn't caught any more after that, even though Pops told me they didn't live long anyway. It seemed selfish to catch them like that, just so I could watch them glow up close.

Ian leaned in, his breath tickling my face. His lips were my lips, and even the fireflies faded.

My heart pounded and my stomach fluttered and twisted. I loved being with Ian, and I hated myself for it. Because I wanted to be with Luke, too. I shouldn't have been able to even think about Luke when Ian was kissing me that way. His kiss was sweet, lingering and deep, but careful, and not at all the way Luke kissed me. But Luke was trouble—I knew that from the very beginning. And it wasn't just because he told me he was. There was something dangerous about him. All the sarcasm in the world couldn't hide his anger.

Ian stroked my cheek with his thumb, kissing the edges of my mouth, and I found it easier to push Luke out of my head. All I knew for certain was that I liked them both. I liked them both way more than I should have.

IAN

Kissing Jenna was like trying to hold water in my hands. No matter what I did, I couldn't keep her from trickling away. I tried to press her into my mind, form her into some tangible image that I could keep with me even when she wasn't there. I made a memory of her to keep my few remaining memories company. And while my memories were hazy black-and-white photographs, Jenna's were vivid, 3D movies. The more I was around her, the more I listened to Jenna's stories and began to make some of them mine, the brighter everything seemed. The brighter *I* seemed. My blurred edges became sharp and defined. I was afraid of losing that.

I didn't know how much of me was already gone. Unrecoverable. I didn't even know how much of me was really me. The gaps in my memory were bridged by what everyone told me I was. Like a mockingbird, I repeated and mimicked what I heard and was told. I didn't know if a mockingbird even had its own song. I didn't know if I did. I only knew I was a good athlete because everyone told me I was. I knew I was an honor student because everyone told me I was. I had trophies to prove it. I had awards and pictures, but I'd lost the experiences. I wasn't even sure if the things I did remember were my actual memories or just remnants of the stories I'd been told.

This town, and this girl, had such a deep past. There were families who'd been here since this place was just a pit stop, generations in the same place. These memories went back years, and I wanted a piece of that. If I couldn't have my past, then I was going to have a future, and I was going to make sure Jenna was a part of it.

That was one of the reasons I had come straight here after my session with Dr. Benson. We'd spent most of the time talking around the issue, and I couldn't remember anything more than when I first got here. Spending an hour stumbling in the dark made me want to sit in the sun. It made me anxious to find what I'd lost, but it also made me even more determined to make sure I held on to as much of each day as I could.

Being with Jenna helped. She was fascinating to watch because she watched everything. She followed her mother's every movement, from the time she sat down to eat, to each time she went in the kitchen to refill her drink. Jenna steered the conversation away from herself and to her mother, which wasn't hard, since her mom seemed to like to talk, and mostly about herself. Vivian Oliver was funny and witty, but she was sad, even when she was smiling. She reminded me a little of my mom. I could tell that Jenna just wanted her mom to be happy, and that she was frustrated she couldn't do anything about it. I knew exactly what that felt like. It was like trying to tear down a brick wall with bare hands—painful and futile.

I brushed my fingers through Jenna's hair and down the side of her neck. Goose bumps formed under my fingers as I trailed along her collarbone. But it didn't matter how tightly I tried to hold on, she flowed out of my grasp. She kissed me lightly on the lips and smiled. Her smile would cause crops to grow in the middle of winter.

"Now it's your turn," she said.

"To what?"

"To tell me a memory." She asked the impossible, and I found myself wanting to give it to her.

"I'd rather hear yours," I told her. "I like your stories."

"You never talk about your family. I really don't know that much about you."

"There's not much to tell," I lied. "You know the important things."

I could tell she didn't believe me. "Luke isn't important?" she asked, then seemed surprised, like she hadn't meant to say it out loud.

Shock jolted down my spine like electricity.

"Why didn't you tell me you had a brother?" she asked. "A twin?"

I didn't know what to tell her, since there were so many reasons I'd kept Luke a secret and I didn't want her to know about any of them.

"It never came up. How do you know Luke?" My voice was harsher than I wanted it to be.

"I came by a couple of weeks ago to see you. I met Luke instead."

I hated the way she said his name—that she knew his name at all. There was a familiar tug at the back of my brain, a promise of a headache and anger. Then a vague feeling of sameness as the blonde girl appeared in the yard. I knew she wasn't really there, and I wondered if I was losing my mind. She screamed words I couldn't hear. I tried not to lose my temper. This wasn't Jenna's fault. The blame belonged where it always did.

"Luke didn't tell me," I said. Of course not. He knew better.

Jenna straightened her shoulders and turned to face me. "You didn't, either."

She blamed me. Nothing about this was my fault. "You don't know Luke," I said. And it was a good thing. "There's a reason I didn't tell you about him." I didn't need to find all my memories to know Luke had never been able to control himself. It was why we were in this mess. "I was trying to protect you," I told her. And Luke, if I was being honest. As mad as I was at him, I still felt the need to shield him. Even if it was from his own stupid, irresponsible self.

"From your brother? That's ridiculous."

Her voice told me she knew him better than I wanted her to. But she didn't know him at all, not really. She wouldn't be defending him if she did.

The blonde girl danced in the dark spots of my vision, and I realized where I'd seen her before. The picture. I tried to remember her, but before I could even try and focus, she slipped behind the walls of the maze my mind had constructed. I needed to talk to Luke.

"I have to go," I said, standing up and causing the swing to rock back. I should have known something was different. Luke hadn't spent nearly as much time in his room as usual. And while he normally reveled in his self-loathing way too much, the other day I overheard him whistling. He never whistled.

I wanted to stay with Jenna, but I had to get home. Because I was responsible. Because I did what I was told. Because I wasn't Luke.

SIXTEEN

IAN

I felt a headache coming. It was just a scratching at the base of my skull, but I knew it would be a clawing before I could get home. They'd been getting worse, and I was having trouble sleeping. I didn't know if it was the headaches or the dreams. Both were painful. I kept having the same dream. Nightmare, really.

I dreamt I was in the tree house, the one Luke had built when we were kids. That memory hadn't disappeared—I had a picture of it in my room. I wasn't sure if I really remembered the tree house, or just the picture. In my dream I was in the tree house. Jenna was there, taking the thing apart. She removed boards, first from the roof, then the walls, and finally, from the platform where I stood. I screamed, because the tree was too high and I couldn't get down. I yelled that she would kill me as the floor got smaller and smaller. But she never heard me, never looked up. It was almost like she didn't see me. No matter how much I screamed or how loud I yelled her name, she kept working. The air filled with the screech of her prying the nails out of the boards. And then I saw what she was doing with them.

She was handing them to Luke.

He was in another tree, one that was bigger and stronger. Jenna handed him the boards, and he built a new tree house. For her. With her. I woke up just as Jenna took the last piece of wood from my house; I woke up right as I was falling out of the tree.

This dream had been trying to tell me what Luke wouldn't. We'd always just known things about the other. Luke had felt the pain of my appendix bursting. I gripped the steering wheel. The idea of Luke spending time with Jenna made me dizzy. She said they'd only met once, but that was once too many. She knew about him, and I couldn't take that back. It couldn't be fixed. But I could make sure it didn't go any further than that.

Luke was in his room when I got home, but I went to the living room first. The box of pictures sat underneath the window, but I couldn't find the blonde girl. I flipped through every single album, but she wasn't there. Someone, probably Mom, had removed those pictures, erasing her from our ink and paper lives. I didn't know why, but I could guess who was to blame.

Luke was the reason for every bad thing that had happened recently. I was having a hard time remembering the good times, since my past was fuzzy and out of focus. But the last few months were all jagged edges and dizzying drops, and Luke was the cause. He was the reason our parents divorced. If he hadn't hit Dad, if Dad hadn't hit him back, then Mom and Dad wouldn't have split up. Dad wouldn't resent me as well. If it weren't for Luke, Mom wouldn't be depressed. I wouldn't hear her crying herself to sleep at night, helpless to fix it. I wasn't going to let him take away the one solid thing in my life. He wasn't getting Jenna.

"We need to talk," I told him through the locked door. I had no idea when we'd started locking one another out. We'd shared a room for years, until we were fourteen, and there'd never been any locks between us. There'd never been any secrets either. A lot had changed since then.

The door opened. Looking at Luke wasn't really like looking into a mirror; Luke's face was usually twisted in a mocking way. He always looked like he was waiting to start something. This time it was my turn.

"Well, hello there, brother," Luke said. "Long time no see."

"Cut the crap, Luke. Why didn't you tell me about Jenna?"

His eyes flashed surprise before his mask of arrogance slid back into place. "Why didn't you?" he asked. "Afraid of a little competition?"

I clenched my fists. I couldn't hit him, no matter how badly I wanted to. I was the good twin. I wasn't supposed to get angry. I wasn't supposed to want Luke as far away from me as possible. But I was getting sick of trying to be that Ian.

LUKE

I knew something was up when Ian banged on the door. He hardly ever came to my room anymore. I'd been asleep, but when he started hollering, I pulled out of my stupor.

He knew about Jenna—sort of. He knew I'd met her. I admitted it. He hollered some more. Good thing Mom was still at work. She really hated confrontation. That was why she'd left Dad instead of hanging around and trying to work things out. Not that anything could be worked out with Dad. He made sure he was always right, even when he was wrong.

"Don't you realize how lucky you are?" I said. Ian was acting so unbelievably selfish, which was totally out of character. Usually that was my role. "You don't have any idea what it's like to live with this kind of guilt. You have no idea what it's like to remember and know it's your fault. You're lucky you have no memories." God, I hated him for that. And myself for feeling that way.

But I didn't want Ian to remember that night. He hated me enough already, and that was just for the divorce. For my behavior. If he knew what I'd done, who he'd lost, he'd never forgive me. And I didn't think I could stand that.

"Are you kidding?" His voice rose several octaves. "I have no memories which don't include you. I have no life that isn't part of someone else's. I have a three-month gap where I remember absolutely nothing. I know what you've told me, what Mom and Dad have told me, but that isn't a whole hell of a lot. I want a life that doesn't include you."

I couldn't blame him. I'd want the same thing. Hell, sometimes I did want the same thing. But there wasn't anything I could do about it.

"Stay away from her," Ian told me. "She deserves better."

I knew he was right, but I didn't want him to be. Jenna wasn't mine, but I couldn't stand the way Ian talked about her. Like she was his. I didn't want to think about her smiling at him, kissing him. Ian was exactly who Jenna should have been with. He was everything she should have wanted, and if I cared about her at all, everything I should have wanted for her. But I didn't. I shouldn't have wanted her, not after what had happened with Ian's last girlfriend. I didn't deserve to be happy, but all of a sudden I wanted to be. "And you think you're better?"

"I always have been. Just stay away from Jenna."

I nodded, but I knew I wouldn't. I couldn't. Even if I wanted to. And I didn't.

SEVENTEEN

JENNA

This time, when the phone rang in the middle of the night, I knew who it was. Ian was the responsible one, the one who made sure I was home by curfew. Luke snuck me out of the house. I was surprised to find I'd sort of been expecting the call. Or maybe just hoping for it.

"Can I come up?" Luke's voice was rough and quiet, reaching into my chest and wrapping itself around my lungs. I didn't even let my mom in my room, and I'd never had a boy in there. I didn't know if I wanted him to see me that bare.

"Sure," I heard myself saying. My brain had not made that decision—the words bubbled up involuntarily. But if I thought too hard about it, like I usually did about everything, then I knew I would say no and probably regret it. I was kind of tired of being so responsible. "Meet me at the back door."

The house was dark and seemed abnormally silent. I held my breath as I tiptoed past Mom's room, convinced she would hear me breathing.

Luke stood underneath the floodlight on the deck. His hands were in his pockets, and he was scowling at the ground. Maybe he was having second thoughts, too. It was bad enough, sneaking into my house in the middle of the night. The fact that I was seeing his brother only complicated matters. And intensified my guilt.

But the grin he gave me when I opened the door didn't have a trace of remorse in it. It was arrogant and sexy, and even a little sad, but not in the least repentant. It was also infectious—I had to smile back.

I leaned out the door. "If you wake my mother up, I'm telling her you broke in."

He followed me up to my room. My heart slammed against my chest. Taking him into my room felt like handing him the keys to my diary. It felt like standing naked in a room full of beautiful people. It felt deliciously real.

I shut the door behind us, staying as far away from the bed as possible. I'd just crawled out, and the sheets were suggestively rumpled.

I felt trapped under a microscope as Luke examined my room, looking at the pictures tacked to the bulletin board and taped to the mirror. When he leaned in to get a closer look at my cross-country ribbons, I pulled the comforter over the tangled sheets. I didn't want him getting any ideas. I kicked a bra under the bed seconds before he turned around.

"I normally don't let people in here," I said, "so be gentle."

His grin was wicked. "I'm always gentle the first time."

I glared at him, and he walked over to my record player. "This is awesome," he said.

"My grandma gave it to me when I was eleven." It had been sitting in her shop for a couple of years, and she said she got tired of dusting it. I think she just got tired of me playing the same two records over and over again every time I was there.

His hands fluttered over the needle, and I could tell he wanted to touch it.

"Go ahead," I told him. "Just keep it down."

I sat underneath the window as he flipped through my small collection of records. I'd dug them out of boxes and bins from the back of the store. Most of the old stuff in my room had been discovered back there. I liked finding things.

"What's up with the little ones?" Luke asked, holding up a record. I couldn't see which one it was.

"They're forty-fives. Single songs," I explained, my head leaned against the wall.

He placed the record on the player and turned it on.

"If you scratch it, I'll have to kill you," I said.

"Then I guess I'd better be careful."

He placed the needle on the record, and familiar static filled the room. Then violins. I sat up and looked at him. He'd put on "Smoke Gets in Your Eyes." My favorite song.

"I've never heard this song before," he said.

"You've got to be kidding." How could anyone *not* have heard this song? It was a classic, and in about a hundred movies.

He sat down beside me, his knee touching my knee, his shoulder touching my shoulder, his head leaning back next to mine. We were silent. I breathed the music, my eyes closed, my lungs emptying and filling with the swell of the melody. Somewhere in the middle of the song, Luke reached over and wrapped his finger around mine. Right then, I didn't need anything else in the world. I forgot to be self-conscious and anxious and guilty. I forgot to be anything but next to him, our fingers twisted together, our breathing synchronized.

We didn't move when the song ended, just sat still and listened to the scratch at the end of the record.

"Are you a vampire?" I asked after the silence demanded it be filled.

I could feel his chuckle. "Would you like me better if I were?"

I didn't answer that. My feelings about Luke resembled a thousand-piece puzzle tossed down the stairs. I wasn't sure I'd ever be able to figure out how they all fit together. "We almost always hang out at night," I said instead. "When do you sleep?"

"I don't know anymore. Do you want me to leave?"

"No," I whispered. While I wasn't certain about what I did want, I was sure about what I didn't. And I didn't want him to go anywhere.

Luke looked up at my ceiling, finally noticing all the words hanging over our heads. I knew it was stupid, but I used to think that sleeping underneath the words of great writers might help me become a great writer. "*Carpe diem*," he read, picking one that spanned both sides of the vaulted ceiling. He turned his head toward me and raised his eyebrows in a silent question.

"I know," I said, pulling at a loose thread on my shorts. "I'm a terrible cliché. My English teacher made us watch this old movie and the scene with this quote was pretty cool. 'Seize the day' and all that. It reminds me to be at my best every day—that way I'm always improving. Better runner, better student. Better daughter." Although I was pretty sure that last one was a lifelong pursuit of failure.

"I think you missed the whole point," he told me.

"I'm sorry?" I didn't exactly enjoy being told I was wrong, but definitely not when I knew I wasn't.

"My Latin teacher," he began, but stopped when I gave him a strange look. "I went to school. I took Latin. It's not like I was always a juvenile delinquent."

When I looked doubtful, he grinned. "Okay," he admitted, "I was usually doing something I wasn't supposed to, but I rarely got caught." There was an edge to his voice. "My dad made us take Latin," Luke said. "Anyway, my Latin teacher said it's more accurately translated 'enjoy today.' I like that one better. 'Seize the day' puts too much responsibility on a person. Grab the day. Do great things. Change the world. I don't need that kind of pressure. Now, 'enjoy the day'?" He raised his eyebrow. "That I can do." He nudged my shoulder. "You should try it sometime."

"I'm enjoying myself right now," I said.

The smile he gave me was like watching the sun creep out and spill light over the mountains. It chased away most of the shadows that had been clouding his face.

"And what are you going to do once you're *better*?" he asked.

"I don't know," I said. I wasn't going to toss out the truth so carelessly. The truth was something I couldn't get back. The uncertainty of whether or not I could actually do all that I dreamed left me feeling like I was being tossed around an angry ocean with nothing but a pair of Floaties.

Luke saw right through me. "That doesn't sound like you."

"I know." I gave him a partial truth. "But this one life isn't going to be enough. There's so much I want to do, and I know I won't be able to do it all. I want to live in a big city and write a novel. I want to own a horse ranch in Wyoming. I want to work at a museum and a magazine and a surf shop. There isn't time for me to be all the different people I want to be."

"That's why you have to start early," Luke said.

"All of my different versions live other places," I told him. "All of my planning and all of my *better* are because all I really want is to get out of here."

"Trust me, it doesn't matter where you go," he said. "You'll still be you. You can't escape yourself."

Now he was missing the entire point. I wanted to escape Solitude and my family's dysfunction. I wanted to find myself. "Who said I wanted to?"

"You do," he assured me. "We all do, on some level."

I wondered which part of himself he was trying to escape, but I didn't ask. He reached up and tucked a strand of hair behind my ear. "When I was little, I used to believe that if you wanted something bad enough, you could will it to happen. If you focused on it and wanted it enough, it would come true."

"And you don't believe that now." It wasn't a question.

Luke shook his head. "No. Well, at least not for me. For you, yes. You are so amazing—the world would be crazy if it didn't do everything it could to make you happy. You deserve it."

"And you don't? You're—"

He put a finger to my lips, stopping my words. His eyes were so sad that my heart ached. "No," he whispered, his voice hard and edged with wire, "I deserve many things, but happiness isn't one of them."

I wanted to weave happiness together and wrap him in it like a blanket. I wanted to pluck it like a fruit and feed it to him. But I couldn't. I kissed him instead, and the world shifted just a little.

LUKE

Jenna was so quietly hopeful that it hurt. I found myself hoping a little when I was with her, which was dangerous, because having hope only hurt in the long run when things fell apart. And they would. They always did.

But then she kissed me. Me. Luke. Without any provocation on my part. Her skin was earthy and absolutely amazing. Did she kiss Ian like that? I tried not to think about it.

Her cheeks were flushed when she pulled away, her eyes bright. Damn it.

"Why did you come over here tonight?" she asked. "Really?"

I grinned. "Wanting to see you isn't enough?"

Jenna's hazel eyes searched my face. Her intensity unnerved me. I was fascinated by the fact that she was willing to look past the Luke I normally threw at everybody. Jenna saw everything, and that scared me.

I sighed. "My dad called this morning. He talked to my mom for a little while, then Ian. Not me. He didn't want to talk to me." I didn't want to care. I wanted to hate the bastard, but I couldn't.

"Why?"

No. I wasn't going to tell her yet. Someday maybe, but not yet. "I just can't quite be the Luke he expects me to be."

"He probably just has a hard time telling you how he feels."

I tried to keep my voice down; I didn't want to wake her mother. "He doesn't have a hard time telling me 'You're such a screwup,' or 'You'll never amount to anything until you learn a little responsibility.'" I was disgusted at myself for telling her these things. "And then Ian came home yelling, and I needed out."

"Sorry, that was my fault," she said. She was wrong about that. "I asked him about you. It's just weird that he wouldn't tell me he has a brother."

"Nothing about our argument was your fault," I told her.

She didn't believe me, and I didn't want to get into the catalyst of our family fights. "Here," I said, pulling a pebble out of my pocket. "I've got a trick."

"I'm sure you have more than one," she said.

I had to laugh. I showed her the pebble, then made it disappear. She waited patiently until I pulled it from behind her ear.

She grinned and clapped. "Dazzling trick."

"I'm very good with my hands," I said, reaching out to rub her arm. "And at making things disappear."

She slapped my hand away. "I'll take your word for it." She took the pebble from me. "Do you always carry rocks in your pockets?"

I decided to let that one go. "I found it in the yard. I thought it was interesting." It was a bad habit I'd had since I was a kid. I stuck all sorts of things in my pockets—bits of glass, marbles, sometimes even frogs and lizards. Mom nearly had a heart attack once when she was doing the laundry and a grass snake crawled out of my jacket.

"Stay right there," Jenna said.

"I'm not going anywhere," I promised.

She disappeared behind a huge heavy rug that obviously served as her closet door. She banged around in there for a minute, then came out carrying a beat-up shoebox.

"You're not going to make me play dress-up again, are you?" I teased.

She folded down next to me, cradling the box like it was the most important thing in the world. She set it down between us and removed the lid.

There was a speckled bird's egg with a tiny hole in the top, half a wooden bird, some old keys, a single chopstick. An old pipe—that had to have been her grandfather's. There were several rocks.

"I'm a magpie," she said.

"Or a serial killer," I amended.

She ignored me. "I pick up most of this stuff on my runs."

I couldn't categorize her. In the shop, I had a place for tools and one for nails, a place for scrap wood and useable wood. Everything was organized according to function. But I had no idea where Jenna belonged. Just when I thought I had everything tidied into a pile, she scattered my conjectures. She wasn't any one thing; she was all good things put together, and put together in a way that was only *her*. Everything I built had the same basic components-- wood, nails, screws, wood glue. But there were a million and one possibilities as to what it would be when I was finished. I could take those things and make a bookshelf or a drawer to hold my socks. And while I couldn't entirely identify all the pieces that went into forming Jenna, I liked who she was when they were all cobbled together.

"I told Ian I'd stay away from you," I admitted. Jenna seemed to make the truth appear. It wasn't going to be pretty when all of it did.

"Do you want to?" she asked.

"No. And I don't like being told what to do."

Her gaze made me feel like I was standing in the sun. "So you're only here because you're not supposed to be?" she asked.

I couldn't tell her why I was really there. "Aren't you?"

She shook her head. "Not anymore."

I cupped her face in my hand, her skin warm and alive in a way that caused my fingers to tingle. She parted her lips, and as I leaned in to kiss her, I half-expected her to swirl away in a cool breeze. But she didn't, and my head was full of nothing but her as her lips formed around mine. She stole my breath, and when I pulled away, I expected to see my heart beating frantically in the box next to the other things she'd claimed her own. It felt as if the answer to all of life's questions was cupped in my palm. I knew it couldn't last much longer. I was going to screw it up. I always did.

EIGHTEEN

JENNA

Luke wasn't there when I woke up the next morning. I was curled into a tiny ball underneath the window, and someone—Luke—had covered me with a blanket. There wasn't a note. He'd slipped away like a ghost, leaving me to wonder if he'd really been there at all. Maybe it had only been a delicious dream.

I tried not to think about either one of them. I attempted to clean my room, but that didn't last long. I kept seeing things Luke had touched—my record player, the blanket, me. There were dark places in Luke, holes that I couldn't fill and that he seemed determined to fall into. But for some reason, I couldn't walk away.

Ian was the safe choice—sweet, considerate, motivated. He was going to be an architect. He was a good student and an athlete. He was interesting. Ian was everything everyone expected me to date. My friends liked him. I was comfortable when I was with him. Responsible Jenna would choose Ian.

Luke brought out my darker side, the part I wasn't sure I wanted people to see. He challenged me, made me angry and giddy all at the same time. Luke had secrets, and when I was with him, it was harder to forget mine. If I chose

Luke, I felt I would be choosing the me that was unstable, the one who thought dark and scary things, who wondered what it would be like to stop playing it safe all the time. Luke was dangerous because he made me want to find out who I really was instead of molding myself into the person I should be. Choosing him would be a bad idea. But not choosing him felt like betrayal.

Responsible Jenna drew me toward Ian, who was solid and balanced and everything I might have needed and should have wanted. And sometimes did. But irresponsible Jenna, irreverent and unthinking Jenna, wanted to push against boundaries and see what was over the fence. That Jenna was attracted to Luke, who hinted at something wonderful but guaranteed trouble and was everything I wanted but didn't need.

I gave up trying to clean my room and went to work. July was just a few days away, and it felt it. The thermometer at the bank was already close to ninety degrees. Nobody came in all morning, and Mops put out the lunch sign early.

I climbed the twisted metal staircase and stepped into her small apartment. It was lived-in, which was the way I liked things. I hated how neat Mom kept our house, like some kind of dysfunctional dollhouse. I didn't exactly fit in with Mom's flower-print sofa and frilly chairs. My room and the kitchen were the only two places in my house where I was really comfortable.

But every room in Mops's house was comfortable.

Her tiny apartment smelled like pinto beans, which were in the Crock-Pot next to the stove. "You're in charge of cornbread," she told me. I pulled most of the stuff out of the fridge and went to work while Mops washed the squash she grew in a tiny patch behind the store. I loved cooking with Mops. She'd taught me how to fry chicken, chop an onion, knead dough. It was also when we had our best talks. It was easier to open up when my hands were busy.

"Your mother tells me you have a boyfriend," Mops said. The metal bowl clanged loudly as I dropped it on the linoleum. I scooped it up and set it on the counter before turning to look at Mops. "When did you talk to Mom?" They were mostly avoiding each other these days.

"I saw her this morning at the Shell station. I was out of milk and she was getting gas." That made sense. Mom was very into appearances and probably went out of her way to make the conversation look good, since Walt Labatut, who ran the Shell station, gossiped worse than an old woman.

"He's not my boyfriend." I wasn't sure which one I was talking about.

"Touchy," Mops said.

"Can we talk about something else?" *Anything else, please.*

"I was about your age when I started dating your Pops." Mops's voice had a lilt to it, almost as if she were singing a song and longing was the melody. "He sat next to me in English and kept trying to copy."

"Did you let him?" I took the preheated cast-iron skillet out of the oven and filled it with the batter. The hot grease in the bottom of the skillet popped and sizzled.

Mops smiled slyly at me. "What do you think?"

I slid the skillet into the oven and closed the door, setting the timer. I stood up and surveyed Mops. If she was this feisty when she was old, I couldn't imagine what she'd been like in high school. But I also knew how persuasive Pops could be.

"Yes," I decided.

"Well, you're wrong." She dipped the squash in egg and rolled in it cornmeal before tossing it into the hot grease on the stove. "And he failed the first semester." Mops poured us both glasses of iced tea and we sat down at the small kitchen table. Purple marker covered the right side of the table where I'd colored outside of the lines.

"I let him sweat it out a bit, then told him I'd tutor him. We were going steady less than a month later." Mops's face was a mosaic of joy and regret when she talked about Pops.

"But how did you know?" I asked.

Mops looked at me. "He made me laugh. He made me smile, made me want to be a better person. Sometimes I would look at him and my heart would literally hurt because I loved him so much and I didn't know how to contain it, what to do with it. I wanted to protect him and scream at him all at the same time. And he put up with me, which helped." She winked at me.

"What happened?" I asked. They'd stopped living together when I was seven. And while there had been love, there'd also been a whole lot of anger.

There was a lifetime in her sigh. "We stopped being good for each other. Life tore us down, and we couldn't even put ourselves back together, much less each other. It was nobody's fault, but we were both to blame. I never stopped loving him, but I pulled myself out of that hole we'd climbed into, and he wouldn't even try." She got up to flip the squash and spoke with her back to me. "Pops wouldn't let me help him. I couldn't live with him. I refused to watch him destroy himself and take me down in the process."

Exactly. I loved my mother, but if her drinking kept getting worse, she was going to ruin both our relationship and our futures.

"Your mother never forgave me for moving out. My heart wanted to stay with him, but my head wanted to stay sober. I knew I couldn't have both."

"Your head is always right?" I asked.

Mops turned down the burner and came back to the table. "No. There's no *always* in life."

"Sometimes I wish I were seven years old again," I admitted.

"Why?"

Because back then Pops was still alive and my mom still climbed into my quilt tents. Because my biggest worry had been whether or not Santa knew about my latest crime. Because I'd still believed in magic. "Because life wasn't so complicated then," I said.

Mops reached over and patted my hand. "It sure doesn't get any easier, either."

Great.

IAN

"What happened the night your dad and Luke got into the fight?" Dr. Benson was supposed to be helping me recover my memories and figure out my headaches. He wasn't doing either. He made me talk about what I did remember to see if it sparked what I didn't. I spent half the time desperately shifting through the maze in my mind and the other half wishing I were anywhere else.

"You need to talk to Luke about that," I said for the second time. We'd spent most of the session talking about how I felt about the move and the divorce. I felt they were both Luke's fault. Exploring that any further was just going to lead to a dead end.

Dr. Benson nodded and leaned back in his chair. "You're right. But I can't make him attend his appointments, and I can't make him talk to me even if he does."

No one could make Luke do anything he didn't want to. It was probably one of the reasons Dad always lost his temper with Luke. Luke couldn't be ordered around like the rest of us. Dad commanded, both at work and at home, and he'd grown used to having things his way. He issued the orders. He wasn't questioned. Mom had done what he said mainly to keep life peaceful. But Luke was the one person Dad couldn't really boss around, and Dad hated that. Funny, considering those two were so alike. Dad didn't take shit from anyone, and neither did Luke. I was like my mom. But the peace was becoming impossible to keep.

"You don't think it would be easier if you just told me what happened?" I asked.

Dr. Benson's face tightened. "No, I don't. Sometimes forgetting is your brain's way of healing. When you're ready to remember, you will."

"Are you sure?" I needed to know that I could reach this goal.

Dr. Benson frowned. "No. The brain is a complicated system."

"And doctors don't know as much as they pretend to." They guessed. Sometimes they groped in the dark. It didn't matter how many degrees he had hanging on his wall. I had to figure out a way to get better on my own. And I would.

"We don't know everything, no," Dr. Benson admitted.

"I'm sorry." I smoothed over the tension out of habit. That had always been my job. "Do you remember high school?" I asked.

Dr. Benson looked surprised. He paused, and I wasn't sure he was going to answer the question. "Parts of it," he said finally.

"Why is that?" Why did some things disappear while others remained burned into our brains?

"Not all parts are worth remembering, I guess," he said.

That was what I was afraid of. Maybe my missing months weren't worth it either.

"Who did you take to prom?" I asked him. I thought back to the picture I had seen, the one of the blonde girl laughing. Happy. Why couldn't I remember her?

"Mary Beth Anderson," he said.

"Why do you think you remember that so easily but not other parts?"

"Because Mary Beth Anderson is now living in my old house and getting a sizeable portion of my income." Dr. Benson smiled at me. "Why are you asking me this?"

Because collecting other people's memories was easier than finding my own.

"I keep seeing a blonde girl," I told him. "Like a hallucination or something."

Dr. Benson's face was guarded. "Go on."

"That's it. I saw a picture of her at my house, though it's suddenly disappeared, and twice she's shown up, standing in front of me."

Dr. Benson smiled. "See? You're remembering."

"But I'm not!" Didn't he see that? "I have no idea who she is."

"Don't force it," Dr. Benson said. "You'll remember when you're ready."

"But what if I don't?" I asked.

Dr. Benson shifted in his chair and tilted his head to look at me. "Ian, we've only just started. Give yourself time. "

I didn't know how much longer I could afford to wait. There were so many things I wanted, and most of them started with recovering what I'd lost. Memories. My family. Myself. I was tired of stumbling around in the dark.

The timer went off. "That's it for today." Dr. Benson and I both stood up, and he clapped a hand on my shoulder. "I'm proud of you," he said. "You're getting there."

Sometimes it didn't feel like I was getting anywhere at all.

"I'll call your mom, see if she can talk Luke into coming."

I shrugged. "Maybe." But I wasn't counting on it.

I hadn't spoken to Luke since our argument. I hadn't even seen him. And while he'd promised he would stay away from Jenna, I knew him well enough to know he was lying. I just didn't know what I was going to do about it yet.

Mom was pulling weeds in the front yard when I got home from my appointment. It was late afternoon, but it was murderously hot and her face was red and streaked with sweat and dirt.

"How'd it go?" she asked, leaning back on her heels.

"Fine." I always told her it went fine. I wasn't sure if there were a more accurate response. I was still having headaches. I was still having bad dreams. I still couldn't find all of my memories. But I hadn't choked the incompetent doctor, so I guessed that meant things were going fine.

"Your dad called again," Mom told me.

That was new. We hadn't heard from him in weeks, then all of a sudden we get two calls in two days. "About?"

"He finally got hold of the superintendent this morning. The state athletic association is going to vote in a couple of weeks on whether or not you're eligible to play football."

"Oh." I should have known. Dad was only interested in how many passes I could complete. Yesterday all he'd wanted to talk about was what I was doing to stay in shape. I figured the vote was probably a technicality at this point; if Dad wanted me to play, he'd make it happen. He could be very persuasive. "You need help?" I asked.

Mom looked surprised. "Sure."

We knelt in the dirt on either side of the porch steps, pulling the intruding weeds and tossing them into a pile behind us. "I could just mow," I offered. The weeds were thick and tall. It would have been easier to just chop everything down and start again.

"No, I want the bushes and flowers. I think there was some pretty nice landscaping here, before it all grew up. We have to thin these out to see for sure."

The yard was wild and unruly, bordered by woods and a broken fence. There was a pond out back. It was nothing like our yard in Massachusetts. The weeds there shriveled up from Dad's glare alone. Everything had been tidy and orderly. Dad always made sure there was nothing troublesome in our yard. And if anything did show up, he tossed it out.

"Dr. Benson knows what I can't remember, doesn't he?"

Mom stared at the pile of weeds in her hand. Just when I thought she wasn't going to answer, she nodded.

"Why doesn't he just tell me?" I asked. "Why don't you?"

When Mom turned to look at me, there was so much heartbreak in her face that I immediately regretted the question.

"It's that bad?" I whispered. My brain was a maze of twisting corridors separating me from the truth. And since Luke didn't seem the least bit interested or capable of fixing what was broken, that meant I had to do it. The only way I knew how to repair the cracks was to remember what had shattered us in the first place.

I needed everything to lay flat. I had to replace Kyle Couty as starting quarterback. That was going to be nearly impossible because of small-town politics, but if I succeeded on the field, my family would be less fractured. My parents had spent their lives putting themselves into Luke and me, making sure we were successful in everything, and Luke had thrown that back in their faces. I wouldn't. I would show them that everything they'd ever done wasn't a waste. Maybe if I worked hard enough, those skeletons in the basement would finally disintegrate and Mom could stop worrying.

"It's that bad," she said. Her voice broke, and she wouldn't look at me. I couldn't stand to see her so sad.

I changed the subject. I told her about Kyle and Steven. I talked about Repete's and the lake. I put just enough hope and enthusiasm in my voice that she didn't warn me to be careful. I made sure she heard the unspoken promise—that things were going to be fine, that I was going to patch everything together, that I was going to be what she'd always hoped I would be. Mom worried she hadn't done the right thing by dragging us down here. I would show her it was going to be okay no matter where we were. Because I would make it that way. For all of us.

"It's going to be great," I promised Mom. There was a sizeable pile of weeds behind each of us, and we'd managed to clear out most of the bed in front of the house. The ones on the sides taunted us, but we wouldn't be able to tackle those tonight. Small steps. Everything could be accomplished with small steps forward.

Mom leaned back and smiled at me. It reached her eyes for the first time in months. "I know it will be," she said. She stood up, stripping off her gardening gloves and dropping them on the porch. "I'm glad you've met some friends."

She disappeared into the shadows, and I scooped up the weeds and tossed them into the garbage can. The screen door slammed as Mom stepped back outside. She sat down on the top step and handed me a glass of ice water. Nothing had ever tasted so clean.

A small puff of air became a slight breeze and dried the sweat on my skin. Two squirrels chased each other up the trunk of the large oak tree at the end of the driveway. One of them leapt from the oak toward a thin branch on a nearby pecan tree. He soared through the air, completely oblivious to what would be a fatal drop if he couldn't catch the limb. He landed on the very tip of the branch, which dipped and bounced, then he shot into the thick leaves at the top. The other squirrel fussed and barked from the safety of the oak.

"I love you," Mom said. "I haven't said it enough lately."

She hadn't said it at all lately. "I know you do," I told her. "Me too."

She leaned over and kissed my cheek. I couldn't remember the last time she'd done that either. "Now go take a shower. You smell like a goat."

I laughed. "You don't exactly smell like roses."

She slapped the side of my leg. "You got some stuff in the mail, too. I put it in your room."

The house was cool and quiet. Luke's door was shut when I passed, and I felt no inclination to open it. There was a large stack of mail sitting on the corner of my desk, and all of it had been forwarded from Massachusetts. Boston University. NYU. Colorado State, Virginia Tech, Baylor. They topped off an already large stack.

I had to do it right if I was going to make it right. Everything was going to have to be perfectly put together by the time I graduated. Because college was going to be how I surgically removed Luke from my life. His grades were bad and his record worse. There was no way he was going to get into college. So everything was going to have to be lying flat by the time I left. And it would be, no matter what I had to do to make that happen.

NINETEEN

JENNA

Steph called on Friday afternoon and invited Ian and me to play laser tag in Middleton with her and Steven. She misinterpreted the hesitation in my voice, thinking it had to do with the plans when really I was afraid of calling Ian and getting Luke.

"Please," Steph begged, "if you don't come, Steven is going to make me invite Kyle and Dani, and I have so totally filled my quota of Dani Peters."

I laughed. I'd filled my quota for the summer after five minutes.

"Sure." The answer came easier than it should have. What was wrong with me?

I called Ian before I could change my mind. There was a wild moment of uncertainty when he answered, because for a second I wasn't sure if he was Ian or Luke.

"Ian? It's Jenna."

"I was just thinking about you," he said. He sounded like he was telling the truth.

"Steph and Steven want us to go play laser tag in Middleton," I explained.

There was a beat of silence, then Ian spoke. "I'd love to see you again, if that's okay with you." His sincerity solidified my guilt, especially since, after hearing his voice, I really wanted to see him again too.

"Let me just text Steph and see what time and everything. I'll let you know."

An hour later, I was sitting in the back of Steven's Jeep Cherokee on our way to pick up Ian. Steph and Steven were arguing over the radio station. I chewed on my lip and picked at a hangnail and prayed silently over and over again that Luke wouldn't be home when I got there.

Steven tapped the horn as soon as we pulled in the driveway, and Ian met us in the front yard. His blue polo shirt made his eyes bluer than I would have thought possible, and he smelled like soap and aftershave. My heart flopped over when he leaned in and kissed my cheek.

It was like he'd been a part of the group since its inception. He teased Steph about her emo choice of music and talked football with Steven until I thought my ears were going to bleed. There were no shadows in his face or disappointment in his eyes. No mocking smile. Instead, there was laughter and possibility and hope. I didn't have to be a mechanic when I was with Ian; he wasn't broken.

Middleton was an hour away and our closest link to civilization, but it only pretended it was a city. It had plenty of businesses and a little traffic. There were movies, restaurants, even a community college, but Middleton was still a child, all bony knees and scraped elbows. While it was the biggest place I'd ever been, it was really just an overgrown town that sprawled across more land than it needed. But it wasn't Solitude, and that fact made it a little endearing.

Ian absorbed everything. He was like a wide-eyed kid looking at Christmas lights. He wanted to know what certain buildings were and how many times I'd been there and why that restaurant had closed if I thought they had the best seasoned fries. I saw Middleton in a whole different way when Ian looked at it, because he really looked at it.

Ian was solid—he was sure about his future, his place, maybe even me. The fact that he'd been tossed into a new environment didn't seem to unsettle him at all. And while I'd lived around here my whole life, I wasn't sure about anything.

The list of things I didn't want was getting more concrete, while the things I was certain of kept shifting. I didn't want to settle when I didn't have to. I didn't want to wake up twenty years down the road and realize I hadn't done any of the things I'd said I would. I didn't want to trade happiness for convenience. I didn't want to have my choices taken from me or let someone else determine what I ended up being, or let fear keep me from making a fool of myself if that was what I needed to do. And I didn't want to lose either one of them.

The Middleton Laser Tag Center was in an abandoned Walmart building in the older part of town. A skinny boy with glasses checked our vests and made sure our guns were working. There were two other groups of people going in, all about our age, and Steven took charge like he always did when Kyle wasn't there to do it for him, declaring it a battle between the sexes. Steph and I were on a team with five other girls, two of which looked slow. I was pretty sure we were going to get our butts kicked.

When the door shut behind us, all I could see was blackness and glowing paint. The boys shouted insults from the other side of the room—they sounded like they'd known each other for years.

We scattered as the buzzer sounded. I tore down a long hallway and cut underneath a bridge. Footsteps pounded in front of me, but a high wall blocked my view, and I didn't know if it was a teammate or not. I backed up against the wall and held my breath, easing around the corner. I shot a boy I didn't know and his vest beeped loudly.

"Gotcha!" I laughed. He raised his gun, and I tore off in the other direction.

The room filled with shouts and loud beeps. I didn't hear Steven creep up behind me, which was a miracle considering how big he was, and he shot me in the back and took off in the other direction before I could shoot him in return.

I found a small fort with a door and a window; it was the perfect place to wait in ambush. I slipped inside and crouched down, listening to the beeps and trying to decide how many points we were behind.

I aimed my gun out the window and shot Steven as he ran by. His shocked look morphed into an arrogant grin. He aimed at me and missed before Steph shot him. He turned and ran after her just about the time Ian snuck into my hideout.

He held up his hands in surrender. "Truce?" he asked. He eased closer to me, ducking his head toward mine. "At least long enough for me to get a kiss?" he murmured.

I grinned. "Not a chance." His vest beeped as I shot him in the chest and climbed out the window.

It was glorious sprinting through the dark. I pounded up ramps and across bridges, neon paint a blur as I whipped around corners. I earned more points for our team than I lost.

"You're dead," Steven said as he shot me again. Before I could raise my gun, he sped off.

I flung myself into a black corner at the back of the room, stalking him. He was quick. I heard him tear after another girl on our team, and I waited for him to come back around.

I was standing in almost total darkness. There wasn't any paint on this part of the course, and the only light was the occasional glow from the team base when someone earned a point. When I thought I heard Steven coming, I leaned away from the wall and poked my head out to look.

Someone stepped right up behind me. Strong arms encircled my waist, and a hand clamped down over my mouth. He dragged me around the corner and turned me around, pressing my back against the wall.

He put his hands on either side of my head and leaned in. "Surrender," Ian whispered in my ear. He brushed his lips across my neck.

"Never," I told him. My voice was breathy and rough.

His lips were a whisper on my jaw.

"Is this your idea of coercion?" I teased.

He kissed me then, deep and real, wrapping his arm around my waist and pulling me into him. I put my arms around his neck, my gun clattering to the floor, and curled the fingers of my right hand around the hair at his collar. I forgot about the game.

It was Ian who pulled out of the kiss, his forehead against my forehead, nose to nose. He put his gun against my chest and pulled the trigger. My vest lit up and beeped, and the alarm went off on the boys' side, signaling their win and casting a bluish glow over us.

"Game over," he said. His wicked smile was just like Luke's. Same scar. Same reflection. I wondered what else they shared. Besides me.

IAN

The restaurant was crowded and we had to wait thirty minutes for a table. Steven kept replaying our victory and

Steph argued with his assessment. I held Jenna's hand and snuck glances at her when she wasn't looking.

The hostess finally squeezed us into a tiny table near the bathrooms, which didn't bother me since that meant I was forced to sit close to Jenna. Her leg ran the length of mine underneath the table, and our arms kept bumping into each other. I couldn't forget the shape of her lips in the dark. I refused to let that one disappear into the folds in my memory.

The restaurant had gotten noisy by the time the waitress brought our order, especially a group of adults at the bar who were laughing loud enough that we had to lean in to hear each other. Jenna's hair kept brushing across my face. I wasn't complaining.

"Jenna," Steven said, pointing over to the group, "isn't that your mom?"

Jenna's face went still. There was absolutely no expression in her eyes as she stared at her mom, who had just leaned out from behind a post. Shot glasses were upside-down in front of her. When I reached under the table and squeezed her knee, Jenna turned to me and forced a smile. "She's going through a phase," she said. "We keep thinking she'll grow out of it."

But I could tell Jenna was upset. She got quieter as the group got louder.

We were waiting on the check when Vivian spotted us. She was headed to the bathroom, her heels tapping over the restaurant noise. Her eyes got big when she saw Jenna. She smiled, then stopped and leaned against the back of our booth.

"Jenna! And Ian! What are you guys doing here?"

"I could ask the same thing," Jenna said, her teeth clenched.

Vivian dismissed Jenna's tone with the wave of a manicured hand. "Oh, I'm just hanging out with some friends."

Jenna eyed the table. "I don't recognize any of them."

Vivian ignored her. "Steph! I sure haven't seen you around much. How's the squad?"

"Great, thanks. We're going to Florida for camp this year." She looked excited about it.

"When I was captain," Vivian sniffed, "we always went to camp at the university. It definitely wasn't a vacation. But we were good back then. Disciplined. That was the best time of my life." She eyed us grimly. "Enjoy it while you can." She turned to Steven. "Now aren't you William Nelson's son?"

"Yes, ma'am."

"Steven, is it?" When he nodded, she winked at him. "I think Jenna had a little crush on you in middle school."

"Mom, please." Jenna didn't sound so much embarrassed as angry.

"Oh Jenna, Ian doesn't mind. And a little healthy competition never hurt anyone."

Jenna tensed. "You should probably get back to your friends," she said.

Vivian waved her hand again. "They'll wait. Now Steph, your hair is always so beautiful. You'll have to tell Jenna your secret. She obviously can't do a thing with hers."

Steph looked uncomfortable. "I don't do much with it," she said. "Just good genes, I guess."

"Oh, Jenna has plenty of those." She laughed. "Though sometimes you can't tell."

Jenna's face was steel, and anyone looking at her would think she wasn't in the least bit bothered by her inconsiderate mother. It was obvious to me the comments had more to do with Vivian's insecurity than any of Jenna's flaws. Vivian had spent her life being the center of attention and didn't know what to do when she wasn't. It had nothing to do with Jenna, so she shouldn't have taken it personally. But her leg was trembling next to mine.

The peacemaker in me wanted to step in and smooth over the cracks. But I wasn't sure how, and besides, Jenna didn't give me a chance.

"I need to use the restroom," Jenna said, standing up and brushing roughly against her mother. "Come with me." She grabbed Vivian's arm before she could protest.

"My dad says that family has always been a little unstable," Steven said once Jenna was gone.

I knew what that felt like.

I glared at Steven and headed to the back of the restaurant. I didn't want Jenna to have to deal with it alone.

JENNA

My mother had picked at me until I was frayed and thin, and I knew if I didn't get away from that table, I'd snap. I grabbed her arm, not caring in the least if I hurt her, and dragged her to the bathroom. She was surprisingly steady on her stiletto death traps.

I pulled the door hard and peeked underneath each stall, grateful that the bathroom was empty. My mom checked her makeup in the mirror. I locked the door so we wouldn't be interrupted.

Mom looked up when she heard the lock, her lips puckered as she applied more lipstick.

"How could you do that?" I asked. "How could you embarrass me like that in front of my friends?"

Mom waved her hand in my face, dismissing me as always. "Teenagers get embarrassed over everything." She turned back to the mirror and checked her face.

"Not everything, Mom, just you." Mom rolled her eyes at me. She wasn't listening. She never listened.

Mom finished touching up her face and turned around to glare at me. "When I was fifteen years old, my mother showed up to cheerleading practice drunk and in her bathrobe. She dragged me out of the gym and yelled at me for five minutes for not picking up my room before practice. Now *that* was embarrassing."

"It's not always about you!" I shouted. "You always have to one-up everyone with your sob stories. You're always dismissing what I'm going through." Her story was always worse, her feelings more valid than mine. Just once, I wanted her to actually hear what I was saying and not try to talk over it.

"You're being overly dramatic. All I did was stop by and say hello to you and your friends. It would have been rude if I hadn't." She widened her eyes. I couldn't tell if she actually thought she was innocent or if she believed playing dumb would help the lie go over better.

"No," I argued, "what you did was let everyone know I'm not good enough."

Mom frowned at me as she put her lipstick back in her purse. "I never said that."

"You didn't have to."

Someone banged on the door. "Jenna?"

"Go away, Ian." Everything was bad enough without him being right in the middle of it.

"Are you okay?" he asked.

Nothing about this was okay. "I'm fine," I said through the door.

Mom nudged me away from the door. "I need to get back."

More injustice flared. "Is this what you're doing every time you say you're working late? Throwing a few back with your friends?" I was snarling.

"Don't talk to me like that. You have no right to tell me what I can and can't do. I'm the parent, not you."

"Then act like it," I said.

Mom ran her eyes over me, reducing me to nothing, making me conscious that there was a hole in my shorts and that the soles of my shoes were separating from the uppers. "I'll see you at home."

She unlocked the bathroom door and pushed past Ian. A wave of laughter and noise rolled over me, receding as the door shut. I wanted to hide inside the silence.

TWENTY

LUKE

I woke up early on Monday to a quiet house. Sunlight poured through the kitchen window, and the honey-colored cabinets helped bathe the room in a warm, golden light. I'd finished all of the boxes and most of the doors, and the kitchen was transformed. Funny how some old pieces of wood made a place home, and made me feel a part of it. The cabinets were my signature on the house. I liked being a solid part of the house where Jenna had spent so much of her time.

I headed out to the shop, the dew dampening my shoes and grass sticking to my ankles. It wasn't even seven-thirty yet, but it was already hot. I flipped on the fan, the blades struggling to push the heavy air out of the opened doors.

I had a few pieces of wood to plane in order to finish the last of the cabinet doors. I stacked the wood next to the planer and turned it on. It rumbled in my feet. I fed the wood into the big machine, stripping away paint and time. The dark, rough wood became smooth as I ran it through, caught it, and ran it through again. I grabbed the last piece. It was damaged and took longer than the rest. Amazing how many layers of crap could develop over the years. I thought the board might have had a touch of rot inside, but it didn't, just a fracture along the bottom. Sometimes boards got broken, but that didn't always mean they were rotted all the way through.

I used all the clamps in the shop and set the doors to the side. I had two more to do once the clamped ones dried. I picked up the cracked board and examined it again. The grain was interesting. The cypress was a beautiful color, rich lines of gold and blond swirling around an almost white oval in the top center of the board. The bottom half of the board was useless, but it would've been a shame to throw the entire piece out.

My mind scrambled through possibilities for its use, something beautiful from the brokenness. When I saw the door molding I'd torn out of the kitchen, I knew exactly what I wanted to create. And who I wanted to create it for.

There was hope in the fact that even damaged boards could be salvaged.

It was well after lunch by the time I got to a stopping point. The house felt emptier than usual. Mom had agreed to work even though it was the Fourth of July, since she didn't really have a family to celebrate with. Apparently Ian and I didn't count. Dad was off in Massachusetts strutting around in his uniform and accepting gracious comments about his service to our country. What about his service to our family? Going AWOL wasn't exactly honorable behavior for a distinguished veteran of the armed forces, and he'd been absent from the family for a while now. I hoped he enjoyed all the prestige that came with his title. I really hoped he was lonely as hell.

Ian didn't seem to want to celebrate with me either, since he was holed up in his room and ignoring my attempts at conversation. I ate lunch alone at the tiny kitchen table and wondered if anyone would hear me if I screamed. I hadn't met a single other person in this town. That was why I cleaned up, took the truck, and headed to Jenna's. I needed someone to verify that I still existed, and there was no place I felt more alive than with Jenna.

I didn't call. I should have, but I didn't want to take the time. Or risk her telling me no. She didn't expect anything else from me anyway. I always just showed up.

It took forever to get through town. The streets were crowded with sweaty kids and red-faced parents. Red and white streamers hung still in the absence of a breeze, and several signs promised family fun at the town fireworks show.

Jenna probably wasn't even home. Or she was having some big family barbeque or something. I knew she wasn't just sitting around hoping I'd show up. The last time I'd seen her, I slunk out of her house before she'd woken up. I hadn't said goodbye. I hadn't talked to her since. I wasn't good at feeling this way. It was completely new territory, and I was hopelessly lost.

But Jenna's Bronco was parked in the driveway. Maybe Fate wasn't quite the bitch I believed her to be. She'd been almost kind to me lately.

I pulled to the curb two houses down and reached for my cell before I remembered I no longer had one and I'd forgotten to take Ian's. I was going to have to go to the door. I hoped her mother wasn't home.

She was. I heard the staccato of her heels on the tile floor before she opened the door. It was the first time I'd seen Jenna's mother, and there was some resemblance. She grinned at me. "Ian! Please, come in."

I didn't correct her, just stepped inside the front door and stood awkwardly to the side. Thankfully, it didn't take Jenna long to appear.

She had a scowl on her face when she walked into the room, but that changed when she saw me. I had to take a deep breath, even though I doubted she knew with any certainty which one I was. It made me ache. I didn't want Jenna looking at Ian like that. I didn't want her even thinking about him when she looked at me, but that was unavoidable.

Vivian clapped her hands together in delight. "This is just perfect! Now you have a date to the party!"

"What party?" I asked.

Jenna grimaced. "Some lame party with a bunch of old people I don't really know that my mom thinks she's dragging me to so that I won't have to spend the Fourth by myself. But I'm not going."

Her mom ignored her. "I told her to invite you, Ian. Susan is just dying to meet you," she said.

"He hasn't done anything wrong," Jenna said. "He shouldn't be punished."

"So you'll come?" Vivian asked me, as if she hadn't heard a word Jenna had said.

"Well…" There was no way I was going to that party. "I kind of had a surprise planned for Jenna," I lied.

Vivian's eyes widened with interest. "Really? How romantic. Well, far be it from me to ruin the perfect surprise. You two have a good time, but don't stay out late." She turned to Jenna, whispered something in her ear, and left the room.

"My hero," Jenna said, throwing me a smile. "I don't know that I would've survived the evening."

"Glad to be of service."

"So where are we going?" she asked, opening the door and stepping out onto the front porch.

Was she so eager to leave with me because she thought I was Ian? I had no plans—my only thought had been to see Jenna. Now that I'd accomplished that, I was winging it. I followed her down the steps.

"Aren't you afraid you'll be burned by the sun?" Jenna asked.

I stopped. "You know who I am?"

"It's pretty easy to tell you two apart now."

"How?" I was interested in how this girl, who I'd known less than two months, had managed to figure out something that even my own parents had trouble with.

"Your expressions," she said simply. "Ian's eyes are a bit wider and his smile is pretty open. I never have to wonder what he's thinking. You slouch," she said, opening the passenger door of my truck, "and I never have any idea what you're thinking."

"Good," I told her, climbing in the truck and turning the ignition. Because I was usually thinking all sorts of things I shouldn't. I pulled away from the curb and headed into the sun.

JENNA

Seeing Luke shouldn't have made me feel better. I should have felt infinitely worse, should have hated myself for being so happy to see Luke after I'd just been out with Ian. And kissed Ian. And liked kissing Ian. But my weekend had been long and treacherous, since I wasn't really speaking to Mom and she seemed to have forgotten that she'd done anything to earn my anger. I was a little surprised when Luke showed up at my doorstep.

I shouldn't have been. Luke always managed to surprise me. But he'd never knocked on the door before. He seemed more at home in the shadows than the sunlight. I didn't know why he was trying to hide from everyone but me. It couldn't only be about whatever he'd done in Massachusetts. Whatever it was, it couldn't have been that bad.

Luke obviously wasn't perfect, but he was wonderful in a flawed way, which I thought might be the best way. I never knew where I was with Luke, which made me both frustrated and interested. Luke was a riddle I wanted to solve.

I had no idea where we were going, and I was beginning to suspect Luke didn't either. I really didn't care—I was content just to be with him.

"Fourth of July—love it or hate it?" Luke asked.

"It's looking pretty good so far," I said.

He smiled and reached across the seat to take my hand. I could feel the calluses on his palms and across his fingers. I was glad Luke wasn't perfect, because that meant I didn't have to be perfect either. Perfection was more pressure than I needed. I didn't have to be worthy to live in his flawless little world. He didn't make me think about the things I didn't have, the things I wasn't. He didn't want me to reinvent myself to fit, because he didn't exactly fit either.

"It's okay," I said, answering his question. "Um, I like the whole premise of the thing, you know, celebrating independence. It's like the Founding Fathers were rebellious teens who wanted to get away from the authority of their parents. I can understand that." I wanted independence more than anything. "And it was fun when I was a kid. We ate hot dogs and Mops made homemade ice cream with a churn and everything, which was incredible, and then I got to run around the yard with sparklers."

"I hate sparklers," Luke told me. "What a bust—all light and no bang. I like the ones that make a lot of noise. Ian and I used to have bottle rocket fights."

Typical boys. "I don't really like fireworks all that much. I like the really big ones that the town sets off. They're gorgeous. But someone else lights them. I don't like being up close to all that noise. That, and Tommy Johnson set me on fire with one once."

"Really?"

I rolled my eyes. "We were like thirteen and Steph had a party at her house. It was supposed to be all grown up—my mom made me wear a dress." I hated wearing dresses. They showed everyone just how skinny my legs were. "There was a DJ and everything, but the boys wouldn't dance. The girls were trying to act all grown-up, but some of the boys had brought a bunch of bottle rockets and started shooting them at everyone. I didn't even notice when one landed on me—not until it blew up."

"It hurt?" Luke asked. His eyes were soft, like he was really worried I'd been injured.

"A little. It scared the crap out of me. And my dress caught on fire. Just the top part, and just for a second. Becca threw punch on me and put it out. But the dress was ruined, and my stomach was burned. I had a bunch of little blisters. And I went home early in a tattered dress."

"I would have kicked his ass," Luke said. I believed him.

"Thanks. Not necessary at this point, but I appreciate it anyway."

"Okay, so no bottle rockets. Not," Luke added, throwing me a wicked grin, "that I'd be too upset if your shirt went up in flames."

I glared at him. "Please don't set me on fire just to get a glimpse of boob."

When Luke laughed, the air seemed lighter. It was so rare that he completely let his guard down, threw his head back, and just laughed. It made me wish I were wittier so I could hear that laughter over and over. I wanted to record it and put it on repeat; Luke's laughter was a song I could dance to.

"So, are you going to tell me where we're going?" I finally asked.

"Not a chance."

"Do you even know where we're going?"

"Not a chance."

I liked that Luke was sarcastic and smart and a little sad. Today, I liked the dark pools I could see beneath his eyes. I liked that he was a little broken. I was a little broken myself. Luke seemed to know me without having to strip me bare. He didn't seem interested in taking me apart and putting me back together in a way he thought worked better.

"Pull over," I ordered.

"Why?"

"Because obviously I need to be captain of this little adventure, otherwise we'll never get anywhere."

He eased the truck onto the shoulder of the road. "So where are you taking me?"

"A secret place," I said. "I never take anyone there."

"Should I be afraid?" he asked as we got out and switched places.

I adjusted the seat and rearview mirror. "Probably."

"I normally don't let girls drive," he told me. "Be gentle."

I grinned at him. "I'm always gentle the first time."

LUKE

Jenna drove us to the old train yard. "Um, I hate to break it to you," I said, "but this place isn't exactly a secret." Graffiti was spray-painted on several of the buildings, and there was trash everywhere. Bottle rockets exploded somewhere in the distance.

Jenna hopped out of the truck. "I run here all the time, and I've never seen anyone else. It's private property."

"So we're trespassing?" I grinned.

She ignored my obvious enjoyment of her lawbreaking. "Sort of," she said. She dug around in the backseat of the truck, and I had no idea what she was looking for until she pulled out the blanket from our picnic.

"Is that for my dead body?" I asked.

"Maybe," she said. "It depends on your behavior."

Those odds were never in my favor.

We walked through the huge train yard. It had its own water tower. There were warehouses and walls that were once buildings but now seemed to defy gravity by remaining upright. It was a shame they'd let this place fall apart rather than finding some other use for it.

Jenna stopped in front of a large, dilapidated building at the far corner of the property and climbed through the window. I followed. It was dark and damp inside. There were piles of leaves in the corners, and an old metal desk with two legs. It didn't really look like a place many people would enjoy hanging out. Jenna walked through it like she owned it, ignoring the dirt and rot; I wondered what she saw instead. She climbed a rickety staircase.

"So, this is where the cute girl-next-door lures the unsuspecting hero to his death."

Her laugh echoed off the walls and swirled through the cavernous space. "I would hardly classify you as the hero."

"I saved you from torture and certain death not even an hour ago. Would you like me to drop you at that party?"

"Okay, okay, I'm sorry." She held up her hands in surrender. "You can be the hero today."

I'd take it.

The second floor was even more damaged. The floorboards were warped and swollen with moisture. There was an enormous hole in the roof, the edges ragged, the sky peering down at us. Something—a tree, a tornado, neglect—had worn it away, leaving a gaping hole large enough to fit a car through.

I helped her lay out the blanket. "Is this like your seduction kit or what?"

She pushed me and grinned. "Sometimes I come here to escape."

We sat in the middle of the room and watched the sky darken. Without my self-revulsion to cloud everything, we talked. About everything. About absolutely nothing.

We talked about music and books, places she wanted to go and places I'd been. About stupid things we'd done when we were kids—I had more of those than she did. I loved watching her. Most of the time, she had this perfectly crafted poker face and I had no idea what she could possibly be thinking. But sometimes everything was in her face.

Jenna was hell-bent on escaping Solitude, but this place seemed created for her. Not the town or the people, but the landscape. She seemed sculpted to run through these woods and dive off the cliffs and sit cross-legged in a condemned building that only made her more beautiful. I wanted to capture and bottle her, because I knew that the world would try to tear her apart, and I couldn't imagine her losing all the possibility she had built up inside her. I wanted to build her a new world, construct it from everything she thought the world was, so that when she emerged from this place, all bright and shiny, it wouldn't tarnish her. I didn't want Jenna to have to become something else. I didn't want this Jenna destroyed. I knew enough of the world to know it was a very real possibility.

Jenna's head nestled into my shoulder as we stared at the sky through the wide-open ceiling. Jenna was so still and silent. I felt her heart pounding against my side, listened to her breath come and go in rhythmic simplicity. There was a faint rumble of thunder in the distance as the day faded away.

"This is nice." Jenna sighed. "Peaceful. No one knows where we are. I can kind of forget everything else that's out there."

I was trying to. I didn't want Ian's presence, real or feared, to break the spell. I just needed Jenna all to myself for a little while longer.

Thunder rumbled again, and a few raindrops plopped on the roof while a few more found their way through the hole, splashing on the floor and echoing through the building. I loved summer storms. This one was easing up on us, just a smattering of rain, a riff of water, which played off the percussion of our breath. My chest felt tight, like my ribs had shrunk, and while I couldn't be positive, I was fairly certain that it was happiness. I was a little surprised that it would visit—I thought I'd killed it for sure.

JENNA

The cicadas began a low murmur, which rose higher and higher until it was a roar. When it started to rain, the frogs joined in. An uncivilized symphony. The chirps and croaks of the frogs replaced the strings of the crickets and rattle of the cicadas; occasionally, the bullfrog added his bass. Bottle rockets popped closer to town, repeated over and over in a chorus of destruction. I took Luke's hand. This feeling was unknown to me. It was anxiety and contentment and rightness all spun together like a colorful thread. I wanted desperately to hold on to it forever; I prayed the thread wouldn't break.

This perfect moment hadn't been made or created—just found. It wasn't pulled off a shelf or chosen off a menu.

We'd discovered it, stumbled over it without having known it was even there. Like swimming in the lake on a hot day when the water was uniform, flat, glassy, and hot under the sun, and then unexpectedly swimming into a cool spot. It was the goose bumps that appeared, brought on by the thrill because it felt so good, and the fear that came with not knowing how deep it went or how long it would last. It was exactly like that.

There was an explosion of color, a flicker of red on Luke's face, followed by dull pops. The fireworks had started. I saw the bursts before I heard them, multicolored flowers that branded the sky, briefly illuminating the room where we lay, a room which had slowly gotten dark as time passed, oblivious to the fact that there were two people who wanted it to take its time and not move so quickly. I closed my eyes and saw colors on the backs of my eyelids.

The fireworks didn't last very long. They died out in a loud, fiery finale; red and silver sparkles reached their pinnacle, scattered, and trailed down the night sky, leaving Luke and me in complete darkness. I listened to his breathing, slow and deep, and imagined a world where I didn't have to worry about anything. I didn't have to worry about tearing brothers apart. I didn't have to feel guilty that I was the kind of person who would do that sort of thing to begin with. I didn't have to worry about scholarships or tendonitis or my mom. Especially not my mom. In my fictional life, I had a mother who still wore birthday tiaras and was so busy being proud of what I could do that she didn't even notice what I couldn't. In my fictional world, my mother didn't drink. She didn't gulp whatever liquor was handy when she thought I wasn't looking. She didn't fall asleep on the couch with her mascara running down her face. In my imaginary world, I wasn't pursued by that demon. In my imaginings, I could breathe.

TWENTY-ONE

JENNA

It started raining pretty hard, dripping then pouring through the roof, so we threw the blanket over our heads and raced to the truck. The packed dirt had turned into slippery mud, and it splashed my shins and coated my shoes. Rain found its way around the blanket, wetting my hair and running down my face like tears. I laughed as Luke slid through the mud, righting himself at the last second. His hair was plastered to his head and his shoulders were soaked and the grin on his face defied the weather. By the time we were in the truck, the rain had already tapered to a drizzle. It stopped completely as we pulled out of the train yard, as suddenly as if God had shut off a faucet.

I was craving onion rings, so we headed to Jimmy's Dairy Bar. It was packed. Luke pulled his truck into one of the last open slots.

Red speaker boxes shone under lighted menus. Eighties music played through the speakers in the eaves of the narrow building, but it was hard to hear over the car radios and the yelling back and forth. It looked like the majority of the senior class was there. A lot of them had just come from the lake. Melanie Overton was strutting around in very short shorts and a bikini top. She'd finally gotten boobs, and she was having a hard time corralling them.

"Ian, man, where you been hiding out?" Steven stuck his head in the truck window. "We've been at the lake all day," he told me. "You guys should have come."

"Actually," I said before I even really thought about it, "this is Luke. Ian's brother."

Luke's hand tightened on the steering wheel, then relaxed as he forced a smile. "Hey."

"No way!" Steven hollered. He leaned in to get a closer look. "That's freaky identical." He turned and shouted across the parking lot. "Amber, Kyle, come see."

I wanted to beat my head against the dashboard. I should have kept my mouth shut. But Luke was going to have to meet everyone eventually.

"Dude, guess who this is?" Steven pointed at Luke like he was some freak of nature.

"Um, Ian, right?" Kyle asked. He looked bored.

"Nope." Steven was enjoying this way too much. I rolled my eyes. "It's his brother."

"No way," Kyle said. "Weird."

"I believe twins are fairly normal," I said. They were being ridiculous.

"I guess," Kyle said. Dani and Amber were sizing Luke up. I didn't like it.

"Where's Ian?" Dani asked me.

I shrugged. I didn't feel like explaining myself to them. I shouldn't have to. Luke still hadn't said anything; he looked really uncomfortable.

"Having your cake and eating it too?" Dani asked. Amber giggled. Luke's jaw clenched. "I guess it *would* be hard to decide." Dani gave Luke a suggestive smirk. "Are you two completely identical?"

Kyle grinned. "Dude, you'd better hurry and pop that cherry before your brother does."

Luke was out of the truck before I knew what was happening, way before I had time to get offended or embarrassed. Dani screamed as Luke reached over and grabbed Kyle around the throat. He picked him up off the ground and slammed him against the side of the truck. Kyle's eyes were wide, his face red. No one had ever gotten the best of Kyle before.

"Apologize," Luke growled through clenched teeth.

Steven tried to step in, but Luke pushed him away.

"Apologize," Luke said again, quietly.

"Luke, really, it's fine," I said. "He's a dick. I don't really expect him to act any other way." Luke was really scaring me.

We had a crowd now, and it was pretty telling that no one else tried to help Kyle, not even his friends. I didn't blame them. Luke looked crazy.

Kyle pulled at Luke's hands.

"Luke, seriously, put him down," I said. "He can't breathe."

Luke set him back on his feet and let go of his throat, keeping a hand pressed tight against Kyle's chest. Kyle coughed. "You're an asshole."

"Let's just go," I said. Luke's silence was more unnerving than anything he could have said. "Please?"

Luke let Kyle go. He looked surprised to see me standing there. Kyle swung at him then, but Luke stepped out of the way and punched Kyle in the stomach. He folded in half.

"Break it up!" The manager came out of the building and eyed Luke. "Or I'm calling the cops."

"We were just leaving," Luke said. He climbed back in the truck and started the engine. Everyone backed away fast—they weren't so sure the crazy new guy wouldn't run them over. I wasn't so sure he wouldn't either. I realized there was a lot about Luke that I didn't know.

LUKE

I blew it. I knew I would. I lost my temper and turned into the old Luke. Give me a tiny bit of joy, and I'll shatter it.

It took me awhile to calm down. I tried to relax, taking deep breaths and trying to rid myself of that shadow, the ugly Luke who was always lurking in the corner. The one who had destroyed his life and the lives of everyone around him. Jenna didn't say a word. After a few minutes of quiet, I managed to push that other Luke back into his hiding place. I wished I could kill him, get rid of him forever, but I knew better. He was always going to be just over my shoulder, watching for his opportunity to step in and screw everything up. Or maybe that was the real me, and this "nice" Luke was just smoke and mirrors. I wasn't sure anymore. About much of anything.

"I'm really sorry," I told Jenna. She had no idea how much, and I couldn't explain it to her.

She didn't answer, just looked at me like she wasn't sure who I was. I wasn't sure either sometimes.

I took Jenna home. I knew I needed to apologize again, but I also knew it wouldn't fix anything. I'd taken a perfect day and trashed it. I was sorry Jenna had had to see me like that. I was sorry that I'd flashed out and turned into the old Luke. But I wasn't sorry for hitting that jerk, and I wouldn't have taken it back if I could. I wished I'd punched him in the mouth. He deserved it. But I deserved worse because I was indeed trying to take Jenna for myself. Not that she was something to claim. No one was ever going to possess Jenna. But I found myself jealous of the time she spent with Ian and wishing she would stop. But I wouldn't ask. I was afraid of her answer.

Her mom's car was in the driveway, but the house was dark.

"Do you want me to walk you in?" I asked.

"No, it's fine." She tried to smile at me, but it didn't reach her eyes. "I'll see you later." She slid out of the truck. I watched her walk across the shadowed lawn and open her front door. I didn't pull away until the door shut behind her.

I hated the fear and uncertainty in Jenna's eyes, and hated it even worse that I'd put it there. If Mom found out, she was going to chain me up in my room. I was supposed to be on house arrest, so I was glad the cops hadn't been called. I didn't need to add assault to my already long list of offenses. The old Luke had done plenty of community service and met numerous times with probation officers. Better that Jenna not know about that. But it didn't matter. All the hope in the world meant absolutely nothing if I couldn't behave myself. And I was obviously still having serious problems with that.

This was the first time I felt bad for something I didn't regret. I pressed down on the accelerator, hoping speed would blow the shards out of my head. I couldn't understand why I always did things I didn't want to do and couldn't do the things I knew I should. I didn't want to lose Jenna. I should have walked away. It was too late for either now.

I was almost home. The pavement turned to gravel, and I took a corner too fast, almost fishtailing into the ditch. Something clattered to the floor. Jenna's phone. I hit the brake. I didn't want to face her, but I knew I was going to. Maybe I just wanted an excuse to go back. I turned around and headed to Jenna's house.

Sarah Guillory

The lights were on when I parked in the driveway. I knocked on the door, but nobody answered. When I heard a crash, I didn't wait for an invitation.

I smelled vomit as I stepped through the door. There was an empty vodka bottle overturned on the carpet, and a half-empty bottle of rum sitting on the coffee table. Wads of tissue were everywhere. There was no sign of Jenna or her mom.

"Jenna?" Banging came from an open door off the living room. I walked into the dark room and toward a rectangle of light.

Jenna's mom was laid out on the bathroom tile, her face pale, her hair tangled; Jenna was trying unsuccessfully to pick her up. The sick smell was even stronger in there.

Jenna jumped when she heard me, and her surprise quickly turned to anger. She wiped at her face—I was pretty sure she'd been crying. "What are you doing here?"

"You left your phone," I said, holding it up. "Is she okay?" She didn't look okay.

"She's fine," Jenna snapped. "She passed out."

"Can I help?" I laid Jenna's phone on the dresser and stepped into the tiny bathroom.

"No," Jenna said. She looked fierce, her eyes hard and jaw sharp. Then she sighed and stood up. "Help me get her to the bed."

I brushed Jenna away when she tried to help. "I've got it," I said. I scooped her mom up off the floor. She weighed almost nothing. She looked less like Jenna up close. I laid her on the bed and stepped back.

"Thanks," Jenna said. "Wait outside. I'm going to get her changed."

I went into the living room. I knew Jenna didn't want me there. She didn't want an audience to her pain. I understood that perfectly. But I couldn't make myself leave.

190

Jenna looked years older as she emerged from her mom's room, and I got a glimpse of what she would look like as an adult. The world was already chipping away at her, and there wasn't a thing I could do about it. I was stupid to have wanted to create a perfect world for her. I'd never be enough for that.

Jenna seemed to have forgotten I was there as she walked into the kitchen and returned with paper towels and a garbage bag. She started cleaning up the vomit next to the couch. I threw away the vodka bottle and some tissues.

"All of it," Jenna said, finally acknowledging my presence. "Throw it all away. Even the tumbler."

I tossed the rum and the red cup while Jenna sprayed something on the carpet to get rid of the smell, and then we were in the kitchen, rummaging through the cabinets and fridge, looking for the rest of the alcohol.

"Sorry about all this," Jenna said, even though I was the one who needed to apologize. "I guess I should have mentioned it up front. Hi. My name is Jenna. My mother is turning into an alcoholic. What's your dysfunction?"

I flinched—that one hit a little close to home. I set the bag, now heavy with some wine and whiskey, outside the back door and joined Jenna in the living room. She folded onto the couch and draped a blanket over her feet. She looked exhausted.

"I'm the one who needs to apologize," I said, sitting next to her.

"Yeah, what was that all about anyway?" Jenna asked.

She looked at me, waiting for my explanation. I didn't want to tell her anything. I wanted to tell her everything.

"The old Luke," I said finally. "He's a bastard. I don't like him all that much."

"Yeah, that was pretty intense," she said. "Not that Kyle didn't have it coming. He's been needing someone to take him down a notch or two for a while now. He's going to make your life miserable," she told me.

I didn't laugh, although the idea that the arrogant prick could somehow make my life any more miserable than it already was seemed absurd. "I can handle it," I said.

"And while I'm not a fan of your method, I do appreciate you sticking up for me."

"I've always had a little trouble with my temper. Got me into more scrapes than I can remember. I didn't like him talking about you like that—thinking about you like that."

"Just promise me you won't get into any more fights on my behalf."

I didn't know if that was a promise I could keep. A fight between Ian and me was pretty inevitable at this point. But I wanted to stay with her, so I would promise her anything. I nodded instead.

It was getting late and I knew I needed to leave, but I didn't. I couldn't.

Jenna leaned forward and looked at me. "What do you want to do after high school?" she asked.

That was a loaded question. I knew what I wasn't going to do. I wasn't going off to college—I'd probably screwed my grades up too much for that anyway. I wasn't going to join a frat or tailgate. I wasn't going to do any of the things that Ian was. He'd followed the rules and gained it all. I'd been stupid and irresponsible and destroyed my future.

"I have no idea," I admitted. "You?"

"I used to have all these plans," she said. "But now I don't know."

"Why?"

"My mom." Her voice was heavy. "My mom is screwing everything up. Her drinking is getting worse, and I'm afraid about what's going to happen if I'm not here."

"You can't stay here just to take care of your mom. You'll regret it forever." I had experience with regret.

"I know. But I can't leave her alone if she's going to drink herself to death."

"She can't ask you to stay here and take care of her," I said. "She's a big girl."

"If I'm not here, there won't be anyone to put her to bed, or roll her over to keep her from choking on her own vomit, or help her get better instead of worse. I feel responsible."

"She's your mother. It's *her* responsibility to take care of *you*. Period."

Jenna looked down and picked at the edge of the blanket. Her voice was soft, hesitant. "I don't want to end up like her. I feel so bad saying that out loud, because she's not a bad person. But I don't want to get stuck here. I don't want to become an alcoholic like the rest of my family. I know I'm going to make mistakes, but I want them to be my mistakes." She sighed. "But I'm scared to go off somewhere far away all by myself, even though it's exactly what I want. I want to meet new people and do new things. I want to see the world. But I'm afraid of failing and being really lonely."

I reached over and ran my finger down the side of her face. "You aren't ever going to be lonely. No matter where you go, people are going to line up around the block to be with you."

Jenna's laugh was beautiful. "You're just saying that so I'll sleep with you."

I loved being with Jenna. "Maybe. But it's the truth, too."

She shook her head. "It's easy to live in a tiny town and talk about what I'm going to do. Actually going out and doing it is a different matter completely. Sometimes I get scared." She pushed her hair behind her ears. Her face was as far away from afraid as it could be. "It's like right before a race. I've been planning my strategy for weeks and I'm focused. My arms and legs practically hum with motion, ready to jump and push the second the gun fires. I chew on the end of my tongue and look down the tunnel. I don't even notice anyone else, because it isn't a race against them. It's a race against myself, to see if I can be better, faster, stronger than I was yesterday. And all I can see is the course in front of me. I'm ready."

She looked ready to face anything, no matter what she believed. She put so much pressure on herself to be perfect, to be better, and she didn't even realize how wonderful she already was.

"But when the gun goes off," she continued, "in that nanosecond between hearing the gun and jumping across the line, I only feel fear—because I have no idea how it's going to end. Weeks of training and mental preparation all come down to that one single moment, that one race on that one day, and what if I fail? Of course, once my legs jump and I'm in motion, all that doubt goes away and I just run. But sometimes it feels like there's an eternity in that nanosecond."

I wasn't a runner, but I knew what she meant. I knew exactly how long a split second could be. "Come on."

Jenna gave me a half-smile. "Where are we going?"

I took her hand and pulled her off the couch. "Temperance movement."

JENNA

Luke grabbed the bag full of alcohol, and we climbed in his truck. I rolled the windows down and turned up the radio as we pulled onto the highway, hoping the music would fill my head and push out all my unwanted thoughts, willing the wind to snatch them up and blow them away. I smelled freshly cut grass and baking asphalt and summer.

We drove out of town, letting the warm breeze blow the night off us. The headlights caught snatches of conversation between trees. Luke waited until there was nothing but stars and countryside before opening the garbage bag of liquor. He stopped at the stop sign at the end of the dirt road and handed me one of the bottles.

"Hit the sign," he said.

"With this?"

Luke's stare was penetrating. "Hit the sign."

I leaned out the window and tossed the bottle. My aim was off, and it slammed against the green pole instead, but there was a satisfying sound of shattering glass. It felt a little like success.

Luke drove again, gaining speed, and I pulled out a bottle of rum. I held it out of the window by its narrow neck, then tossed it up as I passed a speed limit sign. Dead on. This time I laughed. Luke drove faster and I kept smashing the bottles, tossing out the whiskey, and the Chardonnay, and finally the Merlot, which left a crimson smear on the white wooden sign advertising cattle for sale.

"Sometimes you just have to release the pressure," Luke said.

And that's exactly what it felt like. By the time we'd made it almost to the lake, the bag was empty and my head was lighter. Luke understood. He didn't have to say a word—it was carved into his every pore, and if I knew nothing else, I knew we felt the same. Somehow, Luke knew what it was like to be in my skin.

Luke pulled up at the cove. Our spot. He grabbed the blanket, which was still a little damp from the rain, from the backseat and spread it on the soft dirt. We lay down and counted the stars. Luke's chest pressed against my back, his arm around my waist and the other curled underneath his head. I listened to our breathing and felt his heart pound and knew the moment that our hearts were beating at the same time. It only lasted a few beats before mine was a half-second ahead, but in those few beats the world could have caught fire and I wouldn't have noticed.

His heartbeat pushed away my anxiety. His skin blocked out the rift between my mother and me. I knew my problems were waiting in the shadows, ready to pounce, but they weren't gnawing at me just then.

I rolled over and pressed my face into his neck. His skin was warm and smelled like cut wood and soap. I kissed his jaw, and he looked down at me and smiled. I reached up and ran my fingers through his hair.

"Why are you here?" he asked.

The question caught me off-guard. "Do you want me to leave?"

He didn't smile. His face was still and sharp. "Why are you here with me?" He pushed my hair over my shoulder, his fingertips brushing along my collarbone. "You picked the right brother the first time."

"You're right," I said.

He looked hurt, then resigned.

"I picked you the first time I met you," I explained. "At the hospital."

His look was careful. "What are you talking about?"

"That was you at the hospital, wasn't it?" I asked. "Pretending to be Ian?" When he hesitated, I added, "Don't lie."

He just nodded. And I wasn't surprised. I had suspected it that night in my room, the way his hand had hovered over the half-whittled seagull. But I hadn't been sure. I wasn't sure why he hadn't told me either.

"Why lie?"

"I didn't lie," he said. "I never told you I was Ian. If my mom hadn't hollered Ian's name, I never would have told you I was him. He'd agreed to keep quiet so I could pretend to be him and get out of the state. Away from my dad. Away from my life, if only for a little while. I wasn't supposed to meet you. And then it was just easier to pretend that it hadn't been me. Ian is better for you."

I was beginning to believe he was wrong about that.

"I thought about you a lot over those seven months," he said. "I was shocked when I saw you again. I didn't think I ever would."

"Me neither. And then there were two of you and I didn't know what to do."

He put his finger to my lips. "Let's not talk about that right now."

And he kissed me so we didn't have to.

LUKE

I didn't want to fall asleep. I was afraid I would wake up someone else and lose the moment forever. I watched Jenna sleep instead. She was curled into my chest and her hair tickled my face. I wished there was a pause button on the world.

But the clock kept moving forward, and somewhere between ticks, I fell asleep.

I dreamt of my room again, the one with the moving walls. But this time Jenna was with me, and the panic I felt when the walls got closer had nothing to do with me and everything to do with her. I didn't want her to disappear like I always did. I tried to wedge the bed in the corner, but the walls kept moving. Jenna threw books at the wall and tried to find a way out, but there was no door and no window. No escape. Jenna and I stood in the center of the room and watched the walls get closer and closer. When they touched our shoulders, Jenna leaned over and kissed me. The walls stopped. We were pressed together, and the walls were touching us on both sides, but we didn't disappear. It was the first time I didn't wake up from that dream in a panic.

When I did wake up, I knew something had changed. I could feel it in the air. It was like when I was little and woke up to snow on the ground. I'd known even before I got out of bed that there would be a blanket of white on the usually brown, dead grass. For some reason, I could feel the difference in the air. Or those mornings when I would wake up excited and not know why. That was how it was. I was anxious and excited for no reason. No, that wasn't really true. It was because of Jenna.

She was sitting up. "I was watching you sleep," she admitted. "You look a lot younger when you sleep."

"What time is it?"

She looked at her phone. "Almost six."

My time with Jenna was snippets of nights and early mornings, like some crazy dream that comes in pieces. The kind that made me sad when I woke up.

Funny how a bad day could be swallowed up by a sunset and sunrise. Last night I was sure I'd blown it with Jenna, and I knew coming home to her drunk mother hadn't been the high point of Jenna's life. But now it was a whole new day, and there was a feeling that it would be better. At least it was starting out that way. Because we were together. And there was no other place I wanted to be.

The sky blushed as the sun peeked over the edge of the world. Jenna wrapped her arms around her legs and rested her cheek on her knee, her face shining in the early morning light. Glints of gold shone in her hair.

"I had a dream about you last night," I told her. I wanted to take it back as soon as it was out there.

"A PG one, I hope," she said.

"Unfortunately," I admitted. She laughed. "I have this dream all the time, but you've never been in it before." I described the dream to her. "You know, it's normally a nightmare. But it wasn't this time."

"Now I know what you're most afraid of," she said.

"And what is that?"

"Disappearing."

That was exactly what it felt like in Ian's shadow. Jenna saw me even when I couldn't. I didn't know if I was relieved or afraid.

Jenna stared at me for a minute, then leaned in and pressed her head to my chest. I put my arm around her, running my fingers through her hair and pressing her closer to me. I didn't want to let go.

JENNA

Dawn dark felt different from night dark. For a moment, before the sun came up, everything was muffled and still, like the world was waiting for something. Patient, the air was hushed and full of possibility. Then everything exploded in color and sound as the sun popped up over the horizon and the birds started calling back and forth to one another.

Luke's eyes took on all the colors of sky and water and reflected them back. And the longer I stared at him, the less he looked like Ian. Luke held his head differently. He slouched. He had a half-smile that was part smirk, part grimace, and I had no idea if he was being serious, or making fun of me, or hiding something really bad.

But I could talk to Luke—without saying much at all. Stabs of desire cut through me as I stared at the back of his neck, the curve of his shoulder. I didn't have adequate words and only knew it was pure feeling, emotion completely free of reason. It felt like it was going to swallow me whole. I didn't believe people could own one another, but I suddenly felt very possessive of Luke. I didn't want to share him with the rest of the world.

"Thanks," I told him.

"For what?"

"For being here." I reached up and pulled him down to me, trying to tell him without words everything I couldn't say. The kiss was long and lingering and made me ache.

He pulled away and looked at me. "Does this mean you've picked me?"

I smiled. "It was never really a competition to begin with."

TWENTY-TWO

JENNA

The curtain twitched as Luke pulled into the driveway, and I caught a flash of Mom's robe. No amount of fireworks or sunrises or synchronized heartbeats was going to keep the world out forever.

"Do you want me to walk you in?" Luke offered.

"I think that would make it worse," I told him, although I was too angry at my mother to worry about how much trouble I was in. I leaned over and kissed him before he could argue. "Go home. I'll call you later." I hopped out of the truck. "On second thought," I said, turning back to him, "she'll probably take my phone."

"I really am sorry," he said.

"I'm not." I wanted to jump back in Luke's truck and tell him to drive forever. I didn't care where we went, as long as it was away. But I went inside instead.

Mom had positioned a chair so that it faced the front door. Her back was straight and her legs crossed, the top one swinging manically. She clung to her huge mug of coffee like a drowning man grips a life preserver. Or a wino holds his bottle. Her lips were thin, almost nonexistent. "You stupid, stupid girl," she said.

"I'm sorry." Which was a lie. The only part about last night that I was sorry about was her behavior.

"'Sorry' doesn't cut it. Do you know how worried I've been?"

I started to climb the stairs. I was too tired to go into it.

"I'm talking to you, young lady!"

I wanted to tell her that talking involved a two-way conversation; what she was doing was yelling. "And I'm listening," I said instead, turning to face her.

"You're out all night with some boy you barely know, then you come slinking in with the sun, acting like it's no big deal."

"That's some serious bullshit you've got there." She was in no position to start pointing fingers at inappropriate behavior. Especially if she couldn't even remember hers.

"Don't you dare talk to me like that!" she shouted, marching across the room and glaring up at me from the bottom of the staircase. She looked older.

"Like what, Mom? Honestly? God forbid we talk honestly about anything. The truth was you were passed out in your own puke last night and I was here to take care of it. So don't try and make me feel guilty, like you paced the floors, wringing your hands and praying I would turn up alive. You didn't even know I was gone."

"You're grounded."

"Classic. You get drunk and act like an irresponsible jerk, and I clean up your mess and get punished for it. That really sucks."

"Life isn't fair. It's best you learn that little lesson right now."

She had to be joking. "Really? Because life has been completely fair with me, Mom. It's been handing out roses and kittens lately. I'm working two jobs so I'll have money for college. And what are you doing?"

"Working," she snapped.

"Oh, that's right. You're never here because you're 'working,' which apparently means being out with your friends getting trashed. And now you want to waltz in here and pretend like you have some sort of control over what I do. You can't just be a parent when it's convenient for you."

Mom climbed the steps and stuck her finger in my face. "I don't know who the hell you think you are."

"I'll tell you exactly who I am. I'm the girl who always does what she's told. I get good grades. I take care of you when you've had too much to drink. I worry that I can't ever leave here because someone has to make sure you don't pass out and choke on your own vomit." Shattering the alcohol earlier had broken a dam, and the words poured out so fast I couldn't stop them. I didn't really want to anyway. "I'm a teenager with adult worries and problems. I should be allowed to have fun. I should be allowed to make mistakes and be a kid and not have to worry all the damn time. But I'll also tell you who I'm not." I was shouting. "I'm not you! I wasn't out last night getting drunk and knocked up. So spare me the lecture."

Mom's hand flashed out so fast that I felt the sting across my cheek well before I realized she'd slapped me. She'd never hit me before.

"Don't you ever talk to me like that again. Do you hear me?" Mom wasn't yelling anymore. Her voice was taut, a stretched rope between us.

I should have felt guilt. I wanted to regret what I'd said. But I didn't. I was sick of pretending our life wasn't eroding. I was sick of trying to hold it together while it ran through my hands. "I'll be in my room," I said.

"Phone." She held her hand out.

I handed her my phone and headed upstairs. I was suddenly exhausted.

"Maybe you shouldn't see Ian again," Mom called after me. "Any boy who would keep you out all night doesn't respect you."

"You would know." I slammed the door behind me.

IAN

I was drowning in sleep and it felt as if I would never find the surface. Every time I thought I was close to waking up, something would grab me and pull me back under. I dreamt of the tree house again, and then shrinking walls. They pressed against my skull all night, and when I was finally able to wake up, my head was sore.

The house was quiet. Luke's door was shut, and I could hear his faint snore on the other side. I stopped, my hand resting on the doorknob. I missed Luke. I missed our pranks and always knowing what he was thinking. I hated the doors that had shut between us. I turned the knob. He had locked me out, or Mom, or both, and I didn't want to wake him and make him open up. Not yet.

I went downstairs to the kitchen to fix myself a bowl of cereal and walked into a room I barely recognized. The broken kitchen had been fixed, and not just pieced back together. It was a completely different room, all warm and golden. Luke had always had a talent for building, which was lucky, since he was equally talented at tearing things apart.

I sighed and rubbed the back of my neck. If Luke could reassemble this kitchen, I could do the same with everything else. I was more than halfway there anyway. Mom smiled, Dad had called twice, and Jenna was the normal that would camouflage our dysfunction. If I could just get Luke to buy in, maybe I could save him, too. Save myself. Reestablish that connection and find whatever it was that my brain, my mom, and Dr. Benson were hiding from me. Dr. Benson said I would remember when I was ready, and sometimes I thought I almost had it. But every time I tried to remember exactly what had happened, my mind skittered away from it. It was like I was in a maze. I saw the corner, knew I had to turn and go that way if I wanted to get out, but as soon as I did, there was another corner. There was a door somewhere in that maze. I'd caught a glimpse of it once or twice before losing it again. It seemed to move. And while the maze was dark everywhere else, a small strip of light shone from underneath that door. But I couldn't get it open—it was locked tight. I knew my memories were somewhere in there. I just had to find the key.

Jenna's phone went straight to voicemail. I had to see her. Hopefully she wouldn't mind me stopping by. We'd had a great time together on Friday, even though she'd had to drive her mom home and I'd had to ride back with Steven and Steph. I'd wanted to go with Jenna, but she'd needed some time alone with her mom.

It was late afternoon as I drove through town, quiet and sleepy, most people enjoying an extended holiday. I drove by the store, thinking Jenna might be at work, but it was closed. I drove to her house.

Her mom answered the door. She didn't look happy. "She's grounded, Ian."

"Oh, I'm sorry," I said. I had no idea why she was looking at me that way.

"You should have thought about that when you brought her home at seven in the morning. Do you have any idea how worried I was?"

I hadn't seen Jenna since Friday night. And only Luke would have brought her home at dawn. I suddenly remembered looking up from the ground at an angry Luke, and I had an overwhelming sense that this was all just a replay. Somewhere in my memory, I heard the door unlock. I was suddenly afraid to try and find what was behind it.

"Give him a break." Jenna walked into the living room and stood behind her mother. I hadn't moved.

"Don't sass me," Vivian said. "He's half the reason you're grounded."

"Mom, we've been over this." Jenna sounded calm, bored even.

Vivian looked like she wanted to slap Jenna, but she didn't. I didn't think she knew what to say. She just stood there.

"I need to talk to Ian for a few minutes, please. We'll stand right here on the porch. You can even watch us at all times."

I thought Jenna's mom might argue or start yelling and kick me off the porch. She looked like she wanted to. But Jenna was giving her such an intense glare that I don't think she dared. "Two minutes," Vivian said.

Jenna stepped outside and pulled the door shut behind her. "Um, let's sit."

She sat down on the top porch step. I didn't. I walked down the steps to stand in front of her instead.

"I'm sorry," Jenna said.

I didn't believe her. "Luke." It was all I needed to say.

She nodded. There were dark stars at the edge of my vision—another headache. "Behind my back?" I asked.

There were two spots of color on her cheeks, making her eyes seem even greener. "I'm sorry," she said again. "I really like you." I hated the way she was looking at me.

"But?" I was having a hard time staying still.

She rushed through her words. "Just not that way."

"Really?" I asked. "You kiss all your friends like that?"

She looked really uncomfortable. Good. She had no idea what she was doing. I needed everything to lay flat. I needed my mom to be happy and my dad to be proud. I wanted my life back. And none of that was going to happen if she was with Luke. I wouldn't have it. I had done everything right. Luke didn't deserve her.

Her mom beat on the window. "In a minute!" Jenna shouted. She rolled her eyes. "I've got to go. Can we talk about this later?"

I nodded. I had to be careful, and I wasn't sure I could keep things in perspective if I opened my mouth.

Jenna went inside, shutting me out. Tiny dots of color swam in front of me. It wasn't going to hold after all.

JENNA

I usually enjoyed silence. Distance running normally required being alone, just my feet and my thoughts. I loved the quiet of the woods and the stillness of the house at night and the comfortable whisper of rain. But this silence was torture. It left me alone with myself, and right then, I wasn't someone I enjoyed spending time with. That person hurt people. My mother wasn't speaking to me, which was fine, because I wasn't ready to back down either. She had earned at least some of my anger, and she sure wasn't apologizing for her own behavior, past or present.

But Ian hadn't deserved what I'd done to him. I'd hurt him—I'd seen it in his eyes.

My grounding was still fresh enough for Mom to enforce. She took away my keys and drove me to work on Wednesday. It wouldn't last—she couldn't be inconvenienced for long. Not even the radio could drown out the silence as we rode to town. I slammed the door when I got out just to make sure it would make a noise. It did.

Mops left me alone and let me work. She didn't mention Mom, and she didn't lecture me on behavior or responsibility. I loved her for that.

I stayed late at the shop, eating dinner with Mops and then playing cards until nine. After Mops had beaten me twice in a row, I stood up and stretched. "I'd better call Mom." I hated being dependent on others for a ride. I hated being dependent on others, period.

Mops stacked the cards in the center of the table. "Why don't you just spend the night? I can make up the couch."

I shook my head. "That's okay. I can call Mom."

Mops sighed and got to her feet. "I'll take you." She grabbed her keys and purse, then came to stand right in front of me. Her face was full of worry and care. "You know you can stay with me any time."

"I know. And thanks." But as mad as I was at Mom, she needed me.

The house was dark when we pulled up, just a flicker of the TV shining through the living room window. Mops shut off the engine and started to get out.

"I don't think that's a very good idea," I told her. She ignored me. I followed her inside.

Mom was curled up on the couch watching a movie. She'd found a new tumbler. "You didn't have to walk her in," Mom said, not even looking at Mops.

That did it. I was tired of her being so damn self-centered. The world did not revolve around her and her pain. The rest of us were hurting too, and she was to blame for at least some of that.

"It's not Mops's job to chauffeur me around," I said. "Besides, the Bronco isn't yours to take. Pops gave it to me."

"I'm your mother. I can do any damn thing I want."

"How convenient," I said. "I think it's unbelievably selfish that you don't have anything to do with Mops unless you need something from her."

"Jenna," Mops jumped in, "that's not fair."

"Fair?" I was really sick of all the dysfunctional adults in my life talking about fair. "She was so wasted when I got home last night that she'd passed out, puke everywhere. I had to clean everything up and put her to bed. Do you know how ridiculously unfair *that* is?"

Mops paled. "Is that true?" she asked Mom.

Mom held up her hand, dismissing her concern. She always reduced everyone else to nothing. "Don't start. You have no room to talk."

Mops wasn't backing down. "You're right," she said. "Take it from someone who's been there." She lowered her voice. "You know, you're not the only one who lost Pops."

Mom's eyes popped wide as she jumped to her feet and whirled on Mops. "And you think you were the only one who lost Billy? I was just a kid!" She pointed her finger at Mops. "You turned to the bottle and left me to deal with it as best as I could. And I couldn't. I didn't know how. Even once you'd stopped drinking, it was all about your sobriety. You were always too busy being too damn selfish. I got pregnant because I was glad someone was finally paying me some attention."

I stood silently in the middle of the room as years of bitterness shot to the surface.

"Don't you dare blame that on me," Mops shouted. "Your daddy was just as drunk as I was, just as absent."

Mom crossed her arms across her chest, as if she could shield herself from the pain of his absence. "Don't drag him into this—he's not here to defend himself."

He couldn't defend himself, but he *was* here, in every drink Mom took.

"No," Mops said, "you are. You always were. Your daddy could do whatever he wanted, but I was always the one you judged."

"You weren't there for Daddy."

Mops looked at Mom. "Maybe your daddy wasn't there for me," she said.

But I could tell Mom wasn't listening. She'd already decided how she felt about Mops, and that wasn't going to change. Both of them were so intent on making their points that they weren't willing to try and see the other side. "Daddy started drinking because of you," she told Mops. "He joined you. And then, when you got sober and he couldn't, you left."

"Not couldn't, Vi--wouldn't. And what about taking some of the responsibility? He stayed drunk for three days when you told him you were pregnant." Mops ran her hand across her face. "I did everything I could to help him. But I had to start thinking about myself. I couldn't stay sober when he was always drinking."

Mom's laugh was bitter. "You had to *start* thinking about yourself? That's *all* you ever thought about."

And I couldn't keep sane if I had to stay here and try to patch things together. I loved them both, but I was afraid that, if I sacrificed what I wanted to babysit my mom, I'd resent her forever. Mops did what she thought was best, but Pops never got better. Would he still be here if he had?

"You little hypocrite," Mops said. Her voice shook with fury. This wasn't the Mops I knew. "You can't forgive me for my drinking, but you're walking down the exact same path I did. And you think you're better? Don't you remember the things you said to me? Do you want Jenna to feel the same way about you?"

I couldn't voice how I felt about Mom. Watching her destroy herself made me scared and helpless and unbelievably angry. Because she had a choice, and she was choosing wrong.

"I'm nothing like you!" Mom shouted. "I don't show up to her games slurring and tripping over myself. I don't pass out in public places. I've never crashed my car through someone's house."

I flinched. That was cruel.

"Do you think I started there?" Mops asked. She sounded as if she had run through all her anger; her voice became soft and sad. Tired. "Do you think I woke up one day a raging alcoholic? I started exactly where you are. You think you're in control, but that's a lie. You're too much like me. If you don't stop right now, it's going to be too late. It hasn't destroyed your life just yet. It hasn't destroyed your relationship with Jenna. But it will."

"This doesn't have anything to do with Jenna," Mom said.

How unbelievably naïve. Or blind. And incredibly self-serving. "It has everything to do with me," I argued. "Who do you think worries about you? Who covers you up when you pass out on the couch? Me. I have to wake up every day and face the fact that my mother is becoming an alcoholic, and there's nothing I can do about it. I can't fix this." The fact that it was completely out of my control was one of the most terrifying things about it. I wanted to make things better more than anything, but Mom was the only one who could. And she was too stubborn to admit it was a problem. "If you keep getting worse, how am I going to be able to go off to college next year? You already screwed up your own life—now you're screwing up mine."

Mom was white as she turned back to face Mops. "Are you happy? Now you've turned her against me."

Mops shook her head. "You did that yourself."

"Get out." Mom's voice was quiet and cold; it was the scariest she'd ever sounded, and the most serious. "I want you out of my house."

Mops squared her shoulders. "I'm not leaving without Jenna."

I blinked in surprise, then felt anger boiling just under my skin. I didn't want to choose.

"I'm not leaving her," I said. Eventually, yes. But not while she still needed me.

Mom looked smug. Mops walked toward me, her voice pitched low. "I don't think staying is a good idea."

I clenched my jaw. "This is my house. She's my mother." Her drinking wasn't dangerous to me. I needed to be here to protect her from herself. No one else was going to.

Mops put her hand on my arm. "She's not your responsibility."

I jerked away. I was tired of everyone telling me that. Of course she was. "I'm not leaving," I said again.

Mops looked between Mom and me, then sighed. "Don't let her drive."

Mom stormed off to her room.

"I'm just going to run home and get a few things," Mops said. "I'll sleep in the guest room."

"You don't have to stay. She'll be fine." I wondered how many times I'd said that over the past few months.

"I'm staying here for you," Mops said. She reached up and patted my cheek. "Your mom loves you, no matter how she acts. You're what keeps this family together."

I watched Mops pull out of the driveway before shutting the front door. If I was the glue, then I'd never be able to escape.

TWENTY-THREE

JENNA

I made sure Mops was settled into the back room and Mom was sound asleep on her side before I went for a run. I pounded across the ground, shaking the solid mass of worry into manageable pieces that rattled around. I ran harder, hoping the pieces would become sand and trickle away completely. But the fight with my mom refused to break into smaller pieces. It twisted and turned, letting me see different angles. The accusations. Desperations. Fear and worry and complete frustration. Even love. I missed the mom she used to be, like how we'd curl up in our PJs and watch cheesy movies. I missed making tents out of blankets and crawling under them together to eat raw cookie dough. I missed all the laughter, but mostly I just missed knowing she was okay. She didn't seem to miss those things at all.

The crumbling of my family unit should have been enough. But I'd gotten myself into a complete mess with Luke and Ian. That was entirely my fault—I couldn't shift the blame on anyone else. I should have done things differently, but I hadn't exactly planned on any of it happening. That wasn't like me. I was levelheaded and played by the rules. More than anything, I planned my future. And my future didn't involve love—at least not yet. When I was out of this town and on my own, maybe then. But not before. I didn't need to get distracted. I needed to get out before I suffocated.

And then Luke came along and made me realize I couldn't plan everything, that sometimes I had to let things unfold on their own. The surprises, those things that just happened, were some of the best things. Some of the worst too, but if I wanted out, those were risks I would have to take. I didn't want to keep myself in some fragile bubble until everything was perfect and I could emerge fully formed and ready for life. Because if I did it that way, I'd never get to live. I'd never get out of that bubble. Things weren't ever going to go exactly as I'd planned—and sometimes that was okay too.

I left my mother behind. I left Ian standing somewhere in the past. Lost and found—I ran to escape all the worries and in the process caught up with the *me* I was supposed to be. And even though I knew that they were still going to be there when I turned around and headed back, it was enough that, for the moment at least, I was alone.

By the time I hit mile two, my brain had burrowed underneath all that mess and found the quiet stillness that I loved so much. My breath was rhythmic and soothing, and my mind settled down as my body flew over the ground, through the trees, and then out across an open pasture. I thundered across a wooden bridge and back into the woods. I leapt over a log that lay across the path and felt some of me fall away. There was nothing like having a great run. My legs and lungs felt strong; I could run all day. Running made me invincible.

I was surprised to see that my feet had taken me to the pond. I slipped out of the tall grass and stood next to the water. Silence. Sort of. No screaming or accusations. No anger. Just frogs, bugs, and a slight breeze rippling the grass. It was lovely. I scooped up a handful of rocks and tossed them, one by one, into the pond. I must have thrown in hundreds of rocks over the years. Pops had taught me to skip stones out here, though I was never any good at it. I threw them too hard. And I stuck all the pretty ones in my pockets. Mom was always aggravated when they rattled around in the washer.

"Maybe you're the vampire." A familiar voice stabbed the dark, and I jumped. "You're trespassing," Luke said, stepping up behind me.

"Shoot me."

He grinned. "I'm thinking about it."

I turned away from the pond and looked up into his face. Even in the dark, I could see his worry. I just didn't know who that worry was for. "What are you doing here?" I asked.

"I live here," he reminded me. "You?"

I sighed. "I have no idea. I just went for a run and ended up here." I walked to the beaten wooden chairs sitting farther up on the bank. They were gray and weathered, and they leaned back just enough to make them comfortable. I folded into one of them.

Luke sat down next to me. "I went for a walk and ended up here," he told me. "Funny how that happened. So, you got in trouble?"

I nodded. My being grounded was the least of my worries.

"Do you want to talk about it?"

I shook my head.

He reached over and held my hand without saying another word. It was easy to forget everything else. Luke was an island I could escape to.

A whistle rose in the dark, sudden and sharp. Familiar.

"What's that?" Luke asked.

I smiled. "Full House." And memories. So much of me was wrapped up in this place. Would I ever truly be able to leave?

"What?"

"A mule," I explained.

"Like a donkey?"

"Half-donkey, half-horse. He's hollering for Patty, Mr. Simon's horse." I used to feed apples to Patty through the fence. Pops would fuss at me for wasting good fruit on someone else's horse, but I kept doing it. I loved the way her velvet nose tickled my palm. I'd mostly avoided Full House; I never trusted him.

"How do you know that?" Luke asked.

"The mule used to be Pops's. We gave him back to Mr. Simon after Pops died. Full House used to do that all the time when Pops had him. Pop would whistle across the fence and call up Patty, then Full House would lean over and he and Patty would scratch their necks together. I think it's sweet."

Full House whistled again, trying to find Patty. I heard Patty's answering whinny.

"Why does he sound like that?" Luke asked.

I told him what Pops had told me once. "He doesn't know if he's a donkey or a horse. He's both, but he's neither, just like his voice." I turned sideways in my chair to look at Luke. "His real name is Fred, but Pops always called him Full House because he won him off Mr. Simon in a poker game years ago. They were all out at the deer camp one night, drinking and playing cards. The older they got, the less they hunted and the more they drank. Mops said they stopped bringing home deer when they started bringing home hangovers."

Her voice had been equal parts anger and love when telling those stories about Pops. I hadn't understood that then. I was pretty sure I did now.

"Pops didn't need that mule, but he thought it was funny, so he kept it. The mule's kind of mean—he doesn't really like people. But he loves Patty. I think he's much happier now that he's back on that side of the fence."

The wind kicked up again, shushing through the grass, and I lifted my ponytail and let it blow on the back of my neck.

"Do you think we can escape the past?" I asked. Mom had gotten bogged down in hers, and Mops couldn't move on completely because everyone kept reminding her of what she'd been. I wanted to start all over as a girl who didn't have so many family skeletons in the closet. But what if that wasn't even possible?

Luke's face was so sad that I regretted the question. "We can hope," he said. But I could tell by his voice that he didn't really believe it.

I wasn't sure how someone could be both strong and fragile. Luke was solid and broad and sturdy, yet at times I felt he might shatter into a million pieces, leaving me behind to collect them and somehow get them back in order, knowing that I was wholly inadequate and unprepared for such a task.

I leaned my head on his shoulder. My heart squeezed itself against my ribs, all swollen and sore, and I couldn't seem to fill my lungs with enough air. "I think I'm falling in love with you," I whispered. I knew it was true when I said it out loud. I felt it in my skin.

Luke was still, shadows flickering across his face like an old black-and-white film. "You aren't supposed to love the dead."

I didn't have a response to that.

"I'm a ghost," Luke whispered, "a shadow." And in that moment, he felt like one.

LUKE

I was too flawed to love. I was afraid of what would happen if she really did love me. It seemed I always hurt those closest to me.

"Have you talked to Ian?" Jenna asked finally.

"No. I haven't seen him all day, actually. Why?"

"Because I did. He came by the house yesterday, and my mom yelled at him for bringing me home at that hour, and so he knew, but I was going to have to tell him anyway." She sighed, like everything was her fault. None of this was her fault. I would take all the blame. "I broke it off."

"Are you sure?" I couldn't help feeling she was making a mistake. As much as I wanted her to stay, I couldn't stop myself from trying to make her go. "Ian is going places. He'll go to college, major in something responsible. I have no future."

"I don't buy any of that." She reached up and ran her thumb back and forth across my cheek, like she was trying to rub something away.

"I don't deserve you," I whispered.

"No one ever deserves anyone else," she whispered back. "You can't earn a person. They're a gift."

I wanted to believe her. More than anything, I wanted to be enough for her. But no matter how tightly I clung to things, I could feel everything crumbling beneath me.

TWENTY-FOUR

IAN

I locked myself in my room. Luke wasn't the only one who could hide behind barricades. Luke wasn't the only one who was going to get what he wanted. It was time I stopped waiting for things to go my way and started making sure they did. No matter what.

I had to stop wandering in the dark. Mom wouldn't tell me anything—she was still trying to protect Luke. I didn't understand it. I was so careful. I did everything right and it didn't make a damn bit of difference. Mom was still looking out for Luke. Jenna was still looking at Luke. There was hardly anything left for me to put back together.

I'd almost had everything—Jenna in my arms, her lips on mine.

And then Luke had taken it. My anger caused my head to pound, and I closed my eyes and let the ache steer me through the maze. Last night at Jenna's, I'd heard the door unlock and been too afraid to look in and find it. I wasn't afraid anymore.

I turned corners and followed empty corridors. Strips of shadow and light followed more corners and shadow. Always shadows. The corridors were getting shorter and the corners sharper. I caught a glimpse of something moving and began to run.

The maze twisted away from me. There was fabric, then nothing. A flash of arm, then shadows.

I ran past a window. There was a shattered fence and a broken tree. Another corner was followed by another and another. And the door. I pulled up short. I'd found the door with the strip of light. This time, it was cracked open a little, enough that the light lit up the center of the maze. Not enough to see what was on the other side.

But I couldn't open it all the way because the shadow was there, sitting cross-legged in front of the door. And I knew her. I'd seen her at the lake. At Jenna's. But I'd known her before. Of course I did. The girl from the picture. Mandy. Her name made me shudder. Then I realized the trembling was outside of me. The maze was crumbling.

LUKE

Ian was standing outside my room when I came up the stairs.

"You son of a bitch," he said. He didn't sound like Ian at all.

"We're sorry." It was sort of the truth; it was kind of a lie.

"*We?*" Ian flinched. "Since when did it become *we?*"

I sighed. "What do you want from me, Ian?"

"I want you to leave her the hell alone."

"I can't do that." Can't. Won't. It was all the same thing.

I could feel Ian's fury the same way I'd felt his pain and fear when we were kids. But this was much stronger than those feelings had ever been.

"She's mine," he said.

"She doesn't belong to either one of us." That I was sure of.

"Well I'm sure as hell not going to let *you* have her." He shoved me hard in the chest, pushing me out of the hallway and into my room. "Don't see Jenna again," Ian threatened.

"Or what?" I didn't know who the hell he thought he was. He'd never been the one in charge.

"Why don't you push me and see," he said. I didn't like his look, the way his voice hinted at something dangerous. He sounded desperate. "I'm doing everything I can to keep this family from completely falling apart. You've done everything you could to make sure we did. If you know what's good for you, you'll stay out of my way." Ian took a deep breath. "Remember Mandy?" he asked.

I went cold. I hadn't heard that name in over a year. I didn't want to now.

"*I* do," Ian continued. "Mandy was mine. I remember how she died. And that you killed her."

His words reached into my chest and squeezed my lungs. Lights popped behind my eyes.

"How could you do this again?" Ian asked. "I'm your brother." He shook his head, disgust filling his face. "You hurt people. Don't destroy her too."

He didn't have to say her name—it was the only name that mattered to me, and she was the only other person who inhabited my desolate little world.

Ian's smile was sly as he pointed at me. "I know you," he whispered, "inside and out. I know just exactly how to hurt you." He stalked into his room. "I learned from the best."

He slammed the door, and the frayed string that connected us snapped.

I went back downstairs, no longer tired, no longer interested in being holed up in my room. Mom was just getting in from work. She looked exhausted. She looked older than she had a few months ago, and I knew it was my fault. She stopped in the hall, her face hopeful. "Ian?"

When I shook my head, her shoulders drooped forward. She turned her face away from me. "Where's Ian?"

"In his room," I told her.

Mom sighed. I wanted to wrap my arms around her. I wanted to bury my face in her shoulder like I had when I was little. But I was afraid. Thinking she would turn away wasn't easy to take. Knowing it for certain would be unbearable. Most of the time I didn't care what people thought about me. It was how I'd ended up where I was in the first place. But I hated disappointing my mom. I knew that I'd put that sorrow on her face. I wished more than anything that I could take it back. Sometimes I wished it so hard that my chest hurt. But I couldn't go back and change things. I could never change the fact that the accident was my fault. That someone died. That I lost my parents' love. And that they were justified in it.

"I'm going to bed," Mom said. She couldn't stand to be in the same room with me for very long.

"Why won't you talk to me?" I asked.

Her eyes filled with tears, and I prayed they wouldn't spill over. "Because it hurts too much."

The truth was like bathing in tiny shards of glass. "What do you want me to do?" It was a question I wasn't sure I wanted answered.

Her hands fluttered, unable to rest. "I want everything to be the way it was. I want to sleep through the night. I want so much that isn't possible. Sometimes I think I'm losing my mind," she whispered. "I—" Her voice cracked. "I'm going to bed."

She left me standing alone in the kitchen. I knew what needed to be done. It was just that sometimes the right thing felt horribly wrong.

TWENTY-FIVE

LUKE

I put off the inevitable for three days. Three days of me staying in my room and not thinking about Jenna—and trying to figure out any other way. But there wasn't. Ian was right. Jenna needed to be as far away from me as possible. Caring about me would only hurt her. Losing her would be just the sort of hell I deserved.

It was dark when I took off walking. I followed a small path into the woods, where the shadows swallowed me. A couple of coyotes yipped off to my left. I wanted to throw back my head and shout, too. I doubted anyone would hear me.

It was a long walk to Jenna's house. I crossed a wooden bridge and came out in the train yard. I climbed onto the tracks and balanced myself on the rails. I wondered what it had been like when the trains were running. How far away could someone stand and feel the rumble of the train?

I passed the lonely buildings and reached the outskirts of town. There were a lot of abandoned buildings here too, doors nailed shut, windows boarded up, signs hanging and broken. Jenna had told me that, once the trains left, the other jobs dried up too. The small factory in town. Several shops. The end of town closest to the railroad seemed to have boarded the last train out of here. It was depressing.

I cut through the woods behind Jenna's neighborhood, and dogs barked as I eased behind the fences. Most of the lights were off. Jenna was probably sleeping. Normal people were.

But her light was on. I had no idea how I was going to get her to come out; her mom had her phone. Throwing pebbles at her window seemed like a bad idea. That only worked in the movies. If I did it, I was sure to shatter glass.

I climbed the tree instead. It wasn't very big, and I wasn't sure it was even going to hold my weight. But I'd always been good at climbing. I could shimmy up a tree faster than anyone in the neighborhood. It was one of the few things I was better at than Ian. Dad said it was because I was reckless. We'd had a huge tree in our backyard when we lived in Colorado, and I could see the whole neighborhood while no one could see me. I watched Ian and Dad play catch for hours. I watched the teenage girl next door when she lay out in her bikini. I watched Mr. Cutrer sneak out behind his shed and smoke when his wife was watching her shows. I was master of the universe in that tree.

The tree in Jenna's yard was flimsy. I eased out onto the largest limb—it creaked underneath me. I slowly pushed myself onto my toes. Even then I could just barely reach up and tap on the glass. I waited. If she didn't hurry, the branch was going to snap and she was going to find me in the morning, broken into pieces like Humpty Dumpty. I knocked harder on the glass, losing my balance just a bit. I reached out and grabbed hold of a branch, barely catching myself before I plummeted to the ground.

Jenna's face bloomed at the window. She looked nervous—until she saw me. She broke out in a huge grin as she opened the window. "Luke! Get down from there before you break your neck."

"Can you come out?" I asked her. I didn't want to go in. I hoped this would be easier in the dark. "We need to talk."

Her smile disappeared. "Um, sure. I think my mom's asleep. Just give me a minute."

She went back inside and closed the window as I climbed down the tree. I sat on the ground and leaned against the trunk. This was going to be painful, but then again, hurting people seemed to be my specialty.

JENNA

I was barefoot as I tiptoed down the stairs. I eased closer to the wall on the next to the last step, trying to keep it from squeaking. Mom had been in bed for a couple of hours, and before that I'd seen her down half a bottle of rum. I was pretty sure she was out. I probably could have driven a school bus through the living room and not woken her up.

I slipped out the back door and around the side of the house. Luke was sitting underneath a tree, his arms propped up on his knees. His face was even darker than usual, and my stomach tightened. Something was wrong.

"We're back to our midnight meetings," I said, trying to lighten the mood. I sat in front of him, our knees touching.

He raised his face to look at me, and even in the dark, I could see that his eyes were full of shadows. And disgust.

"We can't see each other anymore," he told me.

I heard the words, but I didn't know what to do with them. "Okay," I said. But it didn't really make sense. I knew he wasn't joking because his voice was blacker than I'd ever heard it. But I had no idea where this was coming from. He sure hadn't acted like anything was wrong the other night.

His fists were clenched. "I shouldn't have done that to Ian."

This was about Ian. That I could understand. "Look, I'm sorry it came out that way. I just didn't think it was fair to him anymore."

"It wasn't fair to him to begin with." Luke's voice was quiet anger. "Really, how selfish can you be? What kind of person dates two guys at the same time? And brothers at that?"

It felt like he'd just punched me in the gut. His words cut, mainly because they were true. He had every right to feel that way. But I would not be taking all the blame for this.

"You knew I was seeing Ian. That sure as hell didn't stop you from sneaking over here in the middle of the night and taking me on some moonlight picnic." My pulse raced, equal parts anger and guilt. "You're just as much to blame as I am. Maybe more."

"You've been cheating on *me* with Ian. You've been sneaking around behind *Ian's* back with me. Now all of a sudden you decide you're in love with me, and I'm supposed to know what to do with that? Well I'm sorry, but I don't." Luke stood up to go.

"Why do you push people away? What don't you want them to see?"

The quiet of his voice was worse than any shouting could be. "Don't you understand? We're not good for each other. I don't want someone who tries both boys out until she's sure."

Anger kept me from articulating all the things *I* didn't want.

"You didn't really think you were the first girl who tried us both on for size, did you?" he asked. His crooked grin was harsh. "I kissed his last girlfriend, too."

I didn't know what to do with that. "What happened?" I asked. I was surprised I could speak.

"She died. In a crash I was responsible for. I walked away, but Mandy died."

My first instinct was to run. I wanted to fly through the trees and pretend he hadn't spoken. But the truth was something I couldn't escape. I needed to know more, but I didn't want to know any of it. I tried to picture this girl who had come between two brothers and somehow died. But when I imagined her face, I only saw mine.

"It was an accident," I said. It had to be an accident. A mistake. This was all a mistake.

"Do you think that makes a damn bit of difference?" Luke snapped. "Dead is dead. You can't ever take that back. *I* can't ever take that back!" He stepped away from me. "I told you, you picked the right brother the first time."

And before I could argue, before I could say anything, he turned and walked off. I watched his shadow cross the yard and disappear into the woods behind the house.

TWENTY-SIX

JENNA

Luke was right. I didn't deserve either one of them. Ian was sweet and caring and I'd thrown that right back in his face, sneaking off behind his back with Luke. And Luke—well, it didn't matter.

I wanted my life to go back to the way it had been before the McAlister brothers moved to town, but it didn't. It couldn't. I couldn't erase the past couple of months. I missed them both. I wasn't stupid enough to believe I would get both, or that I even wanted to. After months of not knowing what I wanted, I'd finally found the one thing I was certain I did want, and now I couldn't have it. I missed Ian, too. We'd developed a solid friendship. And I missed talking to Luke and the way he kissed me. I missed that swoop in my stomach, the way I had trouble breathing. Being with Luke was like riding a roller coaster. Not being with Luke was like being forced to ride the merry-go-round after experiencing a roller coaster. I couldn't go back, and I didn't want to.

I tried not to think about him. I wasn't that girl. I wasn't the type to fall in love with the first boy who paid her attention and then be devastated when he moved on. That wasn't me. But here I was, feeling miserable because he didn't want me, nauseated because he didn't feel the same way I did.

I threw myself into work, deciding to finally clean out and organize the junk room in the back. There were years of forgotten and broken items stacked in sealed tubs, rotting boxes, and torn garbage bags. It would've been easier to set the place on fire. If I spent every day for the next year back here, I still wouldn't get through it all. It was the perfect distraction.

I left Pops's boxes alone. Mops and I had agreed that we wouldn't touch them until Mom was ready. It was something we needed to do together. I was pretty sure they'd never get unpacked. Especially since Mom and Mops still weren't speaking.

Mops knew something was up. She let me get sweaty and elbow-deep in a musty old box before she showed up and demanded to know what was going on.

"It's about time someone went through this stuff," I said. "It needs to be organized. You can't find anything in here." I pushed my hair out of my face. The junk pile had gotten out of control.

"Why now? This stuff has been here for years. Why all of a sudden did you decide it needed to be done today?"

"Well, I'll be going off to college soon," I said, "and if I don't do it, no one will."

Mops wasn't buying it. "Tell me what happened."

"I don't know what you're talking about." But I couldn't look at her. I'd never been able to lie to Mops.

"This is about your mother," she said with complete certainty.

It was about my life, which was about my mother and money and the McAlisters. It was about too much alcohol and too much anger and not enough strength to fix either one. It was about plans that fell apart and people who died and the fear that I wouldn't ever escape any of it. But mostly, right then, it was about Luke. It was about finally realizing what I wanted and not being able to keep it.

"Go up front and put out the lunch sign," Mops said.

"It's only ten o'clock," I argued, glancing at my watch.

She winked at me. "We won't tell the boss. Meet you upstairs."

By the time I'd locked the door, put out the sign, and climbed the twisting staircase, Mops had fixed us each a big glass of iced tea. No one made iced tea like Mops—it was so sweet it was syrupy. Perfect. She pulled a package of cookies out of the cabinet and plopped them on the chipped Formica table. Most of my childhood memories included this table. We'd eaten dinner here every night when we'd lived together. Mops's house was bigger then, light pouring in from the windows that lined the east side of the kitchen. Pops's hat was always hanging on a peg just inside the door, and Mops's mean old cat, Dust, was lying on the rug in front of the sink and taking swipes at whoever walked by. That was before everyone moved out and started doing their own thing. Before Pops died and Mom changed. Back when things were simple.

I'd learned to read at this table. I'd colored outside the lines at this table. I'd made messes and glittered Christmas ornaments here, followed it from Pops's house to Mops's apartment. The table, with all its scratches and stains, held a piece of who I was in it. A piece of who we all were. It was scary to think it held my best piece. What if this was all there was?

Mops should have worked for the CIA—she could get anyone to talk. And there must have been some secret ingredient in her tea, because even though I didn't want to talk about it, even though I didn't really want anyone to know about Luke and what I'd done to Ian, I found myself telling her everything. *Almost* everything. I told her about meeting Ian and dating them both, choosing Luke and him dumping me. I skipped over the parts I was trying to forget—mainly those which involved Mandy. I refused to cry. It wouldn't have done any good. Tears never changed a thing.

Mops didn't interrupt once. She waited until I was finished, until I had lost my words and found the silence. Then she patted my hand and sat back in her chair.

"Rejection is never easy. Never. And I'm sorry. I'd tell you he was stupid and a damn fool, but if you care about him, he can't be either. You're too smart for that."

I didn't feel smart. Even though being with Luke was the most natural thing in the world, it made me feel emotions I didn't have words for. Maybe there weren't words to describe how it felt when Luke looked at me or said my name. When his lips touched mine.

When I was ten years old, I couldn't wait to be sixteen. Now that I was almost eighteen, I was already looking forward to my twenties. I wondered if we ever got to the age we wanted to be, or if the minute we were almost there, we started wishing our way back. It was exhausting.

"From what you've told me," Mops continued, "it sounds like Luke feels pretty bad about stealing you away from his brother."

"I'm not a toy. It's not like Ian had me first and Luke took me away. I'm a person, and I can make up my own mind. I chose Luke."

"But it's more than just your choice. It's Luke's too, and I'm sure he doesn't want to hurt his brother. My sister and I fought every day of our lives, but I would've died for her. It's just the way siblings are."

I knew she was probably right. Becca always complained about her little brother, but she adored him. I just didn't know what it was like to have a brother or sister. Most times I was glad I was an only child, but sometimes it was a little lonely having to put up with my mom all by myself.

"I know it hurts, but stressing and worrying about it won't make it any better," she said. "You just need some time. If it's meant to be, he'll come back."

I didn't know if I wanted him to. After everything he'd told me, I shouldn't have. I was mad at myself for getting distracted when what I needed to be focused on was saving money and getting into a good school. I wanted my senior year to be productive. I wanted to qualify for state in cross-country. I needed to improve my ACT score by three points at least. I had to make sure my mom was better by the time I graduated so that I *could* leave. And out of all the things I needed to do, none involved Luke. But no matter what my head said, my heart argued. It wanted to hang out with Luke at the lake. My heart wanted to stare at the stars and beat in time with his. Stupid heart.

"Feel better?" Mops asked.

I felt a lot of things, but I wasn't sure better was one of them. I just nodded. Sometimes giving my thoughts a voice scared me.

She smiled. "Good. Now what?"

"Now we get back to work." But I knew that, no matter how busy I kept myself, I wasn't going to be able to ignore the bruises Luke had left. Whoever said words didn't hurt was either a damn fool or a liar.

LUKE

Ian hadn't spoken to me for days—not that I'd tried. I was staying in my room, away from everyone. Sleep didn't come as often as I would've liked, and when it did, I dreamt of tree houses and walls that became mazes with no way out. But I felt weirdly disconnected from Ian, like I'd been snipped in half. We'd always known what the other one was thinking. It had always been like that. I thought it was completely normal until I got older and realized not everyone had that. Not even all identical twins thought the same. But we had.

Ian was always the one person I'd trusted. We'd done everything together—Little League, the tree house, building forts in the woods and damming up a little stream behind our house in Colorado. We'd even gotten chicken pox at the same time. When his appendix had ruptured, it'd felt like someone had shoved an ice pick into my stomach. I screamed before he did. I was outside working on the tree house, and I'd dropped the hammer and hollered. At first I thought I'd somehow stabbed myself with the nail, but then I'd heard Ian scream, and I'd realized that I wasn't hurt. He was.

I ran inside and up the stairs before Mom even made it out of the laundry room. I'd been so scared. Ian had never made a noise like that before, and I knew it was bad.

He was pale, a light sheen of sweat covering his face. He was curled up on the floor, his hands shaking. There was a pool of vomit next to him.

I don't remember much after that. The hospital had been bright and made my eyes water. I must have looked really bad when we got to the emergency room because a nurse took my blood pressure and pulse. I'd fought her for a while. Ian was in the bed next to me, Mom holding his hand. Dad was at the base, of course. They gave me a shot. I slept. I hadn't woken up until Ian was out of surgery. He was groggy and in pain, but he'd pulled up his gown and showed me his stitches. He'd been proud of them.

I'd hated them—they made us different, distinguished one from the other. It kind of scared me how much I cared about that. I hadn't realized how big a part of my life that identicalness was. It just always was. We tricked our teachers. We tricked our parents. When we were little, we pretended Ian was the real boy and I was the reflection. I liked the idea that I had stepped out of a mirror from some other world, like Wonderland or something. But the scar broke that.

So that night, after my parents had fallen asleep, while Ian was still in the hospital, I'd snuck downstairs and cut myself with a knife. It hadn't hurt as much as I thought it was going to, but there had been way more blood than I'd expected. I never forgot the look on Dad's face when he flipped on the light—it still haunted me. He looked dead. All the color drained out of his face, and for a split second, there was absolutely no emotion. Then there was panic. Later there would be anger. He was furious once he'd realized I wasn't going to die.

I'd needed a few stitches, not nearly as many as Ian, and my scar wasn't quite as straight or neat as his. But we were identical again.

But now things would never be okay. Killing Mandy had been bad. It was something I was never going to get over, never going to forgive myself for. I would never be free of this guilt. Ian might have forgiven me eventually, because we were brothers and it was an accident. But taking Jenna was deliberate, and there would be no forgiveness now. For either of us.

TWENTY-SEVEN

JENNA

Time passed slowly when things were broken. I worked and ran more than ever, but nothing helped. As hard as I ran, I couldn't escape. No matter what I did, I still felt empty. I didn't need someone else to make me happy. I cared about Luke, but I didn't need him to live. My life was going to go on without him. I was going to go to college and pick a career. I didn't need Luke to do those things with me. I could do them by myself.

But I wanted him here. I wanted to stop waking up with a pain in my stomach and an ache in my chest. I longed to talk with him, because he listened and didn't judge. Because he understood. With Luke, I was free to be me. I was going to get over him. I was going to move on. I just didn't know how. And Ian wasn't helping.

For the past three days, I'd woken up to roses. The first morning, it was one rose lying on the hood of my car with a note that simply said, "Ian." The next morning, there had been two roses on the doorstep. I didn't call Ian. I'd made too many mistakes already—I was going to do things right. He just needed some time. I hoped we could go back to being friends eventually. But he wasn't being very patient.

Because when I got up on Friday, there were two dozen roses lying just outside my bedroom door. Each one had his name tied to it. My skin was cold. Ian had somehow gotten into the house without my mom or me knowing. I was furious. My house—especially my room—was my safe place, and I hated that Ian had made it feel unsafe. I was angry that he'd violated that privacy. I thought I knew him better than that.

I dug my keys out of the bottom of Mom's sock drawer. She was at work and wouldn't even know I'd taken them. I threw the flowers in the passenger seat of the Bronco and headed over to Ian's. We needed to talk. I pulled out of the driveway and prayed Luke wouldn't be there. I didn't know if I could keep it together if he was. Just thinking about him made me hurt.

I drove too fast. I hoped Solitude's police force (all two of them) were eating breakfast somewhere and wouldn't see me speeding through town. My knuckles were white as I gripped the steering wheel and bumped off the asphalt and onto gravel.

I tried to direct some of my anger toward Luke. Maybe if I hated him just a little, I could forget how it felt when he kissed me, the way his touch made my blood sing. But I couldn't do either.

I slid to a stop in the McAlisters' driveway and scooped the roses into my arms, ignoring the scratches from the thorns. The yard looked much better. Someone had cleaned out the flowerbeds that bordered the porch, and Pops's roses were blooming again. I climbed the steps and banged on the door.

I expected Ian to answer. I found myself hoping that Luke might. I got Mrs. McAlister instead.

"Yes?" she asked. She looked tired. Not "it's been a long day," but more of an "it's been a hard life." I was just beginning to understand that kind of tired.

"Hi, Mrs. McAlister. It's Jenna Oliver." When she didn't say anything, I added, "I met you the day you moved in. I brought a basket." I didn't think admitting to being the reason Ian and Luke weren't speaking would be the best way to begin.

"Of course." She gave me a faint smile.

"Um, is Ian here?"

Her eyes hardened, and she stared at the roses I was holding. I blushed. She pursed her lips and opened the door wider, stepping back to let me in.

I followed her to the kitchen, stopping as soon as I stepped through the doorway. It was absolutely amazing. Luke had completely transformed the room, turning it from broken to beautiful. It was warm and comfortable and smelled brand new. He had somehow managed to capture sunlight; it made me miss him even more.

"Are you Ian's girlfriend?" Mrs. McAlister asked.

I blushed again. "No, we're just friends." She glanced at the flowers. She knew that was a lie. I felt stupid for bringing them. "Well," I hurried to explain, "Ian and I hung out a while, and he's very sweet, a good friend, but, um, Luke and I…" I couldn't finish. Luke and I weren't anything. And I was not going to tell this woman that I was in love with her son.

Mrs. McAlister made a noise like a trapped animal and went completely pale. She gripped the counter behind her.

"Are you okay?" She was scaring me. I dropped the roses on the kitchen table and went to her. "Mrs. McAlister?"

"I'm fine," she said. She sat down at the table. When she didn't say anything, I asked again if Ian was around. I just wanted to talk to him for a minute, and then I wanted out of there. Mrs. McAlister made me uncomfortable.

"Ian isn't here," she said finally.

"What about Luke?" It hurt to say his name. I knew he didn't want to see me, but maybe, if I talked to him, he could try explaining things to Ian.

Mrs. McAlister's lips were thin and white, and she lifted a shaking hand to her forehead. "Luke is dead." Her voice was jagged and raw, and her words lacerated me.

There was a moment when I felt I was drowning. It was hard to breathe, and my ears felt like they were stuffed with cotton. Then I realized I must have heard her wrong. Because for a second, I thought she'd said Luke was dead. That was impossible.

"I'm sorry?" I asked.

"Luke's dead," she repeated. She sounded like she was trying to convince herself.

I realized I was shaking my head. People like Luke didn't just die. It wasn't possible. I mean, this was Solitude. If there'd been an accident or something, the whole town would have known. Luke couldn't be dead. I'd just seen him a few days ago. Why would she tell me that? It wasn't funny.

"I don't believe you."

"Most days it's hard for me to believe, too," she said.

"When?" I whispered. My throat felt like it was closing up, and there was a rushing in my ears. It couldn't be true. Ian would have called me.

"A year ago."

Why was she lying? I started to back out of the kitchen. She was crazy. "That's not possible," I argued. "I saw him a week ago." *I kissed him underneath the fireworks. I kissed him by the lake as we watched the sun come up.*

She shook her head. She wasn't crying, but that almost made it worse. She wouldn't look at me, and her hands continued to shake. "You saw Ian pretending to be Luke. Luke died in a car crash last year."

No. No no no no no no no no no no no. I knew Luke. He wasn't Ian. He couldn't be. He was Luke. She was all kinds of crazy, and I wasn't going to believe her. I couldn't believe her.

"The doctors say Ian has survivor's guilt," she said. Why was she still talking? "The crash—he hit his head. He hasn't been the same. They call it a fugue state. They say he might get better." Then she did look at me, and her eyes were so full of pain that I was the one who couldn't look at her. "He just has to bury Luke." Her last two words came out as a whisper—but they were a physical blow.

BuryLukeburyLukeburyLukeburyLuke. It felt like the top of my head was peeling off. I couldn't stand to be in that house one moment longer.

I turned to go, but Mrs. McAlister grabbed my arm. Her fingers dug in. "Ian doesn't remember the accident. He doesn't know Luke is gone." Her voice cracked. "They were so close."

I didn't know what to say. How could Ian not know he was pretending to be his dead brother? The idea was absolutely absurd. I wanted to argue, but I couldn't form any words.

"Ian has to remember the truth on his own. It's one of the reasons we came here. There's a doctor, Benson, who thinks he can help him. He's going to try hypnosis next. But if we just come out and tell Ian, he could become even more damaged. He might never recover."

She was pleading with me, like my silence could somehow save him. Or help him. Or my slipping up and telling him could ruin him forever. That was too much pressure. That was a secret too big for me to keep. I wished I could go back and unhear everything. I didn't want to know this. It was better when Luke had just dumped me.

I nodded, agreeing to participate in a charade I couldn't understand, then mumbled a weak apology as I stumbled out the door. I didn't even remember the drive home. Five minutes after pulling into my driveway, I had on my running shoes and was sprinting into the trees. There was no way I was going to be able to outrun this, but I was sure as hell going to try.

But running wouldn't save me. Nothing could. I was going crazy. I had to be. It was like someone had shoved thousands of bees into my head, all buzzing and stinging. I couldn't focus. That was the good thing about running—I didn't have to. I let my body take over, and I tried to shut down all competing thoughts. The way he smiled. The way his hands felt on my waist. His lips. It couldn't be true. It wasn't possible. Kissing Luke wasn't anything like kissing Ian. Being with Luke didn't resemble being with Ian in the least little bit. There was no way that Luke and Ian were the same person. There was no way that Luke was dead.

I stopped and screamed. I didn't care who heard me—it was doubtful anyone did. I hit my fist against the closest thing, which happened to be a pecan tree. I was crying, but I didn't even care. It wasn't possible that the happiest moments in my life had been lies. There was no way Luke could be dead. That the boy who understood me so well didn't even exist. How in the hell could Ian not know? This was so much bigger than I was capable of handling. I felt utterly destroyed.

I was screamed out. I gasped for air, wishing that I could hurt something. Tear something else apart besides myself. I wouldn't have minded a little company here in hell.

I would have to be strong enough to deal with this. But I kept thinking of Luke as a separate person—it couldn't be any other way. I still couldn't make any sense out of it. Because there wasn't really any sense to make.

I already missed him. I knew it was stupid. He didn't exist. He was a figment of Ian's imagination. The real Luke was dead. But it didn't feel that way. It didn't feel that way at all.

TWENTY-EIGHT

IAN

Pressure built behind my eyes, and my head and heart both ached. Jenna was still grounded, so I couldn't call her or see her. I waited. I left flowers and hoped she was missing me at least half as much as I missed her.

I was going to be late for my appointment with Dr. Benson, but I didn't care. He couldn't help me anyway. I was too furious with Luke. He was the one person I'd always been able to go to when things fell apart. We'd weathered Dad's storms together. He'd bloodied Brandon Hampton's nose after Brandon had knocked me down on the playground. But Luke had separated me from everything that had ever meant something to me—Mandy, my family, and now Jenna. Luke was no longer something I wanted to fix.

I drove past the school. It was still early, and the football team, wearing shorts and helmets, was stretching in the wet grass. Dad wanted me on that team so badly. I must have loved football once, but somewhere in the loss of my memories, I'd lost the desire to play the game. Now it was only about making my dad proud and smoothing over the cracks that Luke's irresponsibility had caused.

I should have taken a right and gone to Middleton. I shouldn't have skipped the appointment. But I did. I was getting sick of trying to piece everything together when no one else even seemed to care. It was exhausting trying to be good enough to compensate for Luke's bad. For once, I was going to be the irresponsible one.

I took a left and drove through town, ending up in an abandoned train yard I didn't even know was there. The buildings were falling apart. I knew what that felt like.

I parked the truck and walked through the labyrinth of buildings and debris. This place was almost as big as Solitude itself. The door to one of the buildings had been wrenched off, and I stepped inside. It was dim, the light filtered through broken and grimy windows. A rusted lunchbox sat on a dusty table, like someone had just stepped away. I looked around, half expecting footsteps. But I was alone.

I sat in the shadows and tried to pull together everything I could about Mandy. I remembered her blonde hair and the way her laugh went up at the end. But I couldn't remember how I'd felt about her. Had I loved her? Had I loved her before Luke ripped her away? I resented that he'd not only taken her from me, but that he'd stolen those memories of her as well.

But I could recall everything about Jenna. The way the sunlight caught her hair. The way her voice softened when she told stories. And maybe I didn't love her—yet. But I cared about her, and Luke had taken her too. If piecing together my family included forgiving him, then I was pretty sure I was going to fail. Because I wasn't ready to forgive. I didn't know if I ever would be.

I sat in the damp building in the train yard and watched time pass. I didn't want Mom to know I'd skipped my session with Dr. Benson. He'd tell her eventually, but for now there was freedom in making my own choices. I didn't get to do that very often.

It felt like I was standing on the platform watching as, one by one, everything I cared about boarded a train out of my life. Dad, Jenna, Luke, even my memories. But I wasn't giving up. I just had to figure out how to catch the next train.

Mom's car was still in the driveway when I got home. She should've been at work. I parked next to the shop and headed in the house. I heard her before I even opened the door.

"Don't talk to me like that, Scott. I'm doing the best I can. Things were going fine. Good, even. Dr. Benson said he was making progress."

I stopped in the hall. She was talking to Dad. About me.

"I know you don't believe it," Mom snapped, "but that doesn't mean it's not true. Look, I panicked. She came by here, talking about Luke, and I told her the truth."

Mom's voice was shaking, and I could tell she was close to tears.

"I can't do this by myself!" she shouted. She was sitting in the living room, lights off, blinds closed. Her back was to me, her shoulders bowed and trembling. Sobbing now.

"Mom?" I said, slipping into the living room.

She jumped like she'd been shot. "Ian!" She wiped at her face and tried to smile. "I didn't hear you come in." She listened to the phone. "He just got home. Fine," she said, "but be careful." She handed the phone to me. "It's your father."

"Hello?"

"Ian." Dad's voice was clipped and sure.

"Sir?"

"I have good news," he said. "I convinced the board to let you play ball next year."

"That's great," I answered, trying to sound more enthusiastic than I felt. I should have been happier. Everything was falling into place.

"I've already talked to Coach Hall about sending those tapes from your sophomore year. I don't know if that coach there knows what he's doing. He's probably never coached someone with your ability before." I could hear the pride in Dad's voice. The pain in my head dulled.

"But," Dad warned, "none of this matters if you can't get your act together."

"Sir?" I'd *been* the only one keeping my act together. I was the one making sure things didn't fall apart completely.

"Ian, we need to get some things straight." There was danger in his voice, a combination of sorrow and threat. "Your mom and that doctor don't think we should tell you. They believe this whole split-personality bullshit. But you and I know better."

I had no idea what he was talking about or where he was going with this.

"I've let them have their way," Dad continued, "and their way hasn't worked. So I'm going to do this my way, because I'm your father and you need to deal with this like a man. Ian, Luke is dead."

I inhaled and exhaled as if nothing had happened, as if the world was still on its axis and the sun was still going to come up tomorrow. But it wasn't going to be easy to get a grip on the fact that my dad had completely lost his mind.

"I know you remember," Dad was saying. "You went to the funeral. You said goodbye. He was drunk. He was driving too fast and he wrecked. He and Mandy died, but you didn't." Dad sounded angry. "You didn't die! Quit living in your fantasy world. Stop pretending to be Luke. Let him go and move on with your life before you destroy everything your mother and I worked so hard to give you."

The room tilted, and I smelled dirt, grass, gasoline—and blood. Headlights on a broken tree. Fence rails scattered like leaves.

"Ian, do you understand me? Just stop it."

Stop it. Stop it. I could stop it. I could get everything to lie flat. I wanted Mom to be happy and Dad to be proud. All I needed to do was get rid of Luke.

"Yes, sir." I didn't recognize my own voice. Mom reached over and took the phone out of my hand.

"What did you say to him?" She listened. "You bastard," she whispered. She threw the phone on the couch.

I wandered into the hall. There were roses scattered all over the kitchen table. Their red petals were wilting, and several had fallen off, pooling on the floor like blood.

"Ian?" Mom's voice was careful. "Honey, are you okay?"

I rubbed a petal between my thumb and finger. It was velvet. "Jenna was here," I said.

"Yes."

"To see Luke?" I asked. A fist gripped my heart.

"She wanted to see you," Mom said.

"Not Luke? She's in love with him. Not me." I stared at the roses. She'd let them die. I scooped them up, ignoring the sharp thorns, and dumped them in the trash. "Luke killed Mandy."

"It was an accident," Mom said.

"Now you're sticking up for him?" I shouted.

Her eyes were feral. "He's dead, Ian. Dead!"

But I knew better than that.

LUKE

I didn't feel dead. Not anymore. Jenna had seen to that. There had been a few months where I was pretty sure I was. I'd stayed in my room and not talked to anyone and tried to keep out of Dad's way. But a person can only stay locked away for so long. I wanted out. I wanted to build. I wanted to breathe.

Dad had come home in a horrible mood the night we left. FUBAR—that was the word. Ian was in his room and Mom was cooking dinner while Dad stewed in the den. I went to the garage and started working on a shelf for Mom's cookbooks.

I'd been working for about a half hour when I felt someone watching me. I'd turned and saw Dad standing in the doorway, his shoulders slumped. I think that was what had surprised me the most. I'd never seen Dad not at attention. But then I'd looked up at his face, and there was so much grief.

"You shouldn't be out here, Ian," he'd said.

I corrected him. I usually just pretended and went along with whoever they thought I was, but I corrected him and told him I was Luke. He'd jumped down the steps and grabbed me by my shirt.

"Stop it," he'd shouted. He shook me until I thought my teeth were going to fall out of my head.

Glass shattered in the kitchen, and then Mom was in the doorway, her face pale.

"Scott, leave him alone," Mom said.

"Back off, Ruth. I will not have my son fall apart. You're making it worse, encouraging him, taking him to that quack doctor. Luke is beyond our help now," he said, "but Ian isn't."

I didn't know why I snapped. Dad loosened his hold on my shirt and I hit him in the face. His head snapped back, and Mom screamed. And then I was on the floor, blood pouring out of my nose.

Mom was shouting at Dad, calling him a bastard and crying and Dad was in her face, and then we were packing and gone. Just like that. Funny how it only took minutes to destroy something. Mandy had died instantly. My family dissolved in fewer than five minutes. All because of me.

The fight had been three months ago, but I hadn't spoken to Dad since.

Ian was standing outside my bedroom door when I opened it. I didn't know how long he'd been there.

"Dad says you're a figment of my imagination," Ian told me.

I stood just inside my room and glared at him. "Wouldn't that be convenient?"

Then Ian grinned. "Mom told Jenna."

My lungs tightened. "Mom told Jenna what?"

"Everything," he said.

The word was a fist in my gut, and it jarred me awake. *Everything.*

But Mom didn't know everything. I was the only one who did.

TWENTY-NINE

LUKE

Jenna was the one person I wanted to know the truth. If she believed I was dead, I would be. I might disappear completely. And while a year ago that had been my plan, I'd changed my mind. I'd dug my own grave, but now I was afraid to climb in. I wasn't ready to go yet. I no longer wanted to die.

I headed to Jenna's house on foot. It was a long walk, but I needed the time to think. It felt good to be awake and lucid and aware. It was agonizing to know and remember and feel. The smell of blood and gasoline was a pungent memory. I remembered the squeal of tires, the shattering of glass, the sickening crunch as the car wrapped around the tree. And Ian. Oh God, I remembered Ian.

Humans liked to avoid pain. If they could forget it, if they could push past the hurt, then maybe they could be whole again. But it never worked that way. No one could ever be whole again—with or without the pain—because it defined them. And even when the pain left, if it ever did, there was always a scar to remind them.

I had scars, and every single one of them had a hand in making me who I was. Every regret formed me. I'd believed that becoming someone else, forgetting what happened, would make everything okay. Would somehow erase that horrible mistake. Would free me. But I was so completely wrong. I ruined everything. And I lost my brother and myself in the process. I had to tell the truth, because in a few hours I might not even know what it was. I clung to my shred of knowing as if it were my very last possession. And maybe it was. I had to tell the truth now—I wasn't guaranteed a later.

Jenna was sitting on the porch swing in her backyard, a moving shadow in the dusk. I wanted to cross the space between us, but I no longer had that right.

Being away from her hadn't helped at all. I wanted to wrap my arms around her and bury my face in her hair, but I couldn't. I didn't deserve to. I should have stayed away from her to begin with. I knew I was going to hurt her and me. The truth made me ache. I was never going to be able to be with her. Ever. Because of what I was. Because of what I wasn't.

I'd fallen in love with Jenna. I was going to tell her everything I knew while I was still me. And lose her completely in the process.

She saw me as soon as I stepped out of the trees. The swing stopped moving. The world itself seemed to stand still. I hated to ruin it. But that was who I was.

"Hey." I stepped closer to the swing and she tensed. "It's okay," I said. "I just want to talk." The sadness in her eyes made me want to go to her. But the fear in her face kept me away. "I need to tell you the truth."

She looked away. "I know it already."

"No, you don't."

I couldn't stand the heaviness in her voice. "Your mom told me everything."

"My mom doesn't know the truth." I was the only one who really knew what had happened that night, and even I didn't remember it very often.

"Why should I believe anything you say?" Jenna asked. "You've done nothing but lie."

"I've never lied to you," I said. I hadn't.

She clenched her jaw. She didn't believe me. She thought I had control over this.

"Just listen. That's all I ask."

She looked like she wanted to get up and go inside, but she didn't.

I took a deep breath and sat down on the top step. I'd never told anyone this story. I'd been keeping it from myself for a year.

"Everything I've ever told you is true," I began. "Ian and I were best friends. We did everything together. But once we got to high school, things changed. I didn't want to be like him anymore. I was tired of trying to please my dad. Nothing worked anyway. So while Ian was making straight As and helping the football team to a championship, I was getting arrested for underage drinking and breaking and entering. I don't know what was wrong with me or what I was trying to prove. I hated it—and myself. But I couldn't stop.

"Maybe I resented Ian. I don't know. But one night I talked him into going to a party with me. He brought his girlfriend. I drove my truck, although Ian took my keys. He knew I would get drunk, and I did. It wasn't new. I spent a lot of time drunk."

I remembered everything about that party. It was in Lee Davis's backyard. His parents were out of town and half the school showed up. It was mostly upperclassmen, but Ian and I were popular enough to hang out with the older guys. There had been so much booze. Ian's girlfriend, Mandy, had gotten really drunk, too.

I didn't want to tell Jenna the rest. I remembered the lights and the keg. The lack of responsibility I felt once I was on my seventh or eighth beer. I'd been looking for Ian and found Mandy instead. She and Ian were fighting. "I kissed Mandy," I admitted. "Mainly because I was so pissed at him and just wanted to see what perfect Ian would do."

Saying it out loud made it sound even worse. I'd destroyed so many people over absolutely nothing. Jenna hadn't moved, and I didn't want to look at her. I didn't think I could stand to see the disappointment that must have been there. I should have been used to it. Except Jenna was the one person I didn't want to disappoint.

"Ian saw us kissing. He told me he'd trusted me. I told him he shouldn't have. Ian got really drunk after that, and when it was time to go, he wouldn't give me the keys. I was furious—I hit him. His lip was busted and he just sat on the ground, blinking up at me, accusing me. I took my keys and ordered them both in the truck. Mandy sat in the back and cried, but Ian didn't say a word. I tried to apologize, but I couldn't, because we were spinning. The next thing I knew, I was waking up with a pounding headache. I was covered in blood—and only some of it was mine."

That smell. It had been so strong—blood, gasoline, burning rubber. The roof of the car had flattened, and we'd smashed into a huge tree two hundred yards off the road.

"I knew Ian was dead." My voice cracked. It was hard to say those words out loud. I'd pretended it wasn't true for so long that the lie became the truth and his death became the lie. "I knew he was dead because a piece of me was missing."

Jenna was crying. I didn't know if that meant she believed me or not. My throat was tight.

"I wanted to die. I screamed at God. I was furious that he'd taken my brother and not me. Ian deserved to live—I didn't. It was all my fault. I'd screwed up my life. I was failing most of my classes and was pretty sure I wasn't going to be able to get into college. I was on probation for the next six months. I was a screw-up. But Ian wasn't. Ian was going to get a scholarship. Ian was going to be something. I wished I'd died instead.

"And then I realized I could. I could kill Luke. I could keep Ian alive. I could step right into his life and bury the bad twin. When the paramedics came, I told them I was Ian McAlister."

Jenna interrupted, shaking her head. She didn't believe me. "Your parents would have noticed the difference," she argued. "Surely they can tell you two apart."

My parents. "They believed what they wanted to. Luke's death made sense. He'd been too much trouble, brought it on himself. And Ian was easier to love. It didn't take much to convince them I was Ian."

Her eyes hardened. "I was pretty easy to convince, too."

She still didn't get it. "No. Please. You don't understand. At first, I was only pretending to be Ian. It was harder than I thought. I missed him so much. And the guilt—it felt like I was being ripped apart. And then he was there, and I forgot he was ever gone."

She shook her head. Of course she didn't believe me. It was impossible.

"Right now, I'm clear. I remember the party, the accident, the fact that Ian is," I took a deep breath, "gone. But right now won't last forever. Tomorrow, hell, an hour from now, Ian will show up and I'll think he's alive again."

"But that doesn't make any sense!" she snapped.

"I know. I don't know how to explain it. I'm asleep and I'm awake. I don't know how it feels to be Ian, because I'm not. I go into the bedroom in my head."

"And right now?"

"The real Luke is awake. He isn't usually. Ian and the Luke that thinks Ian is still alive are both asleep. Sometimes I know what's going on. I was completely me the first time we met, at the hospital. But most days I'm not. It's like a limb that's been amputated. I know it's gone, but sometimes it still itches, and I convince myself it's still there. I don't know how else to explain it."

I leaned back against the post and stared up at the sky. The answers weren't there.

"My dad thought I was lying," I said, "that Ian was, really, because he thought I was Ian. He thought I pretended to be Luke just to hurt them. But my mom believed Ian. She's a nurse. She took him to a doctor. They diagnosed him, me, with a dissociative disorder. They said the trauma caused a break. It happens, though usually with younger kids and different kinds of trauma. But our connection, my guilt, it was enough."

In the tiny spaces when I'd remembered, I'd tried to learn what I could. But until Jenna, I hadn't wanted to get better. The three months after the accident had been a soul-sucking black hole. I never wanted to be that alone again.

"Of course, they didn't know Ian was the alter ego, not me. Lots of people don't believe in that sort of thing. My dad's one of them. That's why my parents split up. Because of me. Because of how screwed up I am."

I turned to Jenna, my eyes finding hers in the dark. "But whoever that is, he's not Ian, not really. Ian was so much better than that. So strong. I'm not a good Ian. Hell, I'm not even a good Luke."

JENNA

The world came crashing in, rolling me, waves over my head. I didn't know where the surface was—I was swimming in the wrong direction, caught in the current. And then Luke was there to grab me. I could breathe again. And I believed him. I knew I shouldn't, since I couldn't be sure Luke even knew the truth. But he was here, and it felt like the truth. I knew this version was easier to believe because I wanted it to be true more than anything. No, that wasn't right. What I wanted more than anything was for all of this to be a bad dream. I wanted to wake up and realize that none of it was true, that Luke was still Luke and not so damaged. It was almost impossible to absorb everything all at once. It was too much. Instead, I focused on Luke and tugged tight to my chest the realization that he was alive. And warm. And here. I shouldn't have still wanted him, but I did.

I knew about sadness and regret. I was angry with myself for not saying goodbye to Pops. I missed him and felt as if I left a part of me behind, trapped somewhere in that October. But Luke's grief had caused his brain to shut down, caging him in the darkness—a fugue state, his mom had called it. Luke didn't just lose his brother; he lost himself as well.

Tragedy had drawn us together, and it was tragedy that was going to keep us apart.

"What do you want from me?" I whispered. I couldn't fix it. But I didn't know if I could walk away.

Luke stood up and sat on the edge of the swing. My heart pounded in my throat. He reached out and ran his finger along my jaw. I had to focus on breathing. "You've already given me everything." He leaned in and stared hard into my eyes, his hand cupping my face. "Until I met you, I was hoping I'd disappear completely and forget everything. But you." He gave me a crooked smile. "You brought me back to life."

His lips were warm and careful. I felt the kiss in my toes and in my lungs and as a burning in the back of my brain. I curled my fingers in his hair and pulled him tighter to me, and I knew he was telling me the truth. Ian couldn't kiss like that.

Luke held me close, a hug that was more like a grip. I buried my face in his neck. His hands were tangled in my hair, his lips close to my ear. "I love you," he whispered. "God forgive me, but I love you. I'm sorry."

I pulled back and looked at him. "That's not something to apologize for."

He looked down. "But I'm so screwed up."

I'd give him that. It changed everything. But he was here now, and tomorrow was going to have to take care of itself. I put my head on Luke's chest, and he stroked my hair. I tried to forget about the shadow lurking inside him. He was just Luke. I tried not to be sad. No matter what happened, I was going to lose him, one way or another. So I memorized him. The way he smelled, the sound of his breathing, the strength of his heartbeat. His skin under my fingers. I examined the way the veins crisscrossed the back of his hands. The callouses on his palms. The way my head fit perfectly against his neck.

"I might not be myself tomorrow," he said.

I swallowed the lump in my throat. I sat up and rested my forehead on his, our noses touching. "Then I guess all we have is today."

His eyes were intense. "It's all anyone ever has," he whispered.

LUKE

I knew it couldn't last—eventually Jenna would realize how impossible it was. But I was selfish enough not to care. I had her for the moment, and only that moment mattered.

Ian was silent—just a locked door where the illusion lived. I shouldn't have been trying to find him, but it hurt less when he was there. When I couldn't remember, he was really gone. Missing him was like drowning. My lungs felt flooded and my heart pounded like it wanted to wear itself down, beat twice as much, twice as hard, beat his heartbeats, too. It wasn't like losing him all over again. It was like waking up from a nightmare and realizing that reality was even worse.

"You have to tell your mom." Jenna's pronouncement came out of nowhere.

"She wouldn't believe me." She didn't want to. And maybe I didn't want her to, either. Living Ian's life was easier than living Luke's. No. I didn't really believe that anymore. The lie was getting harder to hold onto.

"You're her son. Of course she'll believe you," Jenna argued. "She believed you enough to move here, to try and fix you."

I sighed. Jenna couldn't understand my family. "She moved here to save Ian, not Luke."

She took my hand. "She loves you, too."

I stood up and stepped off the porch. The stars seemed to mock me. "Not the same way she loves Ian. She'll never forgive me for killing him."

"It was an accident." She sounded angry.

"Maybe I wanted him dead," I whispered.

Jenna came up behind me and wrapped her arms around my waist, resting her head in the middle of my back. "You didn't." She sounded so sure. Even I wasn't sure.

Because hadn't I resented him? Hadn't I wished I didn't have a brother whose perfection made me look more flawed, more inadequate? When Ian died, I got a new start. I didn't have to be me anymore—I could step out of myself, shed my problems and become the brother everyone always wanted me to be. The new me had scholarship possibilities and an unblemished reputation, while the old me was buried, flaws and all. At least that had been the plan. I'd watched myself being lowered into the ground. I remembered standing there and staring down into that dark hole, forgetting who I really was. Thinking I really was watching the old version of me being put to rest.

I turned around and rested my chin on Jenna's head. "Haven't you ever wished you could erase your mistakes and start all over?"

"Yes," she murmured, her lips against my throat.

"Well, I did," I said.

"But you didn't," she argued, pulling back and glaring at me. "Luke is still there, still struggling to get out, and you're still carrying that guilt around your neck like some huge stone. You can't bring Ian back by becoming him."

"I tried to be him for three months," I said. "And then I didn't have to, because he was there. It was like I'd been given a second chance to make it right. I don't know if I want to lose that."

"Your mother deserves the truth. It's up to her whether or not she believes it. But she's your mother. You have to tell her before you forget again."

I was afraid to let him go. What if I told the truth and Ian disappeared for good? I didn't know if I was strong enough for that. Maybe I wanted the delusion.

But I had to try. For my mom. Maybe for me. But more than anything, for Jenna. She made me crave freedom and then believe it was actually possible.

THIRTY

LUKE

I didn't know why Jenna was going with me. I wasn't even sure why she was still willing to be around me. She should have run screaming when she found out the truth. When she learned how completely crazy I was. Delusional. Insane. Clinging to a life that no longer existed. Creating my own reality.

But it didn't really feel like that. Ian had been a part of me for so long that it made perfect sense to still have him here. I couldn't lose him completely—he was an extension of me. I'd always had Ian in my head. Having him there now wasn't strange to me at all. It would have been stranger for him not to be. I didn't know if I could survive if he were completely gone. Our lives, our minds, were too intertwined.

In the beginning, Ian was around so much because I wanted him to be. I'd locked myself in my room and refused to come out. I'd let him take over. And then I lost control over it. My grip weakened.

Holding onto this reality was hard, like trying to keep up with a moving train. It hurtled toward the locked door, and I could feel Ian trying to wake up. I wanted to stay, but it was like fighting gravity. I was going to lose eventually. Pain gripped my head.

Jenna shut the back door softly behind her. "Sorry," she said, "I had to steal the keys. Help me push the Bronco down the driveway. If I start it here, Mom will wake up."

I was going to get her in trouble. Again. But I knew I wouldn't be able to tell the truth if Jenna wasn't there. She made me hate the lie.

Jenna climbed in the driver's seat and put the Bronco in neutral. I pushed it down the driveway while she steered. I was sweating and my legs were burning by the time I'd pushed it far enough down the road for it to be safe. Jenna started the engine as I climbed into the passenger seat. I wanted to drive forever. But running from the truth was what had gotten me into this mess, and even though telling my mom was going to be the hardest thing I'd ever done, I had to do it. It was going to hurt everyone, my mother especially. I hated myself for being unable to do anything but cause pain.

Jenna held my hand, grounding me in reality. Holding onto Luke was getting harder. There were spots in my vision, in my memory, and I felt everything sliding away. The backs of my eyes throbbed.

It was late when Jenna turned into our driveway, but Mom wasn't home yet. Jenna pulled up next to my truck and killed the engine. We were silent as we sat in the dark, fingers intertwined.

I wanted to take everything back. I wanted a do-over, a cosmic rewind. There were so many things I would do differently.

"I'm right here," Jenna said. "It's going to be okay."

I loved her for lying. There was no way anything about this was going to be okay. Mom was going to hate me for not being Ian. "You can't take back a lie that big," I said. "It can't be fixed. With that one lie, I destroyed everything. And nothing I ever do will make that okay." But I was going to try anyway.

The house was dark. I flipped on lights and walked into the kitchen, surrounding myself with Luke. Maybe the cabinets would help me hold on a little longer. They were something I had been able to fix. Now the kitchen I'd torn to pieces looked even better than it had before. I wished life worked that way.

Jenna hadn't followed. I found her in the living room, looking at a framed picture on the coffee table. It was a close-up of Ian and me in the tree house. Our arms were slung around one another, and we were grinning, the kind of smile only children could have—absolutely no shadows.

"Ian?" Jenna asked, pointing at the boy on the right.

"Nope. Me. That's Ian," I told her.

She shook her head. "You two really did look alike." She was whispering, like she was afraid she'd wake the dead. I was afraid of that too.

There had never been a Luke without an Ian. Hell, at one point we'd been the same person. One cluster of cells became two clusters of cells, which became us. It was always we, never just me or I or mine. Ours. Us. Even when things started to sour, when we started going in different directions, we'd still been connected. It had never been any other way. I didn't know if it could be.

"Here." I walked to the other side of the room and opened the trunk in the corner. Mom kept the photo albums tucked away. Remembering was hard for her, too. I thought sometimes she even pretended it was true, that we were both still here.

"Do you want to look at some pictures?" I asked, pulling out a couple of albums.

Jenna looked a little unsure. "I don't want to upset you."

"It's okay," I told her. "I probably won't remember it later."

Jenna flinched.

"Sorry," I said. And I was. About so many things.

She sat on the sofa, and I settled in close beside her. I could feel her all along the left side of my body—her arm against my arm, her leg against my leg. I etched her in my mind.

Mom had them organized perfectly. The first picture in the album was a side shot of my mom, pregnant. She couldn't get her arms around her belly. Next was a picture of both of my parents, my dad's hand resting affectionately on her stomach. They didn't really look like my parents. My parents were resentful and sad. Which was mostly my fault.

Ian and me as babies. I couldn't even tell us apart then. I wondered how Mom and Dad had. Maybe I really was Ian. They could have gotten us mixed up when we were three or four months old and I really was Ian and Luke really was dead.

Our first day of kindergarten. Little League. Boy Scouts and school plays. There were tons of pictures of us in front of waterfalls and monuments, the Grand Canyon and German castles. Jenna was fascinated by all the places we'd been.

"I've been everywhere, but I'm from nowhere," I told her. "I don't have a home to return to."

"Of course you do." Jenna kissed me lightly on the side of the mouth and tucked her head into my shoulder. Maybe she was right—maybe I was home.

There was never a picture of just Ian or just me. Birthday parties found us standing right next to each other, identical stacks of presents, identical grins. On Christmas morning, we wore matching pajamas and opened matching presents.

There was a picture of the tree house again. In this one Ian was standing in the tree, holding onto a can with a string. I was on the ground, at the other end of the string, an identical can in my hand. I remembered that day. We'd seen a commercial with the can telephone on it, and Mom had explained that sound ran up the string. Mom had laughed when I asked why people didn't just use their cell phones. Mom had the best laugh—loud and goofy. She would throw her head back and squint her eyes tight; her whole body laughed when she did. I missed it.

Mom explained that, before cell phones and Walkie-Talkies and everything else, kids played with these. Ian had wanted to try it out. I'd thought it was stupid—we had cell phones—but I went along with what Ian wanted. He was my brother—I couldn't tell him no.

Ian wanted to climb up and test it out. I'd stood on the ground with the can to my ear and waited. When he spoke, I wasn't sure if I heard him through the can or just in my head. I had told him it was pointless. We'd always been able to hear one another.

We were older in the second album. I flipped faster, wanting to get done—like ripping off a Band-Aid. Ian and I weren't together in all of these. Hidden behind a picture of Ian in his football uniform, I found one of Ian smiling with his girlfriend, Mandy. God, it hurt to look at that one. I'd killed her, too. There were a few with me—us standing in front of the fireplace with our homecoming dates. Ian was smiling. I was scowling. Typical.

The pictures stopped suddenly. We hadn't taken a single one since the accident. None of the moments since then were worth preserving.

Headlights flashed across the living room. I shut the album and took a deep breath. I pulled Jenna into the kitchen. My fear was reflected in her face.

I heard Mom's key in the door. I listened to her footsteps as she crossed to the hall table and tossed her keys down. She sighed—I imagined her stretching out her back. It would have been a long day. Mom was on her feet all day, fixing people. She must have felt helpless when she couldn't fix her own son.

Mom's shadow grew taller and taller until it bent around the wall and across the ceiling. I reached over and grabbed Jenna's hand. She gave it a squeeze just as Mom stepped into the kitchen. Mom froze, her surprise quickly turning to anger.

"What are you doing here?" she snapped at Jenna. "Don't you think you've done enough?"

Jenna flushed. "Stop," I told Mom. "I want her here."

Mom stepped closer to me. "We came here to start over. We came here for you to get better. She's making it worse."

"Luke," Jenna began, "I should probably—"

Mom was livid. "I told you, Luke is dead!"

It hurt to hear, even though I'd been trying to convince everyone of just that. "I'm not dead." I took a deep breath. This wasn't going to work if I was mad.

"Ian," Mom began, stepping toward me.

My head was coming apart, like one of those bridges that opened in the middle. It felt like I might fall into the gap. "I'm Luke," I said, trying to convince myself, too. "You always assume I'm Ian. I'm Luke."

Mom turned her back to Jenna, her hand settling on my shoulder as she lowered her voice. "Okay. I'm sorry." Her hand was shaking. "Of course you are. You know I sometimes get you two mixed up. You look so much alike." She forced a smile that didn't reach her eyes. "Where's Ian?"

"Sit down," I told Mom. She did. Jenna stood off to the side, her arms folded across her chest. I leaned across the table and looked Mom straight in the eye. "Mom, Ian is dead." I'd never believed I could say those words. There was no taking them back now.

Mom paled, but she didn't move. "That's not funny. You're tired. We'll make an appointment with Dr. Benson in the morning."

"Mom, I need you to listen. Just listen."

I told the story for the second time that night—the kiss, the anger, the alcohol and accusations. I admitted that I'd wanted Ian's unblemished life and I'd lied. At some point Mom started crying and shaking, but I could tell she didn't really believe me.

"I'm sorry," I finished. For killing Ian. For lying. For being me.

"I'm losing my mind," she whispered to herself, staring at her hands. Tears dropped into her palms.

"Mrs. McAlister, please. Luke is telling you the truth."

Mom turned on Jenna. "What do you know about any of it? You weren't there." Her sobs were screams. "You didn't have to watch them lower your child into the dirt. You didn't see grief take the one who remained. You don't know what it's like to see a ghost every single day."

Jenna didn't answer.

"Mom, I know it's hard to believe." My head was nothing but pain now.

"You're sick. You don't know what you're talking about."

"You'd rather Luke was dead than Ian?" I asked.

She clutched her throat and blinked hard. Tears rolled down her cheeks.

"It was easier to believe that Luke was dead. Better." I stood up. I was shaking now. Mom stood up and crossed to me, but I stepped away. "If you'd looked hard enough, you would have seen that it was me. You didn't want to. You wanted Luke to be dead."

She slapped me. Hard. She looked even more surprised than I felt. I pulled my shirt up. "Look," I said. "Look at this scar. Remember? Look hard. It looks nothing like Ian's scar. Nothing."

Mom was shaking her head back and forth, staring past me.

"Or these cabinets!" I threw my arm out. "You know Ian couldn't have done this—he was failing woodshop until I built that damn birdhouse for him!"

Mom stopped looking past me and through me and around me. Her eyes jerked side to side as she examined my face.

"Or the time I came home drunk and drove over the mailbox. Remember that? Ian was out with Mandy and Dad was in the field. You promised you wouldn't tell if I promised I wouldn't do it again. Only one of us held up our end of that bargain." My throat was tight, the words hard to say. "You made me get up early the next morning and put up an identical mailbox so Dad wouldn't know. You made me go with you to the hospital."

Mom nodded, denial and truth battling in her expression.

"You made me volunteer every Saturday for two months. I hated it. You showed me every drunk driving patient. You made me deliver their flowers and go with you when they needed pain meds. I was standing in the hall when they told Reed he wouldn't walk again." Reed was a high school kid who'd been brought in late one night. Reed hadn't even been drinking. He'd been driving home after a basketball game and someone else had hit him and had stolen his future. He'd been picked up by Chapel Hill the week before. The drunk driver had died on the operating table. "But I didn't learn my lesson, did I?" My head felt like someone had split it with an ax. "Do you remember what you told me that day? 'I can fix drunk. I can handle arrested, suspended, even expelled. But I can't fix dead.'" That had been six months before the accident. "You were right, Mom. I couldn't fix dead."

"Oh my God, Luke." Mom threw her arms around me and cried into my neck. She whispered my name over and over again, her words trying to convince her of what her arms were still unsure of. It had been so long since she'd hugged me. I wrapped my arms even tighter around her.

"Oh God," her voice cracked as her arms dropped to her sides. I didn't let go. "Ian." Her face twisted in agony as she pushed away from me. It felt like he'd died all over again. For her, he had. I was empty and caved in, and I wanted to take everything back. I just wanted him back.

Mom swayed, and Jenna rushed forward and put her arms around her. Mom sobbed Ian's name. He heard. Pain shot through my head, and I fell to my knees. Darkness.

JENNA

Mrs. McAlister ordered me out of the house right after Luke blacked out. I wanted to stay and make sure he was okay, but I couldn't argue with her. She looked deranged—not that I blamed her. I wasn't sure if she understood, or even believed, what Luke had been trying to tell her. It was too much—to suddenly be reunited with the son you thought was dead while being faced with the death of the one you thought had survived. I kept waiting for her to snap or go into shock or something. Not that it changed the fact that there was only one, and he thought he was both. I wanted to stay to make sure she was going to be okay too, but she ordered me out, and I was too exhausted to argue.

I drove home slowly, my head heavy and dark. My brain grappled with the puzzle—I had most of the pieces together, but I couldn't make sense of the picture. Ian's death hurt, but then I had to remind myself that I'd never known him. The Ian I knew had been nothing but Luke's guilt, glued together by memories and regret. But it didn't really feel that way.

I was going to have to face the fact that the boy I'd fallen in love with was seriously unstable. Luke was only present in flashes, in stops and starts, in glimpses. The rest of the time he was hidden away somewhere. I imagined him trying to escape his pain, finding some dark place to hole up in while Ian was awake. But I still couldn't imagine them as one person. Every time I tried, I saw twin brothers, two separate people. Ian stood up straight while Luke had a tendency to slouch. Their laughs were different. And Ian had never kissed me like Luke had.

I loved the most flawed boy I could've found, and my loving him wasn't healthy, for either of us. I just wanted to crawl into my bed and forget.

I got home just before dawn. Thankfully, Mom was sound asleep. I didn't want to explain to her where I'd been—not that it was any of her business. And it wasn't like she'd made the best decisions in life. She was not the person to lecture me about restraint.

I put my keys back in their hiding place and dragged myself upstairs. My mind was having trouble holding on to thoughts. My eyes were gritty, and it felt like a thick fog had rolled through my brain. I wasn't going to have any trouble sleeping, no matter how worried I was. My body just couldn't take anymore. I didn't even take off my shoes. I fell face-first on the bed and was asleep almost instantly.

THIRTY-ONE

LUKE

I woke up in my room, but I couldn't remember how I'd gotten there, nor did I have any idea how long I'd been out. It was dark, but I wasn't sure if that meant I'd been asleep a couple of hours or if a whole day had passed. Or more. I'd never been that disoriented. I rolled over and stared at the strip of light seeping in from underneath my door.

Footsteps in the hall. They stopped right in front of my room—two feet made two dark spots in the light. There wasn't a knock or any real acknowledgement that I was in here. But I knew it was Ian.

My dark room was comforting. No one else could get in. It was more like a cell than a bedroom. No window. Nothing hanging on the walls. The only decoration was the picture of Ian and me looking down from the tree house, taken before Dad started sharpening us on each other and trying to make us prove we were the better twin. I got sick of that game fast—it was one I couldn't win. And I didn't want to compete with Ian all the time. Dad had never understood the twin thing. It was more than being brothers.

I didn't know Ian had left until I heard him coming back. The shadows reappeared, just two gray spots underneath the door. Why didn't he knock?

But he didn't. He didn't even try to talk to me. He just started hammering.

I got up and walked over to the door. "What are you doing?" My door rattled each time the hammer struck, and for a second his hammer was in sync with my pulse.

Ian didn't answer. He hammered louder, paused, and then placed something against the door before starting up again.

"Ian?" I tried to turn the doorknob, but it was stuck. "What the hell is going on?"

Silence. Then, "You're trying to get rid of me."

"Ian, what are you talking about?"

I jumped as the hammer struck the door—loud and violent. I was surprised the wood hadn't splintered.

"You can't fix this," Ian said. "Jenna picks you and all of a sudden you think you have everything under control. That you can make everything okay. But you lost that right when you killed Mandy. I have a chance at a normal life—as long as you aren't in it."

I grappled with the knob, but it wouldn't turn and my hands were sweaty and kept slipping. "Ian," I warned.

More hammering. "Mom said she told Jenna everything. I just have to change Jenna's mind. I'm sure it won't be that hard."

I broke out in a cold sweat. I beat on the door with my fists and hollered his name. He waited until I stopped yelling before continuing, as if I hadn't said a word.

"I warned you. I told you to stay away from her. Things were getting better. *I* was getting better. She made me whole and then you took her away." His voice was conversational and pleasant, like we were discussing the possibility of rain or what we wanted for dinner. "You don't listen. You never think of anyone but yourself. But I do. And I'm going to make sure you can't tear this family any farther apart. You owe it to me, and to Mom and Dad. You broke us. I'll fix everything."

I twisted and tugged at the handle. I focused on turning it. I pictured the latch pulling away from the door. I concentrated so hard that my head ached. It turned, but it didn't open. It was then I noticed that the door opened out into the hall. I tried to push it but it struck something and stopped. I rammed my shoulder against the door but it wouldn't budge. I peeked through the small crack and realized what Ian had been doing. There were boards nailed across the door. I couldn't get out.

"Let me out, Ian. We need to talk."

"I'm through talking to you."

I watched his feet recede. I hollered his name until my throat was sore, but he was gone and I was locked in the room I'd created. It shouldn't have been possible. It also didn't appear possible to escape, but I was going to have to figure that out. Before it was too late.

JENNA

The sun was low when I woke up, and my muscles resisted as I stretched, as if it had been years since I'd moved. Shards of last night pierced my skull; I tried to pretend it had all been a dream, but I couldn't because my chest was nothing but a hollow space with a heart so heavy I wasn't sure I was going to be able to carry it. I rolled over and pulled the covers over my head, thinking they could hide me from reality. They didn't.

I threw back the covers and jumped in the shower. I let the water scald me, turning my skin red. I wanted to steam everything out, clean my brain, but there wasn't enough hot water in the world for that.

The harder I tried to hold things together, the quicker they fell apart. The tighter I gripped, the less control I had. Was that what life was about? Picking the least bad option? Where were the good choices? The easy answers? Where the hell was my happiness? At this point, I would have settled for just a little sanity.

I turned off the water and stood dripping in the shower as my life crumbled at my feet. I'd spent the last couple of years sure that getting out of Solitude was the answer. The idea of going somewhere else and starting all over with new people and a new me helped me wade through the crap and gave me something to focus on. I was going to shed Solitude like a second skin. But that was before Mom fell apart and before Luke showed up and branded my heart— because this wasn't something I could leave behind. Now, wherever I went, I would be different because of Luke. He had seen the parts of me I was most proud of. He made me laugh. He made me furious. He showed me how to string together spontaneous moments until they were a colorful life, and he'd made me want so much more before he jerked the proverbial rug clean out from underneath me. Now I was flat on my back and the wind had been knocked right out of me.

I wrapped a towel around my head and got dressed. I was starving. I headed downstairs to raid the kitchen.

The fridge contained some wilted lettuce, condiments, baking soda, and a swig of milk. Not really the ideal meal. I fixed myself two peanut butter sandwiches and drank the last of the milk straight out of the carton, curling up into my chair and thumbing through a book on India that I hadn't touched in weeks. I tried to pretend like my life was just as boring and predictable as it had always been, but I wasn't buying it.

The house phone rang. "Hello?"

"Jenna. It's Pete. You're not answering your cell."

Obviously. "I'm grounded. Mom took my phone."

"Oh. Look, I know you're not scheduled to work tonight, but I need you. Amber called in sick and Dale is still on vacation. Can you come in?"

Work was exactly what I needed. "I'll be there in twenty minutes," I promised.

"You're a lifesaver," he said.

I threw my wet hair into a ponytail and tucked it up under a Repete's cap. I scribbled Mom a quick note—*Went to work. Buy groceries*—and dug through Mom's drawer for my keys. No keys. I pawed through every drawer and all the cabinets in her bathroom. Nothing. I called her.

"Where are my keys?" I snapped as soon as she picked up.

"You're grounded," she said. There was no need to remind me. She was hard to hear over the background noise—music and the tinkling of glass.

"Where are you?" I asked.

"Work."

I knew she was lying. Her real estate office was never that loud—the phone hardly ever rang. And those were the sounds of a bar. I gritted my teeth. "Pete called and needs me at work."

"Well, you'll have to call Mops and get her to bring you in. I have your keys with me. I found them in a different place from where I left them. You're going to have to earn back my trust. I'll pick you up after your shift."

I wanted to yell at her or throw things. I wanted to tell her she was the one who needed to earn back trust, but none of it would have done any good. "Be there a little before eleven." I hung up and called Mops, pacing the floor until she got there. I was going to be late.

Repete's was already packed when Mops pulled into the back lot.

"You sure you won't need a ride home?" she asked.

"No, Mom said she'd pick me up. Thanks for the ride."

"Any time."

Inside, there were two Little League teams celebrating wins, lots of regulars, and plenty of to-go orders. It was surprising how many pizzas a small town could eat. I tied my apron and jumped into the middle of the madness.

I didn't have time to feel sorry for myself. Pete was training a new cook—Jon, a sophomore—and he was pretty hopeless. He burned several pizzas and left it up to me to explain things to the waiting customers. By the time ten o'clock rolled around, I'd burned myself three times on hot pans and my feet were begging me to sit down. But it was a good tired.

I helped Pete close up. I locked the front door and pulled down the shade. I bussed all the tables, mopped the tile floor, and made sure all the food was stored.

"You're on bathroom detail," I told Pete. "You owe me."

He scowled, but grabbed the cleaner and headed down the hall. Cleaning the bathrooms was something I avoided if I could.

An hour later, Pete and I stepped out into the deserted back lot. One small streetlight tried unsuccessfully to illuminate the alley.

"I've got to drop this off in the night deposit," Pete said, holding up the canvas moneybag. "You'll be okay?"

"Yeah, go on. My mom should be here any second." When Pete looked unsure, I added, "I'll be fine." Where did he think we were? The last crime wave in Solitude involved mailboxes, and the Wiggins brothers had spent a month putting up new ones.

At eleven-fifteen, Mom still wasn't there. By eleven-thirty, I was sure she'd forgotten me and was fairly certain that alcohol had something to do with it. I hated to wake up Mops, but I didn't really have a choice. I started walking.

Gravel crunched as a truck pulled into the lot. I turned, headlights blinding me, and put my hand up to shield my eyes.

"Need a ride?"

I knew that voice. Thank God. I stepped toward the truck and out of the glare. It was the smile that gave him away. "Ian?"

"Disappointed?" He looked sad.

"Of course not," I lied. Because he *was* Luke. And he wasn't.

"Look, I thought we could talk. We never got to finish."

I was uneasy, and I tried to tell myself I was being ridiculous. Ian was sweet. He'd never given me a reason to be afraid. He was just a figment of Luke's imagination. I climbed in the truck and pretended I was okay with Ian. Because no matter who he thought he was, I knew he was Luke.

THIRTY-TWO

IAN

There was pain where my head was supposed to be, like someone had taken a hammer to the inside of my skull. Which, in a way, someone had.

I was the responsible one. I had played by the rules and done everything right. But I wasn't ready to give up. Hard work eventually equaled success. I had remembered Mandy. Her name was salt across a very open wound. I could still salvage what was left of my life. I could still win.

I wasn't a martyr. I had a stack of college brochures promising a future of football games and golden opportunities. I wasn't going to let Luke screw that up.

"Aren't you taking me home?" Jenna asked.

I couldn't afford to lose her too. "Not yet."

I drove into the train yard, the truck bumping hard over the rails. The headlights bounced across the ground before illuminating a building that proclaimed love and a great many other things for some girl named Rhonda. I shut off the engine and leaned across the seat toward Jenna. When she turned to look at me, I pressed my lips to hers. Luke had fed her a lie. I needed to give her the truth.

LUKE

My shoulder screamed as I threw myself against the door again and again. I imagined the door opening inward. I had created this room to keep myself separate from Ian. I had to be able to remodel it a bit now that I no longer wanted to hide. Now that I had a reason to get out. But the door wouldn't budge. I didn't know where Ian was or what he was doing. I wasn't sure what he was capable of. I worried I'd find out too late.

JENNA

Ian's kiss was a current, but my brain and body were on two different circuits. I wanted to kiss Luke, and I was, so my body responded to his touch. But I didn't want to kiss Ian, and I was, and my brain screamed at me to stop. I put my hands on Ian's chest and pushed him away.

His face twisted in agony and desperation, and it was hard to look at that kind of brutal pain, since all of Luke's guilt and grief compounded it. "Pick me," Ian whispered.

His words stabbed at my sanity. "I can't." The hole in my chest waited for me to fall into it. It might have been a relief. Reality played hide-and-seek with my mind. "I do care about you," I told Ian, "but it's because Luke is in there somewhere."

"But he's not supposed to be!" Ian grimaced and rubbed the back of his neck. "I'm tired of sharing a life with him. He hurts people. How do you even know that his version of the story is the real one?"

Because when nothing else about this made sense, Luke did. Because he was the truth I was most able to live with. "I trust Luke."

"You shouldn't. Look what happened to Mandy."

The truth taunted me, continuously changing shape and slipping in and out of the shadows. If truth was supposed to bring freedom, why did it weigh like heavy chains around my neck? Luke felt true, but Ian made me doubt myself. Made me doubt Luke. I hated Ian for that. I hated him for not being real enough for my hate to do any good. Or for being so real he made me forget what I once thought I knew.

I grabbed the door handle and pulled, tumbling backward out of the truck. I barely registered the pain of the fall before I was on my feet and running.

IAN

Dad always said a real man finds solutions, not excuses. Jenna helped me remember, and I couldn't let Luke take that away. Take *her* away. If I was going to have a shot at winning, at pulling my family back together and finding that future they'd always planned for me, then Luke would have to stay in my past. There was only one way to solve this, and only one man to do it.

LUKE

My shoulder throbbed, and my hands and heart hurt. There was a weariness that had nothing to do with my body and everything to do with this room. And while I deserved this cell, I longed to be finally free of the walls I'd put up myself. Walls constructed by guilt and fear and held together with shame. But I'd hidden in here long enough. I wanted out.

JENNA

Moonlight filtered through the broken and grimy windows as I picked my way through the first floor. The room was familiar. A door hanging on its hinges. A pile of old bricks. A warped and broken desk in the corner.

I'd run here to recapture something, but I found that the magic of a moment disappeared as soon as time rushed in. This place wasn't beautiful, like it had been that night. It was broken and scarred. It was lonely.

I climbed the stairs and sat underneath the hole in the roof where Luke and I had spent the Fourth of July. I wanted to forget everything I knew now and live inside that past moment forever. I leaned back and stared at the stars. At least they hadn't changed. There had been a fraction of perfection in that night, a sliver of joy I'd held in my palm before it had cut me to shreds.

I cloaked myself with those memories. Not every single moment with Luke could have been a lie. What did it say about me if it was?

Gravel crunched on the first floor as Ian stepped into the dark building. I took deep breaths and tried to slow my heart. I needed to talk to Luke. He was in there somewhere. I just had to find him.

The stairs groaned. "I just want to talk," Ian said. He crossed and stood in the dim light from the open ceiling, staring down at me.

His smile was sad and asked me what I believed. It wasn't a fair question.

How could I save a boy who'd died before I ever knew him? I couldn't win. No matter what happened, I'd lose.

"Where's Luke?" I asked. I needed to know he was real. I needed to know I hadn't imagined everything.

"In his room," Ian said.

My stomach tightened. "I want to talk to him."

"No."

I stood up. "Then take me home," I said, turning to go. "We can talk about this tomorrow."

Ian reached out to stop me. "What if I don't have a tomorrow?" There was real fear in his voice, and that, more than anything, made me stop. It was hard to breathe around the lump in my throat. "Why can't I have just as much of a chance as Luke? I'm just as real."

I shook my head. I didn't even know if truth existed anymore. Maybe it was a shape-shifter. Maybe it looked different to everyone.

"How can you believe I don't exist?" he asked. "I'm standing right here."

Ian reached out and took my hand, placing it on his chest. His heart pounded underneath my fingers. "Can't you feel that?"

I nodded. I felt the beat of his heart and the warmth of his skin through his shirt. He moved my hand to his face, and I closed my eyes as he leaned into my palm.

"I'm real," Ian whispered. "I'm standing right here."

My eyes were still closed when he leaned down and pressed his lips against mine. I didn't want to see his pain, but I felt it in his kiss. Tears slipped down my cheeks, and I shook my head as Ian's lips moved on mine.

He wrapped his arms around my waist and pressed his chest against mine, deepening the kiss. Panic pounded in my head, and I pushed him away.

"I can't," I said. My voice was ragged and raw. I didn't want Ian to be dead, but I couldn't believe Luke was. I didn't want to mourn for a boy I never knew or lose the one I did. I didn't want this pain.

There was only one thing I did want.

"Luke."

LUKE

Somewhere on the other side, Jenna said my name. It was a plea. I rushed the door, slamming my shoulder against the unyielding wood again and again. I had to get out now.

I put all my weight against the door. I pushed and strained until sweat stood out on my face. "Let me out!" I shouted. "Ian!" I stepped back.

Ian was dead.

That thought was a weight I struggled to free myself from. I shouldn't have been surprised that thoughts had form, considering where I was, but just thinking the words drove me to my knees. I couldn't believe that Ian was gone.

Ian was dead.

It was both truth and lie.

No.

Truth.

"Ian is dead," I said out loud. "I'm sorry." The words choked me. I knelt on the floor and pounded my fists against the door. "I'm sorry, Ian! Oh God."

He was dead. There was nothing I could do to bring him back. No matter how much guilt I buried myself under, I'd never see him again. I could never tell him how sorry I really was.

"Ian," I whispered.

It might have been easier to stay locked in this cell, but I'd spent a year hiding in the dark. I needed to find my way out.

I got to my feet. I kicked at the door and heard a tiny splinter.

"Ian is dead!" I shouted. My voice sounded stronger, but I felt shredded.

It was time to get free of the lies. I wouldn't let my mistakes hurt anyone else.

I took three steps back and ran at the door. This time the crack was louder. I pushed against the door again, and the seam grew bigger. My arms shook and the veins in my forearms popped out. The wood cracked again, leaving me just enough space to squeeze out.

Freedom.

"Jenna."

JENNA

I was halfway down the stairs when Luke said my name. His deep voice caressed it rather than clipping it short. No one said my name like he did.

"Luke." I turned and ran back up the stairs. He was standing in a patch of moonlight, and he ran his hand through his hair. I saw Luke in his face—the worry, the sorrow, the guilt.

"Did he hurt you?" he asked. He took a step forward, then stopped. "Are you okay?" He clenched his fists and wouldn't come any closer.

I crossed the space between us in two strides. "I'm fine," I told him. But it was a lie. My heart ached for the boy standing in front of me.

"I'm so sorry," he said. Relief and revulsion warred in his face, but he finally reached up and brushed my hair out of my eyes. His fingers lingered on my cheek.

"Ian's trying to convince me he's—" I stopped and reached out to touch Luke's face. "Luke, I need to know—"

Luke took my hand away from his face. "You need to get home," he said. "Away from me."

It hurt to hear him say that. I could tell it hurt him to have to say it. He was probably right. But first, I needed to know for sure.

I wrapped my arms around Luke's neck and pulled his face to mine. He hesitated for a moment, his shoulders tense, but then he crushed himself to me, his hands tangled in my hair. I tried to tell him all the things I didn't have words for.

I lost my doubt.

I found the truth.

LUKE

I pulled out of the kiss, but Jenna kept her arms around my neck, her body warm. "Stay," she whispered. Her lips brushed my ear as she spoke.

It was exactly what I wanted. To stay with her. "I don't think I can," I whispered back. I already felt myself slipping away. Felt Ian pulling at me. I didn't know how many moments I had left. Ian was getting so much stronger.

And then he was there, as if I'd called his name.

"You're going to ruin everything," he said.

I'd already ruined everything. This was me trying to hold together what I still could. "Jenna shouldn't be here. This is between you and me."

"You're right about that, brother. I had this under control until you messed it all up. You have to go away—permanently. After everything that's happened, you owe me at least that."

Everyone wanted me to disappear. It had been my plan all along. Things would be easier on Mom. Maybe if I were gone, she and Dad could get back together. Hadn't I wanted to become Ian? Maybe the freedom I'd been fighting for wasn't about forgiving myself but forgetting myself.

Maybe Ian *was* my best version.

"What's going on?" Jenna demanded. She had stepped away and was watching my conversation with Ian. I wondered what it looked like on the outside.

"We're negotiating," I said.

"About what?"

"We both can't—" I sighed. "I had my chance."

"You're going to have to forgive yourself eventually." How could she trust me? I didn't. No one should. "I picked you," she said, "not Ian. Luke can't be all bad."

Ian's anger became a searing pain in my head. "I can make you want to disappear," he said.

"Go!" I shouted to Jenna, pushing her away from me. When she didn't move immediately, I shouted again. "Just go!" My scalp felt like it was shrinking. No, it turned out Ian wasn't my best version after all, but he was the one calling the shots. Lights popped. Colors flowed. Darkness.

IAN

They were trying to get rid of me. He was my brother and I had loved her. Now they were both in it together. More than anything, I needed Luke out of my head. I wanted quiet. I wanted the headaches to stop. I just wanted to be alone for a while, to have a chance to collect and create more memories. I'd do anything to make that happen.

I didn't get why Luke wouldn't go. Why he was fighting me so hard. He'd been hiding in his room for months now. He'd locked himself in—not me. Luke had no right to my life. He really didn't even have a right to his own. The accident had been his fault. We were lucky to have walked away. Mandy hadn't.

JENNA

I tried to run, but I tripped over something in the dark. I banged my knees, and a rock ground into my shin. Blood trickled down my leg.

"Dad says Luke has to go," Ian said, stepping out of a nearby shadow to stand right in front of me. "Please. I need you."

"I can't fix you," I said. *Either one of you.*

Ian's face hardened. "I'm not broken." Ian's fingers dug into my skin as he reached out and grabbed my arm.

"Let go of me," I said, jerking out of his grasp.

"I'm sorry," Ian said, only there was remorse in his voice, and he was Luke. "I'm sorry, I'm sorry, I'm sorry."

I wanted to escape this nightmare. But I couldn't leave Luke alone. He would tear himself apart.

I wanted to help Luke, but I needed to escape Ian. I couldn't have both.

"Shut up!" Ian screamed. "I won't let you take anything else away from me." The softness that usually pushed Ian's mouth into an easy smile had become a jagged edge of desperation. "Maybe you'd like to know what it feels like to lose everything."

Ian's head jerked back, like someone had hit him, then his mouth turned down and sorrow flooded his face. His shoulders slumped forward. "I've already lost it all, Ian."

"You still have Jenna." Ian. His words had taken on a cruelty I'd never heard in them before. "But only because she believes the lies. I can take her, Luke. You know I can."

I tried to be invisible. I could feel my grip on reality slipping. My mind wanted to fold in on itself and protect me from the horror of standing in the shadows and watching Luke lose his brother all over again. It was torture seeing them both cling to a life only one of them could have. For the first time in seven months, I just wanted to go home.

"Don't." Luke's voice was shredded. "Don't."

I stood in the dark and listened to Luke fall apart.

LUKE

I was back in my room. Door locked. Ian was holding me prisoner by sheer will. Not possible, but true.

There were no windows in my room. The door was the only way out. I'd built the perfect cell. It shut me in and the world out. It was a place for me to hide instead of facing reality. But I didn't want to hide anymore. I wanted Jenna. She had torn me apart and rebuilt me. Made me better. She found my best version. Jenna had seen me when no one else could and loved me anyway.

I hadn't been able to save Mandy. I hadn't been able to save Ian. But I could save Jenna. And maybe even myself.

I slammed my fist into the wall, leaving a nice dent in the Sheetrock. Hope. I hit it again, and even in this imagining, pain shot up my arm. I'd made a hole.

"I'm sorry, Ian," I said. "I'm so sorry."

JENNA

"Jenna. You have to get to the truck." Definitely Luke. It felt like I was submerged in some bad dream. I couldn't move fast enough. I couldn't think. I was afraid that, if I did, I would lose it completely. I ran toward the stairs.

"Please." Ian. Damn, they were switching faster than I could keep up. Ian blocked my way out. His eyes were hard, and I knew he was Ian because Luke would never have tried to make me stay.

"Ian, just let me go."

He stepped closer. "There's no other way to fix this." He gripped my arm. "He's trying to kill me."

I no longer recognized the boy who stood in front of me. "No one's trying to kill you."

"If they think Luke's real and I'm the projection, then what do you think will happen? They'll try to get rid of me. There's only room for one of us in here."

He tilted his head, like he was listening to someone, then banged on his temples in pain and desperation. "I don't want to go," he said. "I don't want to forget this. I don't want to forget you."

I wanted to save him, save them both, but I couldn't. I had to remind myself that Ian had been dead for over a year. And Luke needed the kind of help I couldn't give. His phone was in the truck. If I could just get to it, I could call his mom. She might know what to do.

I wanted to forget this entire night, but I would settle for escaping it instead. I stepped around Ian and was almost to the stairs when he reached out and grabbed my wrist. He twisted my arm, sending needles of pain into my shoulder. I cried out in surprise.

"Please. You can help put my family back together."

"You're out of your damn mind," I whispered. The words hurt, as only truth sometimes can.

Ian's laugh made the back of my neck prickle. "If Luke told you everything, then you know that's what he is. I'm the stable one."

Ian's eyes were wild and he was breathing heavy. "Yeah, you look it," I said.

Anger twisted his face, and for the first time, I was truly afraid of just how far Ian was willing to go to hang on to the life he thought he deserved.

"Luke." I hoped he could hear me. "You're better than he is, no matter what you think. He doesn't always have to win."

"I haven't lost yet," Ian said. I looked into his face, looking for any trace of Luke, but there wasn't one. Luke never would have hurt me.

Ian jerked my arm again, and I gasped in pain. Gritting my teeth, I shoved Ian as hard as I could while pulling away from him. The shock on Ian's face ripped through me, and the lump in my throat was equal parts anger and sorrow as Ian lost his balance and stepped backward. I realized too late what was going to happen, and even though I reached out to grab him, my fingers skimmed his arm as his eyes widened and he fell down the stairs.

LUKE

I pounded the wall again and again, and when the hole was big enough, I tore it wider with my hands.

"I miss you," I told Ian. Wherever he was, I hoped he knew at least that much. "I miss you so damn much."

The wall crumbled at my feet, and the harder I pulled, the faster it fell, until all I could do was step back and watch it disintegrate completely.

The rest of the walls followed, tumbling down like ash, the house falling away until the only thing standing was an enormous oak tree supporting a tree house in its thick branches. It looked brand new. Two young boys stood inside the tree house, their arms slung around each other's shoulders. They grinned down at me, and when they waved, I waved back. And then they were gone.

JENNA

Sometimes an eternity existed in a nanosecond. I froze as the crash of Ian's body became a terrifying silence.

"Jenna." Luke's voice, soft and low, floated up through the darkness, and I rushed down the stairs.

His eyes fluttered shut, and I stared in horror at the blood pooling underneath his head. I started shaking. I was pretty sure I'd just killed Luke.

LUKE

In my dream, I had no scars. No pain. No regret. I was just me.

THIRTY-THREE

JENNA

The ambulance was fast. I'd used Luke's cell to call 911, then gone back inside to wait with him.

He wasn't dead. He was broken and beaten, but he was still alive.

Luke coughed and opened his eyes, and in the moment before he spoke, I didn't know which one I'd get.

"Hey," he rasped. "Are you okay?"

Tears. I couldn't help it. I was so glad to hear Luke's voice. "I'm fine. I'm tougher than I look."

"Good." He tried to smile, but it was more of a grimace.

"I am so sorry," I said.

"Don't." He winced. "*I'm* sorry. For everything."

"But I nearly killed you." Him. It would take awhile before I could process what had just happened. It was more surreal than life should be.

"No," Luke said, squeezing my hand, "you saved my life."

"You probably shouldn't talk," I said. He was too pale. "The ambulance should be here any minute." The sirens screamed through the night, an uncommon sound in the quiet of Solitude. They were getting louder.

"I need to say this." He sat up, then swayed a bit; I leaned in to steady him. He propped himself up against the wall. "Thank you for making me want to be me again. For seeing me and for loving me anyway."

"You saw me too," I told him. I leaned over and brushed his lips with mine. Luke.

I visited Luke in the hospital two days later. His mom was keeping him close. I wasn't sure she bought our story about him tripping and falling down the stairs.

I had the Bronco back. Mom's guilt over leaving me stranded had seen to that. Not that she was being reasonable. I wasn't supposed to be here. Mom didn't want me to see "Ian" again for a while. And Luke's mom didn't think I was a good idea, either. But Cathy Anders, sophomore, candy striper, and resident do-gooder, snuck me in and watched for Mrs. McAlister.

I sat in the chair next to Luke's bed. He looked rough. His face was stitched and swollen, and he was covered in ugly bruises. He traced patterns on the back of my hand.

"We're leaving," he said.

My breath caught in my throat. "Why?"

"That should be obvious." His voice was tight, and he kissed me before I could answer. The goodbye leaked through and shredded my heart. "I don't have a choice," he said, pulling away to look at me. "Mom thinks I need distance."

From me. "When?"

"Whenever she says. I'm sorry."

"It's not your fault." Even though we were sitting in the same room, I could already feel him pulling away from me.

"Everything is my fault," he argued.

I sat back. "Your taking the blame for everything is getting kind of old. Sometimes life just gives us crap, and there's nothing we can do about it."

"Sometimes. And sometimes everything that happens is a direct result of a decision. All of my choices were bad ones."

I didn't want him to regret us. I didn't. "All of them?"

He took my hand again. "I'm a selfish bastard, so I don't regret falling in love with you. But because of it, you got hurt, and I regret that very much."

Luke's leaving was going to hurt more than any physical injury. That kind of healing would take time.

He reached up and brushed my hair back from my face. "I'm so sorry I hurt you. Ian says he's sorry too, even if he won't come out of his room."

I jerked back. His eyes were full of remorse.

"He's still talking to you?"

Luke blinked in surprise, then gave me my favorite crooked smile. "Of course. He can't stay mad at me for long. We're brothers."

Driving away from the hospital—and Luke—was one of the hardest things I'd ever done. I wanted as many moments as possible before those moments were gone. But I wanted Luke to heal, however that had to happen. His grief and guilt were so large that I knew it was going to take more than a summer, more than me, to help him figure out how he fit into the world again.

I drove straight to the one person who would be able to understand without me having to explain. I couldn't put how I felt into words—how could I explain that my body was being ripped into pieces of joy and sadness, longing and hope? Because I felt all of those things, and I didn't really know what to do with any of them. With Mops, I wouldn't have to worry about that. She understood without having to know everything. Because I wasn't ready to tell everything.

Becca was due home in a few days, and I knew that I wouldn't be able to keep my entire summer a secret. Not that I wanted to. But there were some things that were too sacred to share, and Luke was one of them. Becca was my best friend, but there were some things she just wouldn't understand. There were some things I still didn't understand. I was pretty sure it was going to take a lifetime before I could see how everything fit together.

I parked behind *Reclaimed* and let myself in the back. Mops was whistling loudly, and badly, as she dug through one of the many boxes we still needed to get to. Pops's boxes sat in the corner, their lids sealed tightly, unopened but not forgotten. I remembered Luke carrying them out to the Bronco at the beginning of the summer, but he wouldn't remember that, because he'd been Ian then. I hurt for Luke, for the half-life he'd been living. He'd made so many mistakes, but he deserved a second chance. Maybe we all did.

Mops turned around and saw me frozen in the middle of all the discarded items, some to toss, some to resell, some we weren't sure what to do with. My life illustrated—there was so much I wanted to let go of, so much I was terrified of losing, so many new things I wanted to find but other things I wasn't ready to release.

Mops didn't say a word, but I saw understanding in her face before she wrapped me in her arms. She smelled like powder and lavender, and I was glad I hadn't outgrown her hugs.

I hated tears. Crying never solved a thing, but I was too tired to hold them back anymore. Mops stroked my hair and let me cry. She didn't try to soothe me or stop me, just let me cry until her shoulder was damp and I had run through them all.

Mops gripped my shoulders and pulled away, her eyes reading my face in the way only she could. She didn't ask what was wrong or what she could do to fix it. She just gritted her teeth and made her assessment. "You need a glass of tea," she said.

It was a start.

She put her arm around my shoulders and steered me toward her apartment stairs. The bell above the front door jingled.

"Go on up," Mops said. "I'll deal with whoever it is."

"Mom?" My mother's voice floated through the store, and we both froze. I listened as her heels tapped hesitantly on the concrete floor. That was new. My mother had always strode with purpose.

Mom stepped into the back room and stopped. Her pencil skirt and silk blouse seemed out of place among the discarded junk.

Her chin wasn't as obstinate as it normally was. Though Mom stood straight and tall, there was uncertainty in her face.

"Hey," Mom said, her eyes darting between Mops and me.

"Vivian." Mops wasn't angry, but I could tell she was surprised. I couldn't remember the last time Mom had been in the store.

"I brought clothes to change into," Mom said, holding up a bag. When neither one of said anything, she set her shoulders. "I thought we could go through Daddy's boxes."

Mops nodded, and Mom went upstairs to change. Mops turned to me and smiled. "It's a start."

THIRTY-FOUR

JENNA

The wooden box was sitting in the Bronco, and I knew what it meant. Luke was gone. He hadn't even said goodbye.

The box was amazing. I ran my fingers around the sides, touching my name and my mom's. Luke had built the box with our height charts. The lid was reclaimed cypress, honey-colored with dark and smudged nail holes, and the grain of the wood was intricate and delicate. He'd used an old hinge to attach the lid, then fitted it with an old-fashioned lock, complete with skeleton key. The key lay next to the box, a large blue ribbon tied around it. I touched every part of the box, imagining his hands constructing it and sanding it smooth. Picturing him placing it in the Bronco. Every tiny piece of me screamed at the injustice of it all. I lifted the box to my face. It smelled like Luke.

I slid the key into the lock and turned, listening to the click. I opened the lid. There was an envelope with my name on it, a small sheet of paper tucked inside.

Jenna,

This is for your dreams. I know it won't hold them for long. It's just a container, somewhere to store them until you're ready to let them out and chase them down. I know you will. You're damn fast.

I'm going to get better—I promise. I'm me a lot more now. Sometimes, like now, I remember. Ian isn't around as much. I'm trying to let him go; I'm just not sure how yet. But I'll figure it out.

I know you'll do something great with your life. You've already done something great with mine. You're an incredibly strong person. I have the scar to prove it. Don't let anyone tell you different. You can do anything you want to—and I know you will. Solitude can't contain you, no matter how hard it tries.

Maybe we'll see each other again one day. But don't wait for me. Don't wait for anybody.

Luke

I called Mops and took the day off work. I drove to the hardware store and bought paint—blue. I took a picture of my ceiling, then covered it completely. I was tired of living underneath someone else's words. I was going to write my own.

AFTER

TWO YEARS LATER
JENNA

Fall always felt like starting over. That first breath of dry air after an oppressive Southern summer was an unburdening. Even the trees applauded its arrival, their leaves welcoming the crisp air with gorgeous color. They had no idea that a week later they'd be raked up and set on fire. Sometimes an ending was really just a beginning.

Becca waited just outside the security checkpoint, and she squealed loud enough that several people turned to stare. I didn't care. She waved her arms through the air and practically jumped on me when I made it through..

"I changed my major," she said, taking mycarry-on and dragging me to the luggage carousel..

"Again?" Becca was in her third semester at the university and had already changed her major four times.

"I'm sticking with this one," she promised. "Anthropology."

"What are you going to do with that?" I sounded just like Mom had when I'd told her I was majoring in English.

She'd said English majors wait tables. I'd said that was perfect because I had a lot of experience in that area.

Becca raised her eyebrow at me. "Become Indiana Jones."

I grinned. "Well, you do look good in leather."

"And I already have the hat."

God, I'd missed her. I was glad she was picking me up at the airport. Mops was too busy cooking Thanksgiving dinner, and Mom was supervising. It made delaying a little easier.

I hadn't seen Becca since May, when I'd come in for a quick visit between terms. I'd only stayed a few days before heading back to Colorado, but it had been plenty of time for my mom's behavior to tie me into knots. I'd told her that, until she stopped drinking, she'd have to deal with a long-distance relationship. I hadn't been back since.

Becca pulled out of the airport and onto the highway, cutting off a green truck and waving when he flipped her off. Same old Becca.

"When did you get in?" I asked.

"Just last night. Early enough to get the budgeting lecture." She rolled her eyes, then turned to smile at me. "Did you bring it?"

I nodded. I had three copies of the student literary magazine tucked into my carry-on, my short story, "Lost and Found," residing on page fifteen. My words. My name. My vulnerability bared to the world. I was nervous that people I knew were actually going to read it. Especially Mom. She'd always been hard to impress. Mom had never read anything I'd written before, and while I didn't need her approval, I wanted it.

Becca filled me in on parties she'd crashed and new friends she'd made. My stories involved a lot of miles run and words written.

"I think you're working too hard," she said.

There was no such thing. And I liked being busy.

"You should come out with me while you're here," Becca said. "One of my roommates is visiting her brother in Middleton. He goes to the community college and is yummy as hell."

"No." This was a short visit, and going out was the last thing on my mind.

Becca's face softened. "You could try."

"No," I said louder. She didn't push.

Becca didn't know everything that had happened the summer she was away, but she knew enough. I kept his name tucked deep inside. I hadn't spoken it out loud since he'd left. Becca had helped me fit together the slivers of my heart that had sheared away that summer, but I was still trying to find all the other pieces.

Driving through Solitude was a completely different experience now that I no longer lived there. I felt a nostalgic tug, rather than the suffocating grip it used to be, as we passed Repete's and the pharmacy. Nothing had changed, but everything felt different.

My house looked the same as Becca pulled into the driveway. My stomach lurched. I hadn't seen Mom in six months, even though she'd been sober for three. I wondered if I could tell a difference. Mom said she'd changed, but I didn't know if I believed it yet.

"Aren't you coming in?" I asked Becca.

She smiled and shook her head. "It's going to be okay." She reached over and squeezed my hand. Funny how she could still read me. Maybe things weren't all that different. "Besides, Mom would have a fit if I didn't get home in time to make my cranberry sauce." She leaned over and hugged me tight. "I'll call you tomorrow," she said, pulling back.

"But you call me if you need anything. I can be here in ten minutes."

She'd proven that before. I wasn't sure I would've made it through my senior year with my sanity if it hadn't been for Becca and Mops.

I slung my carry-on over my shoulder and hauled my suitcase out of the trunk. "Tell your parents I said hey."

"Will do." She put the car in gear and started backing out of the driveway. She was almost to the end when she slammed on her brakes and leaned her head out the window. "I'm glad you're home."

I smiled and waved, not knowing if I was or not. Becca blew me a kiss and pulled out into the street.

I took a deep breath as I stepped onto the front porch and opened the door. Mops hurried out of the kitchen, apron firmly around her waist, and tried to squeeze the life out of me. "I don't think that coach knows what he's doing," she said, brushing my hair out of my face. "Because I don't think you're eating enough."

"I eat more than the entire cross-country team put together," I assured her.

But she clucked her tongue anyway. I set my bags at the bottom of the stairs and wondered what sleeping in my room would feel like. When I turned around, Mom had come into the living room. She smiled at me from behind Mops's back.

Mom looked different. The shadows under her eyes weren't as dark, and her smile seemed to come easier than it used to. But there was still hesitation when she hugged me, a pause that let me know she was wondering if I'd forgiven her. I squeezed her shoulders. I was wondering the same thing myself.

"It smells good," I said.

Mops smiled. "Come on, let's fatten you up."

It was just the three of us for Thanksgiving, but we seemed to fill the entire house. Pops was there too, his memory so present at the table, it was as if he was actually sitting there. He was in Mom's smile. In the food Mops made. She still left the onions out of the dressing because Pops had hated them. But his presence didn't feel haunting, and we no longer tried to step around his memory. Mops told the story about the time Pops caught me trying to smoke his pipe.

"He even helped you light it," she said.

"And then rubbed my back while I threw up," I finished. "I never tried it again."

Mops laughed. "Exactly."

Mom smiled at me. "He would have been so proud of you." She said it without tears. But her hands shook a little, and I knew it wasn't as easy as she was trying to make it seem. I smiled back and reached over to hold her hand. It wasn't much, but it was all I could give.

Mom lay down for a nap after lunch, and I helped Mops clean the kitchen.

"She always like that?" I asked, pointing toward Mom's room.

"It's been a tough three months," Mops admitted.

"I'm sorry I'm not here to help." Guilt caused me to say the words. I should have been around to hold Mom's hand more often, but I was relieved I wasn't. I'd decided two years ago that I was going to love my mother but live my life.

"You *are* helping," Mops said, handing me a dish to dry. "She's so proud of you, even if she won't say it." Mops smiled. "We both are. And you're the only reason she's trying at all."

I took a stack of clean dishes over to the china cabinet and began putting them away. We'd eaten on those dishes every Thanksgiving I could remember. They'd once sat in Mops's kitchen. Now they sat in Mom's.

"It helps that I've been where she is," Mops said. "When things get bad, she calls me."

Such a small thing, but for Mom, it was a huge step.

Mops stepped away from the sink and cracked her back. "I'm beat," she said, smiling. "Think I might lie down on the couch and rest my eyes a bit." She folded the dish towel and placed it on the counter. "Why don't you go for a run."

I'd been dying to. Being back in the house made me antsy, even if things were a little better. And I'd promised Coach I wouldn't get soft over the break. I'd missed out on qualifying for the national championship meet by twenty seconds. I was determined not to let that happen next year.

I carried my bags upstairs and changed into my running clothes. My room looked like I'd never left. My bulletin board was still crammed with old pictures and cross-country ribbons. I stepped into the closet and pulled up the loose floorboard. My old writing notebooks were still there. My treasures were too, hidden now in the box he'd made me instead of the old shoebox I'd used before. I'd tried to leave everything behind when I'd left. Especially him.

I tiptoed downstairs, leaving one copy of my short story in the living room next to Mops and the other on Mom's nightstand. Both were sleeping soundly. I hoped they'd wake up and read the story before I got back.

As I ran away from the house and onto the beaten path through the woods, it wasn't so much an escape as it was a reclamation. Healing was going to take time. But there was hope. I'd chased my dreams all the way to Colorado State

University. I hadn't caught them all yet, but I was going to. I was getting faster.

I wasn't surprised to find myself running toward Pops's house. I would probably always think of it that way, no matter what had happened. The house had been empty since they'd left in the night. They hadn't been able to sell it, but it was probably better that way. Too many memories for other people to keep adding to.

The smell of damp pine needles was so comforting, so very much home, that I wanted to bottle it and take it back with me. I stepped out of the trees and toward the pond. The house looked exactly the same, though the grass needed cutting.

The buzz of a saw cut through the still air, and my mouth went dry.

The shop drew me in. My heart slammed against my chest as I walked closer, and it had absolutely nothing to do with the three miles I'd just run. *Surely not*, I told myself. *Surely not.*

An unfamiliar truck was parked underneath the metal canopy of the workshop, and a new sign hung over the doors: *Solitude Cabinets and Millworks.*

I froze. I wasn't a coward, but in that moment, I was too terrified to take a single step. My mind and heart kept singing his name, a tune I'd wanted to forget, but couldn't. It couldn't be true.

The shop doors opened, and a man stepped through, wiping his face with a towel. He stopped when he saw me, his face registering the shock I felt. There was a hint of the boy I'd once known in that face. He ran a hand through the dark hair that still curled at the edges of his collar. A tiny piece of what I'd lost was found.

"Luke?" I whispered.

He crossed the space between us in two long strides. I couldn't look away. And while his jaw was now covered by dark stubble, I'd be lying if I said those blue eyes weren't familiar.

ACKNOWLEDGEMENTS

I want to begin by thanking my editor, Danielle Ellison, who discovered my book, loved it, and gave it a home. I'm grateful to Patricia Riley, Cindy Thomas, and everyone else at Spencer Hill Contemporary and Spencer Hill Press. They are amazing people to work with and I feel so very lucky. Thanks also to Jenn Rush for designing this beautiful cover.

I want to thank my students, past and present, who always encouraged me and even begged me to print out copies of this manuscript just so they could read it. Thanks to my "crew" – you know who you are. Thank you specifically to Emily T., who was willing to read *Reclaimed* and give me her thoughts, and who has always encouraged me to keep writing.

I am grateful for my critique partners, Abigail and Kate, who went through this book line by line and helped make it so much stronger. They are amazing writers and friends, and I'm so honored they picked me.

Thank you to all of my family for their unending support and love, especially my grandmother, who told me stories, and my parents, who always believed I could do anything I wanted to.

My sister has always been one of my biggest supporters. She is my first reader, biggest cheerleader, and best friend. Thanks, Em, for believing in me and knowing just how to make me laugh.

Finally, thank you to my husband, who has always been so incredibly supportive in every single thing I've ever attempted in my life. He's never once doubted me. I couldn't have done any of this without him.

ABOUT THE AUTHOR

Sarah Guillory has always loved words and had a passion for literature. When she's not reading or writing, Sarah runs marathons, which she credits with keeping her at least partially sane. Sarah teaches high school English and lives in Louisiana with her husband and their bloodhound, Gus. Reclaimed is her debut novel.